DELANEY LYNN

♡ Delaney Lynn

BOOK JACKET DESIGN BY FRED HEIDBRINK

See You Never

Ordering Information:
Quantity sales. Special discounts are available on quantity
purchases by corporations, associations, and others. Orders by US
trade bookstores and wholesalers. For details, contact the publisher.

Editing by The Pro Book Editor
Interior and Cover Design by Fred Heidbrink

1. Main category—Fiction/Romance/Contemporary
2. Other category—Fiction/Romance/Suspense

ISBN: 9798702943596

First Edition

For Mom, Honey, and Papa.

prologue

Ember

I can still remember the day I met Sawyer Christensen at our high school's homecoming parade freshman year. I was invisible, the shy new girl who had to break out of her shell before anyone could really get to know her. My mom's job had caused us to relocate and start over for the first time since my dad died. Not the most ideal situation for someone with an introverted personality.

Sawyer was on the varsity football team, but he wasn't your typical star quarterback who smooth talked his way through the entire cheerleading team. He played the sport because he enjoyed it. He wasn't anything special when it came to his football talents. He wasn't even a quarterback. And although he didn't make it a point to sleep with every cheerleader (per se), he *did* know how to say all the right things. As most would agree, a guy who knew how to make a lady swoon didn't have a hard time getting her into bed.

My mom and I had moved from Milwaukee to Haven Springs, a small town in the suburbs of Chicago where everybody knew everybody. I, however, hardly knew anyone, outside of the few people I met in my neighborhood. But being the new girl in town, I hadn't gone unnoticed.

I remember being so full of nerves on that first day of school. There were so many new possibilities as I was practically handed a new life. I had no idea what to expect, and though it scared the hell out of me as I walked through those double doors that led to my new future, I couldn't help but feel a little thrilled.

A fiery redhead sat beside me in first period. I recognized her from the bus ride to school. Something about her over-the-top personality drew me to her, though I knew I was the complete opposite. She didn't hesitate to introduce herself when she first sat down.

"Hey, new girl, I'm Taylor."

"Ember," I said shyly.

"Do you have any friends here?" she asked.

I shook my head.

"Well, consider me your first. You'll need one to survive high school."

I smiled.

I first noticed Sawyer in the hallway between second and third period. When he passed by my locker, our eyes somehow found one another. I had no idea who he was then, but I couldn't ignore the fluttering in my core that appeared when our eyes locked. If I had to pinpoint the exact moment I fell in love with him, it might have been then. How could a stranger give me butterflies before we even spoke a word to each other? I never believed in love at first sight until I saw him.

Sawyer was tall, though not quite as tall as most of the other athletes at our school. His T-shirt clung to him in all the right places, leaving little to the imagination. Undeniably fit, he had dark brown—almost black—hair that slightly hung over his eyes.

Wow, his eyes. Dark brown like chocolate, and when they gazed into mine, it felt like he looked right through me. Those chocolate eyes instantly melted me as I stood, unable to move as they stared back at me. I couldn't help but wonder if he felt what I was feeling.

I had always considered myself an average girl. Not too pretty, but not ugly either. I was shorter and more petite than most girls in our grade. My thick and wavy hair, a mixture of blonde and brown, hung loosely over my shoulders. My most prominent feature has always been my eyes, which had a unique emerald hue to them. My mom always said my eyes were rare, that only two percent of the world's population has green eyes.

Sawyer and I continued with our frequent hallway glances for nearly two months. He never made it a point to talk to me, and I sure as hell never built up enough courage to talk to him. We didn't have any classes together either, so I often found myself detouring to my locker between every passing period hoping to steal a peek of him again.

The first time we spoke was the day of the homecoming parade. I sat on the curb outside of the school with Taylor and a few of her friends, waiting for the parade to kick off. I saw Sawyer in the distance talking to some of his football buddies. My eyes remained glued to him. He wore his football uniform with those spandex pants that clung to his ass, showing every curve of muscle his legs had to offer. He was *so* attractive.

He turned his head and I snapped my gaze in the other direction, but it was too late. He had already caught me staring. A minute later, he walked toward us with a couple of his teammates, his chocolate eyes fixed on me. I stood as he approached, my legs wobbling, praying they wouldn't give out on me in front of him.

"Hey, Ember," he said.

He knows my name?

"Hey," I said, trying to remain calm.

I picked at my nails, my pesky nervous habit. The way he said my name, so calm and smooth, nearly made me collapse. I didn't know another person could make my heart drop to the floor with just the sound of their voice. I could hardly handle what his stare did to me, but now, he spoke directly to me.

I tried to ignore the intense fluttering in my stomach, but the feeling became more overwhelming as he inched closer to me, merely a step away. If he walked any closer, our bodies would collide. The thought made my heart skip a few beats. I tried to remain calm and focus on my breathing. Sawyer was an all-encompassing being, and when his attention directed toward you, you poured every ounce of yourself into it. I savored that moment and tried my damn best not to buckle under pressure.

Everyone else faded into the background as I concentrated on Sawyer and those mesmerizing eyes staring directly through me. I heard nothing else. I saw only him, so close I felt his breath as it swept across my forehead. I tilted my head back to meet his gaze,

3

but not before I glanced at his lips. They looked soft and plump, the perfect shade of pink. I instantly wondered what it would feel like to kiss him. He smirked as though he knew what I was thinking.

His voice came out raspy. "You're the new girl, right?"

I let out a squeaky "Yes."

He made me so nervous, I could hardly form words. But he didn't seem to care. His smile remained.

"I haven't been able to take my eyes off you, Ember."

What am I supposed to say to that? "Oh," was all I managed.

He chuckled. "How come I haven't seen you outside of school?"

I shrugged. I hardly knew anyone. The only real friend I had made was Taylor, but we hadn't hung out outside of school yet.

"I don't know many people. I just moved here a few months ago."

"Well, we should change that," he said as he showed off his perfectly white teeth.

I blushed.

"We should hang out sometime," he continued. "I want to get to know you, and that's hardly possible to do in passing. It's not nearly enough time to get to know my future wife." He winked.

Wife?

Did he just say *future wife?*

He left me speechless. I had never been speechless before. Only Sawyer Christensen could do that to me.

Sawyer and I dated for six years. We were high school sweethearts and eventually attended the same college. Those six years consisted of a lot of ups and downs. Sawyer became known for cheating on me at parties, and I became known as the girl who always took him back. I didn't want to lose Sawyer. He wasn't someone that you let go of. When we were together, our relationship was unlike anything else. We were inseparable. We were so in love.

I figured having him in some capacity was better than not having him at all. Ultimately, I realized the heartbreak was inevitable.

I understand now how ridiculous that is. After six years of breakups, makeups, and heartaches, I can finally see that I deserve better. I realized that today—this morning, actually.

Sawyer and I always schedule our classes on the same days so we can drive to campus together. We had even been able to register for a few of the same courses this semester. He'd texted me early this morning, letting me know that he is skipping class today because he isn't feeling well. I reply right away.

Me: Sorry you don't feel good. Do you want me to stop over and grab your assignment?

No answer.
I wait a few minutes before I text him again.

Me: I'll stop by and grab it. Hope you feel better. Let me know if you want me to bring you soup or something after class. Love you.

Sawyer and I have been together for so long that I don't hesitate when I walk into his house uninvited. I've done it so many times before that his home is basically my second and vice-versa. Sometimes it already feels like we're married. We talk about moving in together, somewhere closer to campus, and had begun apartment hunting a few weeks back. It's a big step for us, but it only makes sense. We practically live together anyway, and it will shorten our commute.

I pull into his driveway, quickly punch in the garage code, and walk in. I head straight for the stairs that lead to Sawyer's bedroom.

"Hey, it's me. I'm grabbing your assign—"

I look around his room when I realize I'm talking to nobody. Sawyer isn't in his bed. The perfectly arranged bed set gave away that it hadn't been slept in last night. Sawyer *never* makes his bed.

Where is he?

I grab his assignment off the desk, shove it into my backpack, and amble down the hall to see if he is sick in the bathroom, but it's empty.

Maybe he isn't home, but where else would he be?

I walk downstairs and back toward the door I entered, prepared to call his cell, and that's when I see it. That's when I see *her*.

I stop dead in my tracks. She throws herself off him so fast it's almost comical. After a few dreadful moments of trying to catch her footing while also making a valiant effort to cover herself, she eventually wraps a blanket around her bare chest and rushes toward the door. I stand still, undeniably in shock. I catch a glimpse of her long bleached blonde hair as she runs out.

Of course, she's blonde. I look back to where she came from and see him shuffling on the couch. *Found him.*

"Sawyer?"

He stares at me with those big chocolate brown eyes, straight through me, as he always has. He knows what I'm thinking. He always knows what I'm thinking.

Of all the times Sawyer Christensen has cheated on me, I have never seen it with my own two eyes. It is exactly what I need to finally meet the truth. I have been blind to it for a long time, but I know now. I don't care how great he is, or how beautiful his eyes are, or the overwhelming feeling that takes over when I'm in his presence. I don't care anymore. I don't deserve this, and he sure as hell doesn't deserve me.

He sits up on the couch, hastily throwing a shirt on over his head.

Realization hits. *Did I just catch them having sex?*

As if he can read my mind he says, "Ember, it's not what you think. We only kissed."

I gawk at him for a few moments. *Did I really just witness that?* Quickly, rage takes over, forcing words out of my mouth. "Are you even *sick*?"

He says nothing. He doesn't have to. I already know the answer. How can he have a girl over this early in the morning and expect me to believe they only kissed? She was half naked, for crying out loud.

Relationships can't exist without trust, and I can finally admit that I stopped trusting this person a long ass time ago. After all that time, after all that hurt, it's finally my turn. I'll show him what it feels like to be the one left with a broken heart.

"Sawyer, I'm done."

He rushes over to me, nearly tripping on the pillows that spew across the floor. I can see the fear and regret in his eyes. He fears losing me, and rightfully so. But does he really regret it? He'd never thought I would be the one to leave him. Why would he? I love him with all my heart. Or rather, I *had* loved him with all my heart.

"Baby, no. *Please*. We only kissed. I promise. It was so stupid, and I regretted it the second it happened. I was going to tell you. Baby, *please*. I love you so much, you know I can't live without you. I need you, Ember. She doesn't mean anything to me. You have to believe me."

"Fuck you, Sawyer."

I don't give him time to respond. Or maybe he says something else, but I'm no longer listening. I'm done this time. *Really* done. It's as if suddenly all the negative aspects of our relationship aren't being hidden from me anymore: every breakup, every night I'd stayed up crying, every girl he'd cheated on me with. Why had I stayed in this relationship as long as I had?

He follows me outside onto his driveway. I get in my car and slam the door shut. His mouth continues to move as I disregard whatever he's saying. His face is full of sorrow, and I already know he's begging me not to leave. I throw his assignment out the window, continue to ignore him, and drive away.

I drive around aimlessly for fifteen minutes waiting for the tears to come, but they don't. They never do. Why don't I feel sad? I feel…relieved? Is it over? It is over. It is *finally over.*

chapter one

Ember

It is a picture-perfect Friday in May, a comfortable sixty-five degrees, and the bright rays of the sun nearly blind me as they move directly into my line of vision. I love this time of year. The days are longer; spirits are brighter. Spring is the light at the end of a very dark tunnel that is the winter in the Midwest, which seems to have lasted longer than normal this year. The windows of my Dodge are rolled down as my radio blasts the newest Sam Hunt album. I sing my heart out in a pathetic country accent, a little off tune but too happy to care, as I think about how much I've accomplished in the last five years.

I'd recently purchased a charming, three-bedroom/two-bath house back home in Haven Springs after having moved around Chicago and New York. I spent a couple of years living in New York at Cornell University, completing my undergraduate degree. I needed a fresh start, and my breakup with Sawyer had given me the push I needed to transfer out of state to finish school. Then I returned to Illinois after graduating from Cornell and lived in Chicago while obtaining my master's degree. I knew it was time to return to Haven

Springs when I looked over the list of potential jobs I'd set up post-graduation. Of the five interviews I landed, four of them were within twenty minutes of my old hometown. The fifth was only thirty minutes away. If that wasn't a sign that I was homesick, I don't know what was. After securing a job as an assistant English professor at Haven Springs University and making my first mortgage payment, I *finally* felt like an accomplished adult. I have my dream job and my dream home. My life is piecing together rather nicely.

My love life is a different story, though. The only thing that never seemed to fall into place after Sawyer was a new relationship. My best friend Taylor tried to convince me to join a dating app, and call me old-fashioned, but I prefer to meet someone the natural way. So far, I haven't had any luck.

My house sits in the back of a cul-de-sac, in a quiet and quaint neighborhood. The solid brick build initially caught my attention. The three stories lined with rows of brown bricks have a curb appeal that I couldn't turn away from. The massive bay window and warm colored patio were just additional selling points. I hadn't even stepped inside before I knew I wanted to live here, and then walking inside was all the more pleasing. The original chestnut hardwood floors are in pristine condition, and there is a unique iron spiral staircase that leads to the three bedrooms and one of the bathrooms upstairs. I can't deny that the house has character.

I pull into my subdivision after work feeling grateful, for the most part, with the way my life has turned out. I head up my driveway and proceed to grab my things out of the back seat. When I stand up to close the car door, my eyes meet a familiar figure standing on the street, and my whole world stands still. My entire *happy* world suddenly freezes in place.

What is he doing here?

Sawyer's chocolate brown eyes still give me an unusual feeling in my core as we gaze at one another, and I can't tell if it's butterflies or nerves. Likely the latter. His regard alone causes my heart to beat rapidly.

I break my gaze from his for a moment as I take all of him in. In the five years since I've seen him last, he's grown into his muscles and looks manlier now. His hair is cut short, and he is sporting an attractive five o'clock shadow.

He walks up my driveway, eyes still locked on me, until he stands only a few feet away. My legs betray me, sticking in place. I plead with them to move, but they won't.

"Hey, Ember," he says.

My mouth can't form words. I am taken back to that first time he approached me on the curb outside our old high school. His voice is deep and gruff as he speaks my name, and his presence gives me a sense of worthiness. This perfect human is giving *me* the time of day. I quickly shake the thought from my head. Sawyer is *not* perfect. He'd be lucky if I even considered giving him my time after what he did.

"Mallory said you moved back. I tried calling, but I figured my number is probably still blocked." He nervously grabs the back of his neck. "I was hoping we could talk."

Seriously, Mallory? She was part of our friend group back in high school, most of whom chose sides after the breakup. We still have quite a few friends in common after dating for so many years, though, Mallory being one of them. I would like to think she was more my friend than his, you know, with girl code and all, but I question that loyalty now. I can't believe she told Sawyer where I live.

I ignore him and turned away. My legs finally follow through with my thoughts and lead me away from Sawyer, toward my front door.

He follows behind, quickly catching up. "Wait, Ember! *Please.* I just want to talk."

"What could we possibly have to talk about, Sawyer?" I snap.

What could we possibly have to talk about, Sawyer? The first words spoken in *years* to the only man I ever truly loved. The tone of my voice is cruel, and my words come out in an angry rush. I can see the hurt on his face as they gash him like a knife.

What did he think was going to happen? Does he honestly believe he can show up to my house after all this time and expect his charm to work on me like it once had?

"*Please*," he begs.

Shit. Maybe that's exactly what he expects. The way he's looking at me, the way he's pleading. As much as I don't want to admit it, maybe I've always had a soft spot for him, despite the hurt he's caused me in the past.

He's wearing that same look he had the day we broke up. His eyebrows are furrowed, his stature uneasy. I could walk away then, but why can't I now? Maybe because I was full of rage then, and now, I'm happy. I am so happy with my life that not even Sawyer Christensen can ruin that.

"Fine," I say, annoyed. "Come in."

Sawyer Christensen is in my house. *Sawyer*, the guy I dated all throughout high school and even after. The same guy I walked out on after I caught him cheating on me. I never thought I would see him again, and now, here he is, sitting at my kitchen table and drinking the cup of coffee I made him.

I take a seat across from him, ready to get this over with. "Why are you here, Sawyer?"

"I was a really shitty boyfriend to you," he says.

"You can say that again."

He looks away for a moment, his jaw clenching. "I took advantage of how much you loved me because I never thought you would be the one to leave me. I was such a fucking idiot for thinking my immature behavior could last. I never thought I would lose you, Ember."

"And yet, you did." I can't keep the bitterness off my tongue.

He winces. "You know, I was going to propose to you that year. How could I have been so stupid to think I even deserved to marry you? I know we were happy together, but I was so dishonest with you. I lied. I cheated. I was an awful boyfriend." He sighs. "And even after all that, I thought you would *still* want to marry me." His head shakes slightly. "Ember, I am so sorry. I have been wanting to say this to you for a long fucking time. You are the most amazing, kind, and beautiful woman I have ever laid eyes on. You're even more beautiful today than you were the first time I saw you, and I don't even know how that's possible. My life has been miserable since the day you left me on my driveway. I have to try, Ember. I have to try and win you back."

My heart thumps out of my chest. *He can't be serious.* Maybe once upon a time, that was exactly what I needed to hear, but *years* have passed. Where was this coming from?

He continues, "I've changed, Ember. I came here today because I was hoping you might give me another chance."

Another chance?

I can't process his words fast enough. *He wants to get back together.* I can't be hearing him properly. There is no way after all this time that he is trying to win me back. There is no way I can ever take him back. *Is there?*

"I have a boyfriend," I lie.

He swallows sharply. "How serious is it?"

"Pretty serious," I lie again.

He looks profoundly into my eyes, trying to figure out if I am telling him the truth. For some reason, Sawyer has always seen right through me. That man can read me like a book.

"Ember."

Dammit.

"Ember, I have been spending every day of the last *five years* trying to better myself. Trying to better myself for *you.* I never stopped loving you."

His chocolate eyes portray nothing but truth.

"Sawyer, this is ridiculous," I hiss.

"Please, hear me out. I dated a few women over the years, and I compared them all to you. No one came even remotely close. I used those relationships to improve the kind of partner I could be. The kind of man I could be. I want to be that man for you, Ember. I love you. I *still* love you. I've always loved you."

What the fuck?

Is this really happening right now? *How* can he still love me? I am sure that feeling is not mutual. I can't still have love in my heart for this man.

At least I don't think I can.

I take a deep breath before shutting him down.

"I stopped loving you. I have *not* spent the last five years bettering myself for a relationship with you. I broke up with you, *remember?* I did that because I was ready to be done with you, with *us*. Breaking up and getting back together was so easy for you. It wasn't easy for me. I took back more and more of my heart after each breakup. By the time I had enough of your shit, I had my entire heart back. I didn't even cry when I left your house that morning, Sawyer. I was *relieved*."

He shudders.

"But we are supposed to be together..." he whispers to himself.

I don't want to upset him anymore, but he has to know this is a long shot. Though, I can't ignore the familiar feelings in my core as I look at him. He is an extremely handsome man.

I watch him rake his fingers through his hair. He has enormously manly hands. I know what those hands are capable of. I know what they have done to me in the past. I know how they could make me feel. Sawyer was an excellent lover, not that I have much to compare it to. He took his time with me and always made sure to let me know what I did to him. It has been a long time since I have felt those kinds of things. Can we be friends with benefits? Will that sort of arrangement work between us?

No. That wouldn't be smart. You know better, Ember.

Again, I try to let him down easy. "No, Sawyer. We aren't supposed to be together. We dated a long time ago. We are different people now. I'm sorry, but I can't do this. Not again."

I walk toward the front door, hoping he will take the hint that it's time for him to leave, but when I turn back around to face him, he hasn't moved. He stares with a sincere expression on his face. He isn't giving up. Maybe this man really does still love me?

He finally hoists himself up slowly. When he speaks, his voice is quiet. "Please, just give me a chance. Let me prove to you that I'm a different man. I'll do better this time. You have to believe me."

I'll do better this time.

My eyes fall to my fingers as I pick at my poorly crucified nail beds. *There's that pesky nervous habit again.*

There has to be a reason why I'm reacting to him this way. Am I still in love with Sawyer? Before today, I would have laughed at the thought. But now, standing in front of him, the only man I've ever truly loved, I'm not so sure. I can take this slow, stay in control. That way, he won't hurt me again.

I glance back up to him hesitantly and say, "I will unblock your number. I can't promise you that I will respond to your texts or calls, but it's a start, okay? I'm not agreeing to date you. I'm not even agreeing *to go* on a date with you. Right now, all I'm willing to do is unblock your phone number."

A soft smile emerges across his handsome face.

He approaches me slowly, surprising me when he wraps his arms around my frame, embracing me in one of the best hugs I've ever had. I haven't felt his touch in a damn long time, and I would be lying if I said it didn't feel good.

My body relaxes into his chest. I don't return the hug, but I enjoy being held by him for as long as I can. He places a gentle peck on the top of my head.

"Thank you," he whispers.

Now it's time for him to go. Despite my resistance, he has accomplished what he came here to do. Sawyer walks toward the front door but turns right before leaving.

"I'll talk to you soon, Ember," he says with a wink.

I watch through the front window, stunned, as he steps into his car to drive away.

I pull out my phone and find his contact information. After five years without Sawyer Christensen, he has somehow found a way to weasel his way back into my life.

I click unblock.

chapter two

Ember

I'm getting *drunk*.

As soon as Sawyer left, I grabbed my purse and found myself at the first bar I drove past, the Bungalow.

The bar isn't overly crowded, but when I walk in, I can tell it's a Friday night.

"Can I buy you a drink?" asks a scruffy middle-aged man.

"Who am I to turn down a free drink?"

Several hours pass, and I've lost track of how much I've had to drink. My phone dies, so I have no idea what time it is but judging by how the bar is nearly cleared out, I would say it is pretty damn late. The only person left is an old man watching a rerun of the 2019 World Series. I walk toward the graying man, who curses the Astros as they hit a homerun in the second inning. He looks nice enough. The old man might have some words of wisdom for me, which I can really use right about now. I need help with the problems that have evolved out of nowhere, the problems I didn't have until Sawyer decided to show up.

He slams his beer down at the same moment I pull the chair out next to him. We make eye contact. It's as if he assumes a drunk girl is about to bother him with the way he throws those bills down on the table and makes a run for the door. I never knew a little old man could move that quickly.

"Wow, asshole! I didn't want to talk to you, either!" I yell.

How rude was that?

"Do you always pick fights with old men?"

Who said that?

The voice startles me. The deep, raspy words come from somewhere behind me. I turn around. Although the old man and I are the last customers standing, I forgot about the man making our drinks.

It was the bartender.

I stare at him, not responding to his question.

He is tall and muscular. He has the most striking jawline I have ever seen, with just enough facial hair to pull off that sexy 'just got out of bed and didn't have time to shave' look. He smirks at me, which leads my eyes to his lips: his beautifully pink and soft-looking lips. I finally regard his eyes, the most gorgeous crystal blue eyes I have ever seen, with tiny specks of green if you look closely enough. How have I not noticed this man all night? Has he been serving me drinks this entire time?

He is so easy to look at. Almost *too* easy. He is so handsome it makes me dizzy, or maybe I made myself dizzy from turning around too fast. Or the alcohol made me dizzy. Whatever the case, my head is spinning, and it won't stop. His gorgeous face becomes a blur as my body grows heavy. The room spins faster and faster and before I know it, I am flat on my back. Then, I see nothing but black.

When I wake up, I have a splitting headache.

I definitely drank too much.

I was full of so many emotions when Sawyer left that all I wanted to do was forget it ever happened. I thought getting drunk would help me forget, and I guess it did for a few hours, but I'm not sure it is worth this hangover.

When I sit up in bed, I immediately panic.

This isn't my bed.

I look down and see that I am still wearing the same clothes I was in when I went to the bar. I glance at the clock next to the bed. It's nine in the morning. I look around the bedroom. It appears very simple, like a man's room without the help of a woman to decorate it.

Wait, am I in a man's *house? In a* man's *bed? Why can't I remember what happened last night? I remember the old man running out the door, but then everything went black. How the hell did I end up here?*

I slowly get out of bed and tiptoe out of the bedroom. I have no idea who or what I will see when I step outside the room. I don't have the slightest clue whose house I'm in.

The door creaks softly as I draw it open, careful not to make too much noise. I walk into the hallway and find a bathroom directly across the hall and a closet beside the door I exited.

As I round the corner, I walk into an open living room, the kitchen directly behind it. The living room looks cozy, but again, it lacks the decorative touch of a woman. It is clear a man lives here.

I walk toward the only door I can see when I notice something shift out of the corner of my eye. I turn to look, and my entire body tenses as I see a man sit up on the couch. He rubs the sleep from his eyes and looks at me with a smirk. I recognize that smirk.

The bartender. How the hell did I end up in the bartender's apartment?

He must notice the look of confusion on my face because he raises his hands, as if to show that he means no harm.

"You passed out on the floor in the bar. I live right upstairs and figured it made more sense for you to sleep it off here."

"Do you always allow strangers to sleep in your apartment?" I ask.

"Not usually," he says. "Only the pretty ones who pass out in the bar."

Is he flirting? He is flirting. And he thinks I'm pretty? I can't hold back my smile. He is by far the most attractive man I have ever seen in my life.

As if I am suddenly overcome by a wave, embarrassment floods my thoughts. I passed out on the floor in a bar and had to be rescued by an extremely attractive stranger. *Strike one.*

"I'm sorry," I say. "I had a bit of a day yesterday. I'm not usually like that. I hardly ever get drunk."

"Don't worry about it. It happens to the best of us."

I glance around. "So, you live above a bar?"

"Yeah. I own the building and converted the downstairs into a pub. It makes it easier working late nights. Not such a long commute home," he says with a sexy smirk.

"What's your name?" I ask.

"Ace."

Is it possible for a name to sound sexy? Because I think Ace has just become my new favorite name.

"Well, Ace, I'm Ember. And this is probably the most embarrassing moment of my life."

Ace laughs. "I enjoyed the company."

"I could hardly be company when I was passed out drunk."

"You woke up after I carried you up here. Started telling me all about some guy named Sawyer and why you needed to get drunk in the first place. It sounded like you were quite the heartbreaker yesterday."

Oh, my God. He had to carry *me? Then I told him about Sawyer? Strikes two and three, Ember. You're out.*

"Hardly," I say, trying to seem unfazed. "It's been five years. That man is crazy if he thinks I've been holding out hope for my high school sweetheart to come and sweep me off my feet."

Ace looks me right in the eyes and says, "Maybe he's a hopeless romantic who couldn't bear the thought of losing you forever. Maybe you're someone worth fighting for."

I roll my eyes. "Yeah, right."

Ace smiles at me, a picture-perfect smile that is sure to break hearts. He has to have a girlfriend. There is no way someone as good-looking as him can be single. I wonder how his girlfriend feels about letting a drunk girl sleep over.

Not thrilled, obviously.

"What about you, are you a hopeless romantic? Someone worth fighting for?"

He laughs. "Me? No."

"No?" I ask surprised.

"Nope."

"I find that hard to believe."

He smiles. "What is it that you really want to know, Ember?"

"Do you have a girlfriend? She probably wouldn't be too thrilled to hear how her boyfriend had to rescue a drunk girl at his bar and how he let her sleep over after said rescue."

"There's no girlfriend."

"Oh."

"How about some breakfast?" he asks, noticeably changing the topic as he gets off the couch.

When he stands, my eyes immediately fall to the six-pack sketched into his abs. Ace catches me ogling his body, and I quickly switch my gaze from his stomach to his face, but not soon enough. He can't hide his huge grin.

Shit.

I blush. "Breakfast sounds good."

He cooks us eggs, pancakes, and sausage for breakfast. He doesn't wear a shirt the entire time, only sweats that hardly hold onto his hips and urge me to see everything that is underneath. I catch myself continuously checking him out while we eat. I can't help myself.

When I woke up this morning, my first instinct had been to try and get out of this unfamiliar place. I have never woken up in a stranger's bed before, but something about Ace makes me feel comfortable. I haven't tried to plan my escape. Hell, there isn't a girl I know who would ever try to get away from this man. I haven't had sex in over five years. Could Ace be the guy to finally break my dry spell? The thought brings an ache between my legs, followed by a moment of sheer panic. Have I already slept with Ace? He says I woke up once we made it upstairs, so did we…?

"Did we hook up last night?" I blurt out.

He smirks again. "No. I would never take advantage of a drunk woman."

I feel relieved, but also slightly disappointed.

Would a guy like Ace even want to sleep with an average girl like me?

"I appreciate that."

Once we finish eating breakfast, I collect our dishes and load them into his dishwasher. I have every intention of leaving after we eat, but for some reason, I'm still not ready to say goodbye.

As if he read my mind, Ace says, "The bar doesn't open until this afternoon. They say the best cure for a hangover is drinking more. Up for a drink?"

I smile and nod. "But I swear, I'm not an alcoholic."

He laughs. "Don't worry, Ember. You don't strike me as an alcoholic. I'm not one either if you're worried. I mean, I do own the bar and all, but it's more for business purposes."

Ace leads me down a staircase into the familiar scene from last night. The bar is empty and spotless. He must have a cleaning crew come in after hours because it smells fresh of bleach and lemon. I've never had a bar to myself before. It's kind of exciting.

"What's your poison?" he asks.

"Surprise me."

He smiles and mixes things behind the bar.

I glance around and notice how modern the building looks on the inside but remember how ancient it looks from the outside. I know the bar is in the historic district, but you would never know from the opulent red bar stools, a stark contrast to the neutral shades accented on the walls.

"Did you remodel this place yourself? Whoever did, they did a really great job."

He looks up, admiring the space himself as he pours the concoction he made into a glass. "My dad and I remodeled right after I bought the place five years ago."

"Five years ago? How old are you?"

"Twenty-eight. This was my first investment right out of college."

"Impressive," I say. "First investment? What else have you invested in?"

He hands me the drink, and I take a sip. It's spicy. A homemade Bloody Mary and probably the best I've ever had.

"I own a few restaurants in the area. I stop in from time to time just to check on things, but they each have their own managers who handle operations pretty well. I'm the owner and manager at the Bungalow, so I'm here most of the time."

"Wow. Good-looking and successful," I say.

Am I flirting? *Why am I flirting?*

"You think I'm good-looking?" he asks with a smirk.

"Well, you think I'm pretty."

"I think you're more than pretty."

His words send a sudden jolt to my heart that I was sure caused it to stop beating. Ace is a complete stranger, yet his presence so easily makes my chest tighten. Just a few kind words—that's all it took for me to feel like a puddle beneath him.

I can't quite explain it, but I am so drawn to Ace, in a different way than I had been captivated by Sawyer in the past. What is it about him that makes me want more?

He walks around from behind the bar to join me. His knees brush against mine as he takes his seat on the bar stool. Such a small touch, likely an accident, yet I can feel the sensation all the way from my knees to my toes. He's sitting so close, and he smells like fresh pine and peppermint.

"So," he says. "I have to run a few errands today before the bar opens back up, but I would love to see you again, Ember."

He wants to see me again.

I think my heart stopped, but his words only confirm that it hasn't. His closeness makes it beat so rapidly it practically falls out of my chest. I wonder if he can sense my rapid pulse and shortened breath. Do I make him feel the same way? I definitely didn't see my drunken spiral from last night turning into this.

"Well, maybe if you're lucky, I'll stop by your bar again sometime," I say, trying not to sound too excited.

He smiles. "I hope I'd be so lucky."

I swallow the last of my Bloody Mary before I stand to leave. "I should get going, then."

"Can I walk you to your car?"

"Wow. A true gentleman."

He follows into step with me, opens the door to the bar, and holds it as I walk out.

My car is the only one left in the parking lot, outside of what I assume is his own. I stop when we reach the driver's side door and turn to face him.

His beautiful blue eyes lock on mine, the green specks even more noticeable in the sunlight. He lifts one hand and caresses my cheek with his soft, yet manly fingers. His touch takes me by surprise, as does the warmth I feel. I can't even begin to imagine what those hands might do to me.

His fingers stroke my cheek and eventually fall under my jaw. He is delicate and gentle. He slightly tilts my chin up toward him, making our gaze that much stronger.

Is he going to kiss me?

"It was very nice to meet you, Ember," he says, his voice deep.

"It was nice meeting you too."

He smiles. "I know I already said this, but I *really* want to see you again."

I blush and can't hold back my cheesy grin.

"Come back soon, please," he continues. "Bye, Ember."

I choke on my words. "Bye, Ace," is all I could manage at first. I clear my throat. "Thanks for looking out for me last night."

He watches me get into my car and waves as I drive away. My head is spinning, either from the hangover or because Ace is doing crazy things to me. Probably both.

I have the biggest smile plastered across my face the entire drive home. I can't believe a man I just met can make me feel this giddy. I'd only spent a few hours with him, and already knew it wasn't enough. I crave more.

Damn. I haven't felt this way since high school. *How soon is too soon to see him again?*

When I get home, I head straight for the shower. I need to wash the smell of alcohol out of my pores.

This has been the wildest twelve hours of my entire life. My ex-boyfriend from high school shows up, then I get drunk at a bar alone and spend the night with the damn bartender. I didn't think my life could be this exciting after college. Who am I kidding? My life has *never* been this exciting.

I know I have been floating through life the last few years. I haven't been concerned with dating or getting emotionally involved in another relationship, mostly because I never met anyone worth taking the risk for. It seems like any time I would begin to develop feelings for a guy, they were suddenly no longer interested. So, instead, I placed my focus on finishing school and getting my own place, my own independence. But now I have nearly everything I want in life, and the only thing I'm missing is someone to share it with.

In the short time I've spent with Ace, I already feel something for him. Even if it's only a strong attraction, it's *something*. Something I haven't felt in a long time. He is worth the risk.

And then there is Sawyer. I haven't sorted out my feelings toward that situation yet. When he showed up at my house yesterday, I realized he still had a hold on me that I thought I'd let go of many years ago. All the emotions I had toward him in the past came rushing back the second he stood in front of me. It scared the shit out of me. I don't want to love Sawyer again, and I am afraid if I let him in, I will.

Maybe Ace is exactly what I need to rid myself of Sawyer for good. God knows I haven't had any luck with other men in the past. Why couldn't I have met Ace a few months ago?

When I finish showering, I hear my phone vibrate near the faucet. I dry off and glance at my phone.

Speak of the devil.

Sawyer: Hey, beautiful. I hope you had some time to think about what I said yesterday. I meant it, Ember. All of it. I hope you'll give me the chance to prove it to you.

I should've expected a text from him, but for some reason, the small gesture still makes my head spin. I loved Sawyer so much back then, despite what he did. I meant it when I said I didn't love him anymore. I did fall out of love with him, but that doesn't mean there isn't still love there. There is a hell of a lot that happened between us that I can never forget, even if I want to.

I guess texting him back wouldn't do any harm. It doesn't mean we would get back together or that I have to spend any time with him. I take a deep breath and respond.

Me: Hey. I've been persuaded to at least text you back. Nothing more, yet.

He responds back almost immediately.

Sawyer: Yet? So, there's hope. I'll take it.
Me: You can't see me, but I'm rolling my eyes.
Sawyer: You have the prettiest eyes.

Women love to feel beautiful, and boy, does Sawyer know how to make a woman feel worshipped. So worshipped, they fall right into bed with him. I won't fall for it that easily. Not this time.

I spend the rest of the day cleaning up around the house and doing anything else I can to distract myself. I call Taylor so she can talk me out of showing up at Ace's again tonight. Before I can get any words in, she insists that we have a movie night, which is our code for wine and gossip.

It's nearly seven when Taylor's car pulls into the driveway. She walks through the front door like she owns the place, wine and Chipotle in hand. This is why she's my best friend. What can be better than wine and Chipotle?

"Okay, spill."

"Spill what?" I play dumb.

"Oh, *come on*, Ember. You called because you have juicy gossip for me. I can't even remember the last time we had a movie night, and you agreed to it, so I know it must be something good."

"Okay, you're right," I admit. "Sawyer showed up at my house yesterday."

She stops chewing, and her mouth falls wide open. "Shut. The. Fuck. Up. What did he want?"

"He wanted me to give him another chance. He said that he's been 'working on himself' and trying to 'become a better man' so that he could be that man for me."

"Well, what did you say?"

"I told him I stopped loving him and to get out."

"No, you didn't," she says. "You didn't give into him? You're not going to give him another chance?"

She knows me well, and though I know she wishes I would have left him years sooner than I did, she also knows I am a sucker for anything that comes out of that boy's mouth. She was there through all the breakups and makeups. She understands that Sawyer is persuasive, and if he wants me back, he knows exactly what to say to make it happen.

"Come on, Taylor. It's been *five years*. I'm not just going to give him another chance like nothing ever happened. I did unblock his phone number though. That was kind of a big deal to me."

"Oh. You did?"

I know deep down that she wishes Sawyer hadn't shown up, but she also understands that the male population has failed to pay me any attention for a long time. She probably pities me. Therefore, she is happy I am getting some attention, even if it is from Sawyer Christensen.

"Has he texted you yet?"

"Yeah. A few texts saying he hopes I'll consider giving him another chance and how serious he is about this. And, obviously, some flirting. You know how Sawyer is."

"*Wow*. That is not what I was expecting the gossip to be when I walked through the door. I thought maybe you ran into some hot guy at a bar."

"Well…" I say, unable to hide the enormous smile on my face.

"*Oh, my God*. You *did* meet a hot guy at the bar! When?"

"After I kicked Sawyer out, I took it upon myself to go to the bar and get drunk. Apparently, I passed out and the owner, who lives upstairs, took me up to sleep it off."

She stares wide-eyed and completely flabbergasted.

"He was so hot," I say, still grinning.

"What were you thinking? You should have called me if you planned on getting that fucked up! You're lucky you didn't get murdered or raped! Where did you sleep? Did he sleep in a bed with you? Did you guys hook up? What the fuck, Ember? This isn't like you. This is something I would do! Not you! What the fuck!"

I laugh. She's right. "He was sleeping on the couch when I woke up in his bed. I was fully clothed. There was no rape or murder. But Taylor, he was the hottest man I have *ever* seen. He made us breakfast and drinks and said he wanted to see me again, but he didn't ask for my number. Obviously, I know where to find him though."

"Well, do you want to see him again?"

"Of course, I do. But now this stuff with Sawyer and him...It's all so confusing."

"There's nothing confusing about it, Ember," she says sternly. "There's a sexy man who owns a bar who wants to see you again. So, go see him again. There's an asshole ex of yours who doesn't deserve you, but I know he's a smooth talker, so let him smooth talk you. Relish it, girl. Let the men come to you. You deserve it."

We both laugh.

"What bar did you go to anyway?"

"The Bungalow."

"Oh, I went there a couple of months ago with Mallory! The bartender who works there is hot as fuck."

Mallory. "That's the owner. The one who lives upstairs. His name is Ace."

"Damn, Ember! You have to go see him again!"

"I know, but when? I don't want to show up too soon."

"Oh, who cares? He'll want to see you. Clearly, you made a pretty big impression on him. Besides, you've already slept in his bed. Who cares how long you wait? And I'm pretty sure Mallory gave him her number when we were there, and he never called. Obviously wasn't interested."

"Speaking of Mallory..."

I fill Taylor in on how Mallory was the one to tip off Sawyer about where I live, and Taylor sneers.

After several hours, I have a decent buzz going. Once Taylor leaves in her Uber, I finally lay down in my cozy bed. I didn't get much sleep last night, though Ace's bed was extremely homely. Part of me wishes I were back in it.

So much has happened in the last day that it is hard to keep my head on straight. Sawyer consumed my thoughts after he showed up, but now that space is being invaded by Ace. As I shut my eyes and fall into a slumber, I wonder which man I will dream about tonight.

chapter three

Ember

I spend all of Sunday planning lessons for work. A professor's life means working overtime for free. But I don't mind, I love my job.

During my drive to work Monday morning, my phone pings, alerting me of an incoming text. I pull into the faculty's lot and reach for my phone that is buried at the bottom of my purse. The text is from Sawyer.

Sawyer: Good morning, beautiful. I hope you have a great day at work.

Me: Good morning. Thanks, hope you have a great day at...wait, do you work? I don't even know what you do.

The realization that I don't know Sawyer at all really hits me. It has been so long since we broke up. I truly don't know who he is anymore. He could be a completely different person now. Hell, *I* am a completely different person now.

Sawyer: You can't see me, but I'm smiling. I work for my dad's company. Can't escape the family business...But at least I mostly get to work from home.

Sawyer's dad owns a factory that produces marshmallows: *The Plant*, they call it. Sawyer had never expressed any interest in working for his dad, so I am surprised, to say the least.

Me: No kidding, you decided to work at The Plant after all. I bet your dad was happy about that. I'm an instructor now at Haven Springs University.
Sawyer: I can't say he wasn't thrilled. An instructor, huh? You never cease to amaze me.

I smile and put the phone back in my purse.

The school day goes by fairly quickly. I have two morning lectures and a few more in the afternoon. HSU's campus is busy as I stroll across the quad on my way to my last lecture of the day. When I walk into the theater-style seminar room located inside of White Hall, I notice a vast arrangement of flowers mounted near the white board. I freeze in the doorway.
Oh, God.
I saunter to the podium, eyeing the flowers cautiously. I find a card tucked inside the beautifully displayed blooms.

To: Ember Johnson
Thank you for sharing a part of yourself with me. I can't wait to learn more.
From: Sawyer Christensen

Damn.
Sawyer never used to send me flowers. Not once.

I blush as my students walk into the lecture hall, noting the flowers.

"Professor Johnson's got a secret admirer!" yells one of the students.

"He's not so secret about it," I whisper to myself.

I sit at home that afternoon, staring blankly at the flowers. They really are pretty. But what does it mean? It is a nice gesture, and I can't resist the urge to want to openly welcome Sawyer back into my life. But it can't be that easy. I shouldn't think like that. I am much more mature and levelheaded now.

As I stand to move the arrangement to the counter, away from my constant line of vision, I notice a car sitting in my driveway. It takes me a few moments before I realize it's Sawyer.

What is he doing here?

I walk toward the bay window, flowers in hand, and watch as he shuts off the car's engine. He stays seated as he runs his fingers through his hair.

He finally steps out but pauses for a moment before he takes a few paces. He looks deep in thought, like he is contemplating if he should even be here. I can't blame him after the way I acted the last time he showed up.

He finally builds up enough courage to walk toward the house and up the front steps. He waits a few seconds before he knocks on the door. I still haven't moved. I am locked in place, confused about how I feel. Why does he think this is okay?

He knocks for a second time, and I snap out of my haze, put the vase down, and head for the door. I hesitantly place my hand on the doorknob and pull in one swift motion until I am standing face to face with Sawyer.

His nerves are even more obvious now. He's wearing a tight-lipped smile that shows he is happy to see me, but he's also petrified at how I might react.

"Hi," I say.

"I'm sorry to show up unannounced again. I wanted to make sure you got your flowers."

He glances behind me at the beautifully set arrangement I left on the coffee table.

"You could've made sure of that through texts, Sawyer."

"You're right." He grabs the back of his neck with his hand. "I just…wanted to see you again."

I hesitate before stepping aside to let him in. He isn't respecting the boundaries I placed. I told him I was open to texting him, but I haven't agreed to seeing him again. Yet, here he is.

So much for putting my foot down.

"Would you like something to drink?" I ask, trying to make him feel more welcome. He has gone through the trouble of sending flowers to my work. I can at least be polite.

He wavers for a moment, opening his mouth to say something before he shuts it again.

"It's fine that you're here, Sawyer, I'm not mad."

I am a *little* mad, but he doesn't need to know that.

Relief washes over his face. He walks through the threshold and embraces me in another one of his amazing hugs. It is warm and comforting, different than that last hug because this time, I hug him back.

It feels like we are wrapped in one another for several minutes before either of us speaks.

Sawyer breaks the silence when he whispers in my ear, "I've missed this so much, Ember. I could hold you for the rest of my life and never grow tired of it."

I don't say anything. I just let him hold me. Our bodies fall together with perfect familiarity. Despite the uncertainty of what may happen between us, it is time to admit to myself that I miss this too. I'm just not ready to admit that to *him* yet.

We order pizza for dinner. It is nice to be with him again after all this time. He fills me in on his family, and I talk to him about what my mom and I have been up to lately. Sawyer says he moved into a high-rise downtown a few years ago with an insane view, and he makes a promise to show me it sometime. We talk a little bit about college and what made me transfer to Cornell. He says he is proud of me. I don't need his approval, but it feels good to hear him say it.

After dinner, we sit on the couch in my living room and watch the most recent episode of *The Bachelorette*. Monday night television is my guilty pleasure.

We stay separated on the couch with no intention to take our physical interaction any further than the hug that lasted a little longer than it probably should have. Instead, we eat food, laugh, and watch some incredibly hot men fight for a shot at love with *The Bachelorette*.

When the episode ends, I pick out a movie for us to watch on Netflix. About halfway through the movie, I glance over in Sawyer's direction. His eyes are closed, and his breathing is shallow.

"Hey," I whisper, trying to get his attention. I grab his hand and give it a gentle squeeze. "Sawyer, you fell asleep."

His sleepy eyes struggle to open, but once they do, a smile spreads across his face. "I want to wake up to you for the rest of my life." His voice is tired.

I can't help but smile.

His demeanor changes suddenly, and he looks at me nervously. "Do you think I could crash on your couch tonight?"

I don't answer right away. I only look at him as I contemplate if I should say yes or insist that he leave. I am keen enough to know it won't be smart to allow my ex-boyfriend to spend the night, but I also see how tired he is, and he has a long drive home.

He continues, "I really wanted to spend time with you, Ember. I didn't mean for it to get so late. I promise, it won't happen again. I'm just too exhausted to drive home. I'll stay put on the couch. You won't even know I'm here."

I look at Sawyer, sleep still displayed in his chocolate brown eyes. Those eyes nearly melt me, and I know I can't say no. Have I ever successfully said no to Sawyer, anyway? I guess he will be crashing on my couch for the night.

I walk to the linen closet without a word and pull out a clean blanket and pillow. I place them on the couch next to him before I walk up my spiral staircase to bed.

"Goodnight, Sawyer," I say.

He takes that as permission to stay. "Goodnight, beautiful."

chapter four

Ember

I wake up to the smell of bacon. I stroll down the iron steps in my pajamas, an oversized T-shirt that falls right above my knees. Sawyer has clearly made himself comfortable in my kitchen. I watch for a few moments while he moves from the refrigerator to the stovetop preparing breakfast. As I descend the final step, the floor creaks. Sawyer swiftly pivots to look at me, one hand still on the frying pan.

"Good morning. I hope you don't mind that I made breakfast. I usually—" he stops mid-sentence before walking over to the refrigerator, stalling as he looks inside.

"You usually, what?"

"Sorry," he says, staring into the fridge. "You're not wearing any pants. I just realized that you're not wearing any pants and now, I'm very distracted." He peeks around the door as he checks out my legs with a smirk.

I blush but try to play it cool. I can't let him see that his compliments actually make me feel something. I am not prepared for this man to know he still has any type of hold over me. I only want him to know that he has to continue to prove himself to me until I decide whether or not I want to be in a relationship with him again.

Sawyer was always in control, but not this time. This time *I* am in control. I roll my eyes in an effort to seem unfazed and make my way into the kitchen to pour a cup of coffee from the pot that has already been brewed.

"Thanks for making coffee," I say as I sit down at the kitchen table.

"What time do you have to be into work?" he asks.

"I need to leave in about twenty minutes. I teach an early morning lecture."

Sawyer takes a seat beside me at the table. He grabs my hand in his and turns to face me. I instantly meet his gaze. As he looks into my eyes, he studies them with curiosity.

Yes, Sawyer is at my house cooking breakfast. Do I want him here? I can't tell yet. Is it nice to have someone there to wake up to? Sure. Can I get used to this? Maybe. But I don't know how I feel about his spending the night so soon. There will always be love there, that much I've come to realize, but I can never forget our history. There was a hell of a lot that happened between us, and he should know better than to expect anything from me. He is trying to pursue me again, like he has done several times before. I would be lying if I said that I don't like being chased, but how long will it last? It has been a long time since I was in a serious relationship, and I *do* miss this part. I miss getting butterflies. I miss smiling so much.

Shit. I catch myself smiling and try to hide it with my cup of coffee.

Sawyer grins. "Please…" he says in a hushed whisper. "Please don't hide that beautiful smile of yours."

I put the coffee cup down.

"I was thinking…" he says. "Would you like to get dinner with me this weekend?"

Dinner? Like on a date?

A date means that I want to see him again. It means that we are *dating* again. I remain silent, my smile fading.

"Ember, it's just dinner. Please, let me buy you something to eat. It's the least I can do after you let me crash on your couch."

Before I even have time to think my voice betrays me. "Sure."

It doesn't have to mean anything. It can just be a friend buying another friend dinner. Though, I know better. Sawyer has other intentions, and he and I both know he wants it to be a date. I can't help but feel like this whole thing between us is moving too fast, maybe even getting out of hand.

How did I let this happen already? It has only been four days since he first showed up to my house. I was very clear that I wasn't interested in a relationship with him then. How has he already weaseled his way into spending the night and now taking me out to dinner?

Annoyed, I stand up and walk out of the kitchen without even a glance back in his direction. "I have to get ready for work. Thanks for making breakfast, but I don't have time to eat."

When I get to my bedroom, I slam the door shut behind me.

"What am I doing?" I say quietly to myself.

I only have about ten minutes left to get ready for work. In a haste, I choose a cream-colored pencil skirt that goes right above the knees. I pair it with a short sleeve blush blouse that is tucked in at the waist. My hair is in long, naturally loose curls. It falls down the length of my spine and lays freely around me. I slip on the beige heels I wear to work almost every day and make my way back downstairs and into the kitchen to grab my things and get the fuck out of here.

As I pick up my lesson plans and purse off the island, I feel his hands press against me, slowly, as they handle my waist from behind. I tense. It becomes harder and harder to grasp air. How can his touch still leave me breathless? Not five seconds ago, I was aggravated that Sawyer was taking things so fast, yet here I am now, wanting him to touch me. I want his hands to move to the places that haven't been touched since being with him all those years ago.

I squeeze my eyes shut, trying like hell to shallow out my breathing. He pulls me in closer, until my back presses against his chest. My heart only beats faster, louder. I can feel his heart beating rapidly too, as there is no space left between us. We have become one in this moment. One heartbeat. One breath. He lifts his arms around my shoulders and embraces me from behind. I can feel his breath like a light breeze against my neck as he leans in toward my ear.

"You look amazing," he whispers.

He pulls back his arms and deliberately walks around me until we are facing each other. I can still hardly catch my breath, and my heart continues to race. That was the most intimate I had been with a person in over five years, and there was nothing sexual about it. But I can feel it. The sexual tension. The desire. I feel like Sawyer and Ember have become a pair again, and that scares the hell out of me.

He picks up a container off the counter and hands it to me.

"Breakfast," he says. "I hope your day is as good as you've just made mine."

Sawyer scoops up his car keys and begins walking toward the front door.

As he opens the door, I suddenly yell out, "Sawyer, wait."

He turns around, one foot out the door, his hand gripping the doorknob. He looks at me, waiting for me to say whatever it is I need to say.

"Thanks for breakfast," is all I can manage.

He nods and continues his way outside.

Once he leaves, I linger in my kitchen. I need a break for a few days from the whirlwind that is Sawyer Christensen. He is doing weird things to my heart, weird things to my mind, weird things to my stomach. I don't want to feel these things, but I can't help it. I can't tell if he gives me more butterflies or nerves. Whatever it is, I know I'm not ready for it.

I make my way out the front door and into my car. As I drive to work, I decide that I will keep my distance from Sawyer until our dinner this upcoming weekend. That gives me at least a few days to get my head right.

Maybe I need to get drunk again.

I manage to make it the rest of the week without any life-altering events. I text with Sawyer a few times after he leaves Tuesday morning, and we decide on a Saturday night dinner. He wants the restaurant to be a surprise but leaves me with the directions to dress up.

I have another twenty-four hours before I have to see him again. God only knows what a dinner with him will do to me. Will he try to kiss me? Or ask to stay the night again? I don't want him to get the wrong impression, but I have already agreed to dinner, which I know he considers a date. That is as far as I'll let it go. Dinner and that is it.

I stop and pick up a bottle of red wine on my way home from work. I am ready to get comfortable on my couch, drink a little wine by myself, and binge watch TV for the rest of the night. But as soon as I pull into my driveway, I hear my phone ding. It's a text from Taylor.

Taylor: I need a girls' night. Now. Can you come over?

Taylor rarely asks me to come over. Ever since I moved out of the apartment we shared in the city, she's made the drive to Haven Springs frequently to see me. Someone *else* keeps her occupied in Chicago. Taylor has been sleeping with her boss for the better part of the last two years and, although I've warned her that it is probably not the best idea, I can already tell that something has happened and that she needs me. If he's broken her heart, I will be sure to give him hell the next time I run into him. That is my job as her best friend.

Me: I'll be there in an hour. Girls' night in or out?
Taylor: Out. Definitely out.

Taylor's apartment is located inside a fifty-story high-rise that overlooks Lake Michigan. She has an amazing view of the city, probably one similar to Sawyer's. She loves the location, so she moved into a one-bedroom apartment a few floors down after I moved out.

I use the key she gave me to let myself in. Taylor is getting ready in the bathroom when I walk into her contemporary-styled loft.

"I'm in here!" Taylor yells.

She is taming her fire-red hair. I have naturally wavy hair. But Taylor, *wow*. Her hair has ringlets of wild curls that can hardly be controlled, despite her best efforts. Her hair is beautiful and makes her stand out in a crowd of people.

Taylor never has trouble attracting men. Most often, she tries to throw the guys she isn't interested in at me. Taylor and I look nothing alike. If a man is interested in her, odds are that he wouldn't find me attractive. Luckily, we don't have the same taste in men. Taylor has a type, and her type is far different from mine.

"Boss man problems?" I ask as I approach her.

"Do I *ever* have any other problems?" she says, annoyed. "The asshole decided that it wasn't professional for us to have a relationship anymore since he's my boss. What the *fuck*?" She continues to spray something in her hair to relax some of the curls. "But it was acceptable to bend me over his desk for the last two years whenever he wanted, only *now* it's unprofessional?" She turns to look at me. "I need to get blacked out tonight. You ready?"

I nod. I'd settled on wearing a pair of dark blue jeans that feel like they are made for me with a black top that shows just enough cleavage to make it seem innocent.

She grabs my hand, and we go quickly down the elevator and out the door, ready to take on the city.

I've lost track of how many bars we've been to after the ninth or tenth one. I have no idea how much either of us drank either, but that is kind of the point. So far, the night has consisted of a lot of tequila and dancing.

Taylor and I stand near the wooden bar top that houses hundreds of bottles of various liquors as we order another cocktail at the country western bar where we've just arrived. There is an American flag made of beer cans on the far back wall with cowboy boots and other paraphernalia lining the top shelves, and a sea of people spread across the concrete floor gathering around a small stage waiting for the band to play.

"Ember?"

I hear my name called out somewhere among the noisy and eager crowd. I turn around, shocked to see Ace strolling toward us. He looks sexy as hell with his signature smirk and bright blue eyes that dance as they focus on me.

"What are you doing here?" I ask. I can't hide the excitement in my voice or the smile that spreads across my face. "Don't you have your own bar to run?" I tease.

I feel immediately comforted with his familiar scent of pinewood and peppermint as he pulls me in for a hug. The second we make contact, I feel hundreds of tiny goose bumps erupt throughout my body.

Holy shit.

When he pulls away, I can sense the loss of not having his body close to mine anymore. I want it back. I want more than just to be embraced by Ace. *Damn.* I want a hell of a lot more.

"I have other managers to run the bar for me on nights I'm off. Tonight is being covered. I was kind of worried you might show back up at the Bungalow tonight and I would miss you, but now I'm pretty happy that I ended up at this bar. Can I buy you a drink?" he asks right as Taylor hands me the tequila Sprite I just ordered.

He laughs. "Never mind. I see she's got you covered."

Taylor's eyes widen when she sees who I am talking to. She must recognize Ace from her night at the Bungalow with Mallory.

She reaches out her hand to introduce herself. "You must be the bartender from last week. Hi, I'm Taylor. I'm Ember's best friend."

His hand meets Taylor's. "Lovely to meet you, Taylor. I'm Ace."

Ace turns back to me and smirks. He bends down a little so that his mouth brushes against my ear. It sends shivers down my spine. "You've been talking about me, huh?" he whispers.

Normally, I'd blush from embarrassment, but the alcohol keeps my cheeks naturally flushed. He would never know. "How could I not tell my best friend about the attractive man that rescued me during my drunken escapade and allowed me to spend the night in his own bed? I thought chivalry was dead."

He laughs. "Come on. Come with me."

His hand reaches for mine as he pulls me away from the dimly lit bar.

The band members take the stage. The lead singer has short brown hair that is only noticeable when he removes his cowboy hat to speak into the microphone. He introduces their newest single in a deep country drawl as couples make their way to the dance floor. The guitar strums as a low beat sounds in the speakers.

Does Ace want to dance? I will *not* slow dance with him.

"Ace, I'm not dancing with you!" I say as I yank my hand away from his.

He smiles. Damn, I love his smile.

"Come on," he says as he grabs my hand again. "There's a secret hallway over here."

A secret hallway? I tense. *Not here. Please not here.*

"I'm not going to have sex with you in a closet or something if that's what you're thinking."

He looks a little offended. "Really?"

I shrug.

"Ember. You must know that isn't my intention by now. You slept in my bed, and I didn't take advantage of you. What would make you think I'm going to now?"

"The secret hallway you're leading me to."

He laughs. "There's a set of stairs that leads to a downstairs section of this bar. Only the locals really know about it."

"Oh," I say, embarrassed that I assumed he wanted to have sex with me, but also...*disappointed?* I want him to want me, just not here. "But you're not a local."

"No, but my friend is."

I turn to call for Taylor, but she is already strolling behind us with a man she met at one of the other bars. He is cute, I guess. Definitely Taylor's type. He is really tall, has blond hair and olive-colored skin, and is wearing glasses. He has a certain arrogance about him that can't go unnoticed.

Taylor always seems to be attracted to the men that look like they can run an entire corporation themselves. In other words, she is attracted to authoritative figures. Hence, the infatuation she has with her asshole boss.

We all follow Ace down the stairs and into the basement of the bar. The vibe is completely different. There are several black leather sofas spread across the floor with one bar tucked away in the back corner. It is dark, but not too dark. Dim florescent lights illuminate the room. The music playing through the DJ's speakers isn't country. It is more upbeat with a deep bass.

"Thank God for some good fucking music!" Taylor shouts.

She hates country music, so how we even ended up at a country western bar in the first place is beyond me. But I am glad we did because I found Ace. Or rather, he found me.

Ace leads us toward a group of guys sitting on a few of the couches near the bar. He introduces us to each of them, but I don't catch the name of his friend who walked over to talk to Taylor. He looks like he could be Taylor's type as well. Taylor has been attracting men all night, but that isn't anything new. He doesn't look intimidated by the blond Taylor picked up earlier. Things might get interesting for her tonight. I'm sure she revels in the attention and welcomes the distraction.

Ace takes a seat on one of the empty couches and signals for me to join him. I take a big gulp of my drink and prepare myself for the surge of electricity that is bound to run through my body the second I sit near him. Our thighs brush together as I fall onto the cold leather. I can instantly feel the magnetic pull that draws me near him, like our bodies have an invisible force that attracts them together.

Ace puts his hand on my knee. I let out an unintentional small gasp. His eyes dart up to mine, telling me that he heard that.

Shit. Why does his touch have such an effect on me?

He leans in closer and says, "You know, when I saw you upstairs, I thought you were just a figment of my imagination. I have pictured you walking back into my bar every single day since you left. When I saw you up there, I thought I was just picturing that too, but when I got up close to you, I knew you were real. I could smell the floral scent of your perfume."

I smile.

"I want to know you, Ember. I want to know everything about you."

I have spent the week trying to avoid Sawyer when I should have been using that time to get to know Ace and see if something sparked, because clearly something has. Why didn't I go see him? What stopped me?

The way he makes me feel can't be normal. I have never developed such strong feelings for a complete stranger before, not since, well, Sawyer. But this is different. Sawyer and I were kids when we met. I thought it was love at first sight, but it was just a crush that led to something more.

This is not a crush. I don't know what it is, but I know it's different. What do I feel for Ace? We spent one night together, during which I was a drunken mess who had to be taken care of. I have no memory of that night, only the next morning. So, what is it that makes me feel this way? I need to know him. I need him to know me.

He chuckles to himself after a moment. "This is crazy, right? Whatever is going on here? We hardly know each other."

"Well, let's change that," I say with a grin. "What's your favorite color?"

He laughs. "My favorite color is red, but I don't want to get to know you like that. That's surface level stuff. I want to know what you're all about, Ember."

He is right, that is surface level. Why did I ask such a childish question?

I can feel the intensity stirring between us. How do we get to know each other on a deeper level?

He studies my face like he is trying to read my every thought. If only it were that easy. I look away because I *want* to tell him everything about me, but what if he doesn't like me? Right now, I am just the mysterious girl that passed out in his bar. Will he still be interested in me after he learns more? If he finds out I'm normal and boring?

Ace is incredibly accomplished and undoubtedly handsome. I don't question whether he has the ability to pick up any girl he wants in this bar. Of course, he can. So, will I be enough for him? I'm average, with nothing exciting to tell. I live a regular life and, though I am excited about the things I have accomplished, they pale in comparison to what he's achieved.

My words spew out like vomit before I can second-guess myself. "Well, I teach English to college students. I just bought a house. I live alone. I'm an only child. My dad died in a plane crash when I was little, so it's always just been my mom and me. I haven't been in a serious relationship in more than five years. I don't get drunk often, but for some reason every time I'm around you I'm on the verge of blacking out. Red wine is my go-to, but tonight Taylor needed to get blacked out, so we've been drinking tequila. I used to not like coffee, but just started drinking it after college. I don't think I could live without it now. I want to get married one day and have three kids. I don't care if they're boys or girls, I just want them to be healthy. And I don't really know why I want three, I just do."

I take a moment to catch my breath. His gaze is still locked with mine. His eyes watch me passionately as he soaks up every little detail that I share with him.

"Is that the kind of stuff you want to know?" I whisper, feeling vulnerable.

"Ember," he says in a raspy, quiet voice.

He looks down from my eyes to my lips then back up to my eyes. I already know what he's thinking because as I sit here, gawking at *his* lips, I'm thinking too. Maybe he doesn't see me as average. Or maybe he likes average. Maybe a guy like him can be interested in a girl like me.

"I *really* want to kiss you. Is it okay if I kiss you?"

I can only nod. My words fail me and suddenly his lips smash against mine. His touch intensifies my senses, and I can feel it throughout my whole being. When his lips touch mine, it makes my entire body want to implode. I have never felt this kind of rush with someone from a kiss. I can't compare it to Sawyer because frankly, it isn't even comparable. How is this possible? How can a kiss from this man make me feel things I have never felt kissing anyone else?

His tongue slides delicately into my mouth, and my lips instantly part for him. It feels natural, as if we have been doing it our entire lives. Our mouths and tongues fervently feel for one another and work together like they are made for each other.

Everything feels right. It feels safe. I have no ill will toward Ace. He has never hurt me. He has never broken my heart. We don't have a past. This is new, and it is fucking exhilarating.

He moves his hands into my hair and pulls me closer to him until there is no longer any space between us. A moan escapes my mouth, and he only pulls me in tighter. I am practically on top of him, in a very public place, although I have honestly forgotten we are in the basement of a bar. Our kiss slows, but it remains passionate yet somehow frantic, like we have been waiting all of eternity to kiss each other. He gradually pulls away, trying to catch his breath, his eyes full of desire.

"Wow," I say, breathless.

"I've been wanting to do that since the moment I first saw you. If I didn't stop there, I don't know if I ever would have."

It is the most incredible kiss I have ever had. I want more. I *crave* more. Kissing this man is a new experience, and I am not ready for it to be over.

"Where are you staying tonight?" he asks.

I nudge my head in Taylor's direction. "Taylor's," I say. "She has an apartment a few blocks away."

"I'm not going to make the same mistake again, Ember. I can't let you leave tonight without at least getting your number."

We both laugh.

Our kiss spoke for itself. I am undeniably interested, and I won't be leaving this bar without giving him my number. I want to see him again after tonight. I *need* to see him again.

I take his phone and enter in my information. He can't hide his smirk when I hand him his phone back. He places a soft kiss on my forehead. His lips linger, and my eyes shut as I savor the moment. My core flutters from the romantic and sweet gesture.

"Can I walk you back to Taylor's?" He looks at his watch. "The bar is closing now."

The bar is closing? What time is it?

I look at my phone, and sure enough, it is already three in the morning.

"Holy shit," I mutter.

He grabs my hand and leads us back up the stairs, through the secret hallway, and outside into the cool spring air.

We walk in the direction of Taylor's apartment. Taylor ditches the blond she is with and walks back with Ace's friend. I find out from Ace that his name is Jason. He seems nice enough. I'm just happy she has a distraction from her asshole boss.

We made it back to Taylor's apartment building thirty minutes ago, but she hasn't stopped making out with Jason long enough for us to go inside. Ace and I give them some privacy and find a nearby bench to wait on. We've been talking, too afraid to kiss again and end up taking things too far. There is no way we can kiss each other like that again and *not* take it too far.

"You look beautiful tonight," Ace says sweetly. He places another soft kiss on the top of my head.

I smile. We sit close, his arm wrapped around my shoulders and my head resting on his chest. We both look ahead, observing the nightlife as it slows down.

Chicago is like a mini New York City. There are always sirens and horns going off no matter what time of night it is. People are out and about, whether it is four in the morning or four in the afternoon. The hustle and bustle never stops. It is almost as though the city never sleeps, much like New York. However, when you pay close enough attention, the people vanish, and the sounds become fewer and far between.

I can't help but wonder how this happened. How can Ace be thrown to me so easily when I have had so much trouble trying to form relationships in the past? It almost seems too good to be true. *He* seems too good to be true.

"You seem too perfect," I belt out.

"How so?"

"You're still here."

"Where else would I be?"

"People have the tendency to disappear. The good ones at least."

"The good ones?"

"People who don't try and force themselves into my pants."

"That's not me. You know that."

"I know. You're one of the good ones. And you haven't disappeared yet."

"What makes you think I ever will?"

"Because they always do." I shrug. "I like that you know you're hot, but don't have a big head about it. Some guys think they can get any girl they want with their looks, and with the way you look, you probably could. Hell, I *know* you could have any girl you wanted, and maybe you do. I don't know. But you don't act like it."

He chuckles. "I don't have the girl I want, Ember. Not yet."

49

Not yet? Does that mean I'm the girl he wants?

He leans forward and places a soft peck on my lips. I love the feeling of his lips on mine.

"Ember! Let's go!"

I sigh, disappointed. I don't want this night to end.

As we stand, he pulls me in for one last hug. His embrace is the most comforting thing about him.

"Goodnight, Ember," he says quietly.

He holds me tightly, and I never want him to let go. He continues to clench my small body when he whispers, "If you haven't figured it out yet, you're the girl I want. I'm not going anywhere." And with that, he walks away with Jason in the opposite direction from Taylor's apartment.

I can't move. He'd just admitted that *I* am the girl he wants.

I watch as he walks away. I can't peel my eyes away from him.

He wants me.

He looks back and catches me in my spell. He's wearing that sexy smirk, his eyes locked on mine. He winks right before they round the corner.

I am in trouble.

chapter five

Ember

Two Saturdays in a row, I've awakened to a terrible hangover. The difference is that I actually know whose bed I woke up in this time. Too bad I don't feel any better about it. I have a raging headache and the light that sneaks in through the window only amplifies it.

Last night was worth it, though. Taylor needed it. Hell, I needed it too. And if we hadn't gone out, I wouldn't have run into Ace. Then, I wouldn't have had the most amazing first kiss with him. But the word "amazing" hardly seems to do it justice. *Just* amazing? It is more than that. I can still feel the lingering tingle Ace left on my lips.

I roll over to see Taylor still sound asleep with a dribble of drool trickling onto her pillow. I have no idea what time it is or how long I'd slept.

I grab my phone off the nightstand and see that I have several missed messages. The first one I notice is from my mom.

Mom: Hey, Em, just checking in. Thought we might have dinner sometime next week? Miss you. Love you.

I text my mom back right away. It has always been just her and me, at least as far back as I can remember. She is more like a sister to me than an actual mom, especially now that I am older. My mom has always been the *cool* mom, the one who allowed me to have friends over whenever I wanted. I basically had free rein over the choices in my life, as long as they were responsible. I think I turned out all right, thanks to her.

My dad passed away when I was two years old, so I hardly have any memories of him. He was a pilot and an instructor in flight training school. One afternoon when he was with a young student pilot flying one of the smaller aircrafts, they lost control and crashed. Neither he nor the young man survived the impact.

It sucked growing up without a dad, but my mom made up for it. She had the role of two parents, and she kicked ass at it. I would never have known I was missing a parent if it hadn't been so blatantly obvious. My mom kept pictures hanging up around the house of him. She always says I have my dad's eyes. His were a striking shade of green, just like mine.

I know she misses him every day. It is a void that she can never fill. Instead, she loves me more. She's assured me numerous times that she doesn't need a man to make her happy, she is *already* happy. She's already experienced that once-in-a-lifetime love, that all-consuming, all-encompassing love.

We usually spend time together every few days, but I realize now that I haven't seen her in over a week. Not since Sawyer appeared. I have *a lot* to tell her.

Me: Want to come over tomorrow? Love you, too.

I hit send.

My mom responds back right away, and we agree to meeting at my place tomorrow. She doesn't eat meat, so I'll have to come up with a nice vegetarian meal for her. She's never been much of a cook, so she really enjoys my homemade meals.

I scroll through the next few messages and see that Sawyer has texted me a few times. There is also a message from an unknown number. I open Sawyer's messages first.

Sawyer: I miss you.

Do I *miss him?*
I read his second message.

Sawyer: Good morning, Ember. I can't wait for our dinner tonight. We still on for 7?

Fuck. How did I forget I agreed to go to dinner with Sawyer tonight? All I can think about is that kiss with Ace. Sawyer has never kissed me the way Ace did. Of course, I haven't kissed Sawyer in a really long time, so it is hard to remember what kissing him felt like.

I can't bail on him now, no matter how badly I want to. Besides, Sawyer said it was just dinner, but I need to refrain from allowing him to flirt with me. How did this happen? How did I go from being content on my own to *this,* to choosing between two painstakingly attractive men?

Just as I am about to text Sawyer back, I receive another message from him.

Sawyer: Please don't tell me you've changed your mind about dinner?

If only he knew.
I haven't changed my mind about going to dinner. The problem is, I want to go to dinner with Ace tonight, not Sawyer. But again, it is *only* dinner. He won't be getting kissed at the end of the night, and

if he tries, I will tell him that I am not interested. I'll tell Sawyer that I met someone else.

I want the chance to see if this thing with Ace can go anywhere. Maybe Sawyer and I can still be friends. He may not like it at first, but if he wants me in his life, then that's how he will have to take me. As a *friend*.

I look at the time and realize it is later than I thought. Sawyer is supposed to pick me up in four hours.

Shit.

His good morning text was sent five hours ago. No wonder he thinks I am ignoring him. I quickly text him back before I grab my things and head out the door.

Me: Sorry. Late night with Taylor. Just woke up. I'll see you at 7.
Sawyer: Can't wait.

I pull into my driveway with just under three hours before Sawyer is due to pick me up.

The small icon on my phone screen reminds me that I still have a missed message from the unknown number. I forgot to check it in my haste to leave Taylor's. I click open the message. It's from *Ace* and time-stamped from right after he left last night. I feel dizzy at just the sight of his name.

Ace: Hey, Ember, this is Ace. I want you to know that I think you are incredible. I can't stop thinking about that kiss. Please don't make me wait another week to see you. I wanted so badly to bring you back with me, to call an Uber to take us to my place, but I know I wouldn't have been able to control myself around you. You make me feel things no other woman has ever made me feel. I'm trying so hard to get this stupid smile off my face and not turn around to take you home. Home with me. In my bed. Because, fuck, Ember, I wouldn't be able to take my hands off you.

Holy shit. What could that man do to me in his *bed*? I can only imagine, and in my imagination, it is fucking amazing.

Then, I remember what I'd been doing before I read his message.

What the hell am I thinking?

How can I be getting ready to go out to dinner with my fucking ex-boyfriend when Ace is texting me things like that? I love that he feels the same way I do. I love it more than I probably should. And dammit if I don't wish he would've turned around last night and taken me back home with him. I would have given myself to Ace. Whatever he wanted, I would have given it to him. But now I have to go to dinner with Sawyer instead.

I have no idea how to respond to him. I don't even know if I *should* respond. Especially because I am meeting Sawyer in only a few hours. I have to focus on this dinner right now, or else I'll be sidetracked the entire night. I'll probably be distracted either way, but I have to at least *try* and be polite.

I refrain from answering for now. I set my phone on the counter and jump in the shower.

Sawyer pulls up at seven o'clock on the dot. I choose to wear my satin emerald green knee-length dress with a basic pair of heels. My hair is half up, half down with loose curls that frame my face. I don't typically wear makeup, but a fancy dinner is a good enough excuse to throw some on. I am going for soft and subtle.

Sawyer steps out of the car to open the passenger side door for me.

High-school Sawyer would never do that.

Before he opens the door, he gives me a once-over as I walk down the steps toward the driveway. He is blatantly checking me out.

It's fine.

I smile as his eyes meet mine. I worked damn hard to look good for this dinner tonight. I deserve to be checked out.

"I didn't think it was possible for a woman to be so beautiful. How lucky am I that I get to take you out to dinner?"

I blush.

"Pretty lucky," I joke.

What happened to not letting him flirt with you, Ember?

He opens the car door for me, then walks around the front of the car before he opens the door for himself and steps inside. He places his hand on my left knee and gently squeezes. "Thank you for coming, Ember."

I smile and nod.

He doesn't remove his hand from my leg, and I don't make him. What kind of person does that make me? Why am I letting him flirt with me? This is going to be harder than I thought.

He puts the car in reverse and pulls out of my driveway. We make our way to a restaurant in the neighboring town. It is about a fifteen-minute drive before we pull in front of a restaurant called the Lux. This sort of place has a valet out front covered by a dark green awning. Sawyer puts the car in park, steps out, and hands the valet attendant his car keys. He proceeds around the car to the passenger side and opens the door for me. He reaches out his hand and mine melts into his. I get out of the car, holding his hand, and we make our way into the restaurant.

From the outside looking in, we probably look like a lovely couple out for a romantic evening dinner. Little do those people know I had an erotic steamy make-out session last night with a man who wasn't this one.

Ember! Stop thinking about it!

The hostess leads us to a nice candlelit table on the west side of the restaurant. Sawyer orders a bottle of red wine as soon as we sit down, and the waiter appears within seconds to fill our glasses.

"Thank you," I say to the waiter.

He nods and walks away.

Sawyer grins across the table. He has been nothing but a gentleman to me thus far, but I can't stop comparing the things high-school Sawyer did to what grown-ass Sawyer does. For instance, he hasn't checked out any other women in this restaurant, not even the busty blonde who walks by. It looks like her chest is about to fall out of her tight sculpted dress. High-school Sawyer wouldn't have been able to stop gawking at her, but grown-ass Sawyer can't keep his eyes off *me*.

"So," he says.

"So," I say back.

"How was the rest of your week?"

I hesitate before I answer. I don't want to bring up last night's adventures. I have to keep the conversation from going there.

"It was fine." I keep it short. No details mean no questions.

Sawyer talks about his week and how he had to deal with a potential vendor the other day who was a complete asshole. He seems passionate about his family business. High-school Sawyer wasn't passionate about anything except hooking up with girls.

Shit. I did it again.

I see the waiter coming from the kitchen, prepared to take our order. He looks to me first.

"I'll have the baked chicken with asparagus, please."

Sawyer's eyebrows shoot up. "You're not getting steak?"

"No. The chicken sounds good."

The waiter shifts to Sawyer.

"I'll have the ribeye, medium rare."

We fold our menus and hand them back to the waiter. He walks away and enters our order onto a small computer screen that clings to the wall. I have already finished two glasses of wine and can feel the slight buzz.

"I remember your never turning down a good steak," he says.

"And I remember your hating red wine." I lift my wine glass in salute.

He laughs. "Touché." He takes a sip from his glass. "Remember when we went to that restaurant in Old Town and ordered one of every dessert?"

I laugh. I know where this story is heading. "Of course, I remember. How could I forget?"

"How do you think the waiter reacted when he noticed we took one bite of everything and ran out before he could bring us the bill?"

I laugh. "*Pissed!* That was so terrible of us." I take another sip of my wine. "You know, after we broke up, I went back to that restaurant."

"You did?"

"Oh, yeah. I felt so shitty about completely ruining that server's day. I mean, he easily should have made a thirty-dollar tip off us. That's a lot of money for a teenager. And that dessert menu was huge! Anyway, he didn't work there anymore, or at least I didn't recognize him if he did. I ordered a small dessert to go and tipped the guy a hundred. It was my way of saying sorry for being an asshole."

"You're a much better person than I ever was."

"I know," I say. "You were the bad influence. I was the voice of reason. Obviously, I lost my voice that day."

Sawyer smiles. "I miss our adventures, Em."

"You miss stealing food?" I say, kind of snarky.

He shakes his head. "No. I just miss doing things with you. Doing life with you. There's no one in the world like you."

I stare blankly at him, not knowing what to say. This is typical Sawyer and Ember. Sawyer breaks Ember's heart. Sawyer shows up and apologizes to Ember for everything shitty he's ever done. Sawyer tricks Ember into spending time with him. Sawyer flirts with Ember. And before Ember knows it, she is back together with Sawyer. A tale as old as time.

Sawyer readjusts himself in his seat and clears his throat. He looks uncomfortable.

I change the subject. "So, tell me about the girls you dated."

My question catches him off guard. He raises one eyebrow, no doubt curious what my motive is behind the random topic. "Why do you ask?"

"Curious if you still have the same type. Tall. Skinny. Blonde. Big boobs. Kind of like that chick that walked by a half hour ago. Did you notice her?"

Old emotions emerge. I sound like a bitter ex as I spit out the truth. He really always had the same taste in women. Every girl he's ever hooked up with over the years has fit that description to a tee.

I suppose I'm not too far off. I'm the outlier if you lined up all of Sawyer Christensen's hookups. I am more petite, and I don't have a huge chest. I am a C cup at best, but I like to think I fill out my clothing well. Guys have always complimented me on my ass, so I guess I have a nice ass, too. And, of course, I am blonde right now, but my hair color has changed too many times to count since high school.

"Ember," Sawyer says, trying to regain control of the conversation. "The women I dated were nothing like the girls I would fool around with in high school. I had two serious relationships. Both women wanted to take the next step in our relationship, and I wasn't there yet. I knew I would *never* get there with either of them. I dated a girl named Lisa about two years after you ended things with me. After seven months, she wanted to move in with me because our leases were up. I didn't think that was a good enough reason for us to live together, and she took that as I wasn't at the same level in our relationship as she was. And she was right. So, we ended things. About a year later, I met a woman named Beth. We dated for about five months, but I knew pretty early on that things would never progress with her, so I broke it off. I haven't been in a relationship in a little over a year now. And before you ask, *no*. I *never* cheated on either of them." He pauses to take a sip of his wine.

"I'm different now, Em. I really am." He laughs to himself. "Besides, Lisa was a brunette, and Beth had black hair."

His admissions surprise me. The Sawyer I know can't *not* be in a relationship. If he wasn't dating me, he was pursuing some other girl. Maybe our breakup had finally taught him a lesson about commitment. Or maybe he'd been busy enjoying his laundry list of booty calls when *Lisa* and *Beth* didn't work out.

"Tell me about your relationships, Ember."

I clear my throat, taken back by his request. I didn't think it through when I asked him questions about his past. Why wouldn't it lead to questions about mine?

I am uncomfortable admitting I haven't been with anyone since him, so I lie. "I dated a lot of people. Nothing serious and no one worth mentioning, though."

His eyes squint slightly as he studies me, like he is trying to read me.

Dammit. He's trying to figure out if I'm being honest. How does he always know when I am lying?

"Ember," he says. "You haven't dated anyone since me?"

My shoulders drop, and I shake my head. There is no use in lying. "No," I confess.

"Why?"

"I was with you for *six years*, Sawyer. The last thing I was doing was looking for a relationship." It is partly true. I wouldn't have turned away a good thing, but one never came. "I was motivated, independent, and ready to kick ass at life alone. Besides, I never had a connection with anyone that would lead to something more." I want to add, *not for lack of trying*, but that is none of his business.

The waiter interrupts with our meals.

Perfect timing. I am so ready for this conversation to be over.

He places my meal in front of me first, followed by Sawyer's steak. He asks if we need anything else before he retreats toward the kitchen.

Sawyer never took his eyes off me while the waiter stood there. I try so hard not to meet his gaze again. He doesn't want this conversation to be over yet.

But I do.

"Ember, have you slept with anyone since me?"

And there it is. I should have expected as much. I look down, embarrassed about my answer for obvious reasons.

Sawyer was my first, and *only*. I have never been into hooking up with random guys. Sure, I made out with a lot of men. A lot of *attractive* men. But I never went back to their place, and I sure as hell never invited them back to mine. I feel like sex should be had between two people who care about one another. I haven't cared about anyone in that way since Sawyer, so why would I have sex?

"Em?"

I clear my throat. "No. I haven't. Not that it's *any* of your business. But there's no point in lying. You always see right through my bullshit."

He smiles.

"Why are you smiling?" I ask.

"You're right. I do always see through your bullshit. I don't know why you insist on lying to me. It's just me, Ember." He reaches for my hand across the table. "You don't have to lie to me. *Ever*. But, if I'm going to be honest with you right now, I'm grateful and feel lucky as hell to be the only man that's ever been inside of you."

I roll my eyes and take my first bite of chicken.

As soon as we finish our meals, we order dessert. I order a warm chocolate brownie with vanilla bean ice cream on top, and Sawyer orders a cheesecake.

Once the bill is paid, we stand, ready to leave. Dinner wasn't awful, but I am relieved that the night is finally almost over.

As I push in my chair, Sawyer's phone rings. He glances down at the screen, "One sec, I have to take this. I'll be right back."

He walks away in a hurry toward the bathroom. I don't see who is calling, but his face makes it seem like it is important enough to walk away and not take the call in front of me.

I sit back down while I wait for him to return. He is only gone a few seconds when I glance up and see Ace walk through the front door. He immediately spots me in the room full of diners and grins.

What the hell is he doing here?

The initial shock of seeing him quickly vanishes once I take all of him in. He looks good. *So good.* He is wearing dark jeans, somewhat distressed at the knees, and a dark blue shirt that makes his eyes resemble the deep blue shades of the ocean.

He walks toward me, unmistakably excited to see me. "Ember! What are you doing here? You look so beautiful."

I stand as he wraps his arms around me and again, I am captivated by that familiar scent of pinewood and peppermint.

He whispers in my ear, "So damn beautiful." He kisses the side of my head right before we separate.

"I just finished eating dinner. What are *you* doing here?" I ask.

His smile grows wider as he looks around the dining area. "This is one of my restaurants."

My eyebrows raise. I remember his saying he'd invested in a few restaurants, but I never asked which ones. Ace owns the Bungalow *and* the Lux. What are the odds?

"How did you like the food? Are you here with friends?"

"The food was great," I quickly respond, trying to ignore the last part of his question.

His eyes focus on something behind me, and his face drops almost immediately as disappointment floods his expression. He looks back to me, and I can see the hurt in his eyes. Does he think I'm on a date? No, this *isn't* a date. He'll understand after I have the chance to explain.

"No, it's not what it—" I try to say, but before I can get my sentence out, Sawyer returns frantically to the table. *Shit.* Now I have to explain Ace to Sawyer *and* Sawyer to Ace. This is not how I expected my night to turn out.

Before I can justify what I am doing here with Sawyer, and how I know Ace, Sawyer grabs my arm. "Em, we've got to go. There's been an accident. I don't know what happened, but we have to get to the hospital. It's my family. We have to go."

"Oh, my God, Sawyer," I say, blatantly more scared in this moment for him than I was for myself five seconds ago.

Who the fuck cares that I am talking to Ace? And it shouldn't matter that I am at an innocent dinner with a friend. Sawyer's family is in the hospital. There has been an accident. *That* is something to be scared about, not talking to the guy I made out with last night while I am at dinner with my ex.

As Sawyer pulls me out of the restaurant, I turn my head to look back at Ace.

"Sawyer," he mumbles under his breath.

Fuck.

Fuck. Fuck. *Fuck.*

He knows who Sawyer is. He knows Sawyer is the ex who showed up at my house last week. He knows he is the reason I ended up blacked out and drunk in his bar, thanks to my drunken confession after I came to. Sawyer is the whole reason Ace and I ever met. He is probably putting all the pieces together. *And* I never responded to his message from last night.

He looks broken.

I want to go back. I want to tell him it's not what it looks like. But before I can explain to him that I am *not* together with Sawyer, that it is all just a misunderstanding, I am pulled out the door.

chapter six

Ember

We have been in the car for nearly an hour on our way to Oakbrook Memorial. His family had been taken to the hospital nearest the wreck. I can see the worry etched across Sawyer's face. Once upon a time, his family had been my second family, and the thought of anything happening to them makes me sick.

So far, all we know is their car collided with oncoming traffic. The scene is still under investigation and, since it is an ongoing case, they can't disclose any other information to Sawyer right now. We don't know how many people are injured. We only know that his parents were involved in the wreck. Sawyer had tried to find out more from the nurse who called when we were still at the restaurant, but she didn't have any additional information to offer.

Sawyer grips the steering wheel, his knuckles turning white, while his other hand squeezes mine for dear life. He is so afraid for his family, and so am I.

Sawyer's dad helped me get my first job waitressing at his best friend's country club when we were still in high school. And our moms used to be best friends.

Tears slowly descend my cheeks. My fear that something devastating has happened to them can't even come close to what Sawyer is feeling.

Sawyer turns his head for a brief moment. I shift in my seat so that I am facing the window. I don't want him to see that I am upset. This isn't about me. I quickly wipe away at the tears that won't quit.

How pathetic am I?

It is *his* family in trouble and, although I know he is worried, *he* isn't even crying. I need to pull it together.

"Baby, don't cry," he says softly.

Sawyer drops my hand and moves his to my cheek, wiping away at the tears as they fall. "Everything is going to be okay, Em. It'll all work out just fine."

I keep my focus on the trees that sweep past outside, but I can't stop the tears from flowing. The unknown of the situation is unbearable. I hope he is right.

We walk into the hospital gripping each other's hand. When we enter the waiting room, Sawyer promptly finds the nurses' station. He probes for more information on his parents, only for them to tell him they are both in emergency surgery and that we will be updated as new information emerges.

The seats in the waiting room are uncomfortable. There aren't any decorations on the walls and the paint is faded blue. The hospital should at least *try* to make this area comforting. This is a room where families wait hopelessly while praying tirelessly. I try to comfort Sawyer. I stroke his back, hoping it will help in some way. But for some reason, it seems like he is doing a better job at comforting me.

"Thank you so much for being here, Em. I couldn't get through this without you," he says into his hands.

"I wouldn't want to be anywhere else," I answer honestly.

A few minutes go by before two teenagers burst through the double doors. They look frantic, likely what Sawyer and I looked like when we first arrived. The boys look familiar, but it doesn't register who they are until the taller one yells out.

"Sawyer!"

Sawyer looks up from his hands and sees his brothers Eric and Cole walking toward us. Eric is older than Cole by a few years. He looks just like Sawyer, but his hair is a lighter shade of brown. Cole resembles Sawyer in different ways. He is shorter, but his facial structure and hair remind me of his oldest brother.

Sawyer stands up and grips them strongly, hugging them both simultaneously.

"What happened to mom and dad?" Cole asks.

"I don't know yet, buddy. There was an accident. They're in surgery right now, and they'll let us know when they have more information."

Eric doesn't say anything. He glances over in my direction. "Hey, Ember."

"Hey. Long time no see," I say with the best smile I can manage.

Cole's eyes drift to me, a smile displayed on his lips. "Ember!" he shouts as he maneuvers around Sawyer to hug me.

"Hi! Look how big you are!" I say, trying to lighten the mood.

Cole's smile remains, though I see fear in his eyes. Sawyer and I lead both the boys back toward the stiff chairs. I have a feeling it is going to be a long night.

We remain seated in the waiting room for hours. It is the middle of the night, though I am too tired to check the clock for the time. Eric stays quiet in his seat while Cole rests his head against my shoulder as he sleeps. Sawyer asked for an update again a few hours ago, but they still had nothing.

Sawyer, Eric, and Cole have an older sister, Katie, who had apparently moved to Michigan with her husband a few years before. Sawyer called her shortly after the boys arrived to fill her in on what happened. Sawyer said she wanted to drive down tonight, but with it being so late, he encouraged her to hop on the next available flight instead.

A man wearing a white lab coat and navy-blue scrubs walks through a set of double doors on the opposite side of the room. His stethoscope hangs around his neck. He appears confident yet nurturing. His demeanor is intimidating, but in a good way.

The man glances around the waiting room and says, "I'm looking for the family of Elizabeth and Rod Christensen?"

We all stand.

"Are they okay?" Eric blurts out.

"Are you the family?" he asks.

"Yes." Sawyer confirms. "Yes, these are my brothers. And she—" He looks over at me. "She's my girlfriend. Well, fiancée rather."

Girlfriend? Fiancée?

Panic grips me at his choice of words. I am certainly neither of those things.

"I can only allow the family through," the doctor states.

"They are just as much her family as they are mine," Sawyer argues aggressively.

My alarm quickly dissipates when the man nods approvingly and waves his hand for us to follow.

Sawyer squeezes my hand tightly. I understand in that instant that he won't be able to keep it together for the boys if I'm not there. *Sawyer* needs me here.

As we enter one of the sterile white hallways of the hospital, the man introduces himself as Dr. Freeman and asks to speak with Sawyer alone. They continue further down the hallway while I stay back with Eric and Cole. I watch Sawyer's body language as he speaks in private with the man who is likely responsible for keeping his parents alive.

What is he saying?

I see Sawyer's shoulders drop. His head falls back as he stares at the ceiling. I don't know what that means, but I know it isn't good. Sawyer wraps his hands around the back of his neck and slightly turns to eyeball me. I have never seen more dread in his eyes than I do in that moment. He shakes his head ever so slightly, and I instantly know.

They didn't make it.

I don't know what is next for this family, but I do know that I want to help them get through whatever it is. I have to help them. I have to be there for them. For all of them, *especially Sawyer.*

chapter seven

Ember

Blunt force trauma. Apparently, *blunt force trauma* is a sufficient explanation to put on a death certificate. It occurs when an object physically assaults some part of the body. The blunt object in Sawyer's parents' accident was the vehicle itself. The impact from the head-on collision caused his mom's organs to be crushed. Sawyer's dad suffered from severe fractures of the skull. It appears they each died from two completely different injuries, yet the cause had been given the umbrella term *blunt force trauma.*

It hardly seems fair that the deaths of two people like Liz and Rod were given such a broad term for the way they departed this earth. Perhaps a better term is *fucking unfair.* They died in a fucking unfair way. Eric and Cole say they were driving to the movie theater for a date night. Liz and Rod, after being married for twenty-something years, still went on dates.

Isn't that something?

Who knew that keeping their love alive would be the death of them? They certainly didn't, which is why I want to argue with the goddamn coroner that their death certificates should say: *Cause of death: Fucking unfair.*

The accident happened yesterday. The last twenty-four hours have been one hell of a whirlwind. I am supposed to have dinner with my mom tonight, but instead she got a phone call from me explaining the devastating news.

Katie and her husband were on the first flight out of Michigan to O'Hare. We picked them up from the airport this morning and, needless to say, Katie was confused as fuck that I was in the car with Sawyer. Don't get me wrong, she was delighted to see me, but she couldn't hide her uncertainty. I don't blame her, though. I'm still confused myself.

Eric and Cole haven't spoken much since we got home from the hospital. We came directly to Sawyer's parents' house early this morning. Trying to make sense of the accident is nearly impossible.

Eric is almost eighteen, but Cole still has three years before he becomes of legal age. They both need guardians, and Sawyer steps up immediately. He has already called his landlord in Chicago to explain the situation and why he needs to break his lease. He plans to move all his stuff to the house in Haven Springs this week so he can look after his brothers. Katie and Ben, her husband, discuss with Sawyer about moving back home as well, but Sawyer says that isn't necessary. Eric and Cole are good kids, and Sawyer thinks he can handle things on his own.

Sawyer has been stressed all day, though I don't think anyone notices, so when he walks upstairs to his bedroom, I follow. Maybe I can talk with him alone to see how he is truly feeling. He is holding himself together very well, and I am concerned that he might finally break. No one can hold it together this well mentally or emotionally when their parents are killed without warning. He still hasn't shed a tear since he heard the news. I've cried, Eric and Cole have cried, Katie cried the second she got to the house that her parents no longer lived in. Everyone has broken down at one point or another. Everyone *except* Sawyer.

When I step into his room, he is sitting on the edge of his bed staring at a blank wall. I stand in the doorway for a minute before I walk toward the bed, closing the door behind me.

"My parents kept my room exactly as I left it, in case I ever decided to move back home," he says quietly.

I look around. "Yeah. It looks the same to me. You still even have that odd-shaped mirror behind your bed."

I've never understood why Sawyer wanted a mirror above his headboard. It is such a weird place to put a mirror. It isn't like he is going to stand on his bed to check himself out.

He snickers. "You hated that mirror."

"No," I say. "I hated where you decided to *put* that mirror."

He smiles and motions for me to sit next to him on the bed. I oblige.

"How are you holding up?" I ask.

"I don't know when it's going to hit me," he admits. "I feel like they're out of town or something and will be back tomorrow. It's kind of unbelievable to lose both of your parents at the same time."

"Yeah." I grab his hand and squeeze it gently. I want him to know I am feeling these emotions with him, that I am here for him.

"Thank you for staying with me, Ember. I don't know how I'm supposed to suddenly step into the parent role for Eric and Cole, but I know it's what I have to do. I'm so fucking lucky to have you by my side."

I smile. Part of me is still concerned about the fiancée comment he made last night at the hospital. I haven't even agreed to be his girlfriend. Life happens, though. Life *really* happened for this family, and I understand that circumstances change.

Yesterday I was excited about the kiss I had with Ace, but today I am more focused on helping Sawyer get through the death of his parents. I plan to be with him every step of the way and to help work through whatever struggles are ahead. Sawyer was my first and only love, and I can't imagine abandoning him in his time of need. I know he would do the same for me.

Sawyers hand reaches for my face, his thumb brushing against my cheek. He slowly draws me closer. His eyes look from mine down to my lips. I can tell he is about to kiss me. Maybe it's all the heightened emotions I'm feeling from the accident, but in this moment, I *want* him to kiss me.

Before I know it, his lips drift into mine. Every emotion, every sensation, every little thing I used to feel when we would kiss rushed back. It is as if time has been standing still and resumes with the meeting of our lips.

The last five years vanish, a mere figment of my imagination. Kissing Sawyer feels good. It feels *familiar*. We are back to being Ember and Sawyer. Ember and Sawyer are high school sweethearts. They are supposed to end up together. And maybe now they will. Maybe now *we* will.

My lips part to make way for Sawyer. His tongue slides into my mouth. We kiss passionately. He moans into my mouth, and it makes me want to pull him closer. His sounds vibrate in my mouth. I grab the back of his head with both hands and bring our bodies closer together until I am nearly straddling him.

Sawyer inches further onto the bed, bringing me with him. He places me on my back gently as he moves his muscular frame over me, never releasing our kiss.

"Fuck, baby," Sawyer says as he gasps for air.

I don't respond because his tongue is back in my mouth almost instantly. He moves his hands frantically, desperately trying to feel all of me as if I might disappear.

Having no clothes to change into at the hospital, I am still wearing the dress from our dinner. Sawyer reaches for the hem of the satin and places his warm hands on my thighs. His movement is slow as he inches up slowly, not stopping until he reaches the bottom wiring of my bra. He doesn't feel underneath; instead, his hands maneuver back down to the bottom of my dress. He pulls it up slowly, stopping midway, my pink lace thong visible.

He breaks our kiss, and I sigh from the loss. His eyes look down at my body as he takes all of me in. I know he wants my dress off, but he hasn't lifted it over my chest yet. I replace his hands with mine and slowly remove the satin, watching as Sawyer's eyes fill with desire.

I suppose people cope with grief differently. I am not sure how I would react if the roles were reversed. I can't say I would find comfort in bed with Sawyer if I received the same devastating news about my mom. But who am I to judge? Sawyer needs this right now, and I am the only one who can give it to him.

My dress is off, and my body is uncovered, except for my matching bra and panties. Sawyer places small delicate kisses down my cheek until he reaches my neck. I tilt my head, allowing him more access. He works his way down from my shoulder to my chest and doesn't stop until he reaches the top of my panties. He continues to place passionate kisses across my stomach and down my inner thighs until he reaches my feet. Everything Sawyer does to my body is unhurried and gentle. He never takes his eyes off me.

He slowly eases himself on top of me as his lips find mine again. Our kisses become rougher, filling with increasing desire. I tug at the bottom of his shirt. He pulls away from me as he lifts it over his head. He tosses his clothing to the side as he lays his bare chest on mine. The contact of our bare skin sends goose bumps down his back. I can feel them as I desperately draw him in for more.

"Fuck," he moans.

Sawyer suddenly stands, maneuvering to the side of the bed where he removes his pants, leaving them in a puddle of black next to the bed. I watch him. He can't hide the bulge being tamed beneath his boxer briefs. *I* did that to him. Our physical chemistry is undeniable, though I can't help but wonder how we got to this point so quickly.

He lays back on the bed, his back on the mattress, and ushers me on top of him. My legs fall on either side of his body and our chests press together. I feel him hard beneath me, pushing against the sensitive spot between my legs.

Sawyer slips his hand behind my back and unclasps my bra. He softly pulls down the strap on my left shoulder, followed by the right. It falls onto his chest. My breasts are completely bare and vulnerable to Sawyer, to his touch.

He tosses the bra onto the floor as he sits up. His lips fall to my chest as he sucks skillfully on my pebbled nipples. My head falls back, and I moan from the pleasure. He grabs at my hips, his fingers digging into my sides. He moves his tongue along my breasts, not leaving any surface untouched.

I glide myself over his hardness as he continues to slide his tongue across my body. He eventually finds his way back to my mouth, and my lips instantly part to let him in. His hands remain on my waist, assisting in the movement I make over him. Together, we create just enough friction to nearly send me over the edge.

"Ember," Sawyer says breathless.

"Yeah?" I moan.

"I need you to come, baby. Come for me."

It doesn't take long after his plea for the sensation to take over. My entire body trembles with Sawyer beneath me. It has been so long since I had an orgasm caused by a man, it leaves me completely weak. It's as if five years of pent-up tension had been locked away and Sawyer found the key, causing explosions to erupt throughout my body.

Once the trembling subsides, Sawyer moves out from underneath me, my arms still wrapped around him as he gently lays me onto my back. He stands again to remove his boxers. A glance at his hardness tells me just how ready he is, and I ache between my legs with anticipation. He pulls open the drawer of his nightstand to grab a condom. He slides the condom down his length before he makes his way back to the bed. He locks eyes with me as he reaches for my panties.

"I need to be inside you, Ember," he says with urgency.

I don't stop him. I need him inside of me, too. Instead, I reach my arms up and pull him onto me, his weight falling on top of me. It isn't long before he pushes himself inside of me, holding his own weight above me. The familiar yet forgotten pressure makes me gasp. He slowly pulls out before he slams back into me a second time. He splits me in two as he continues to thrust in and out. I wrap my legs around him, and we move in sync.

"Holy shit," he mumbles. "Holy shit, baby."

He continues to move in and out of me, becoming more desperate and frenzied with each thrust. His lips brush along my neck as he kisses me desperately. I can feel his breath on my skin as he gasps for air.

He moves his mouth to my ear, his lips finding my ear lobe as he gently tugs, causing me to moan.

"Ember," he grunts.

His pace quickens before his body tenses above me. I can feel his release as he pulses inside me. I hold onto him tightly until he reaches the end.

His body collapses on top of mine as he places breathless kisses on my collarbone.

"That was mind-blowing," he whispers.

chapter eight

Sawyer

She moved back to the Haven Springs a few months ago. I have had no choice but to do everything I've done leading up to this point. I fucked up big time the day she walked in on me nearly fucking Sarah Stanford, a slutty blonde who has the biggest rack I'd ever seen. Sarah and I hadn't gotten that far when Ember showed up.

I had gotten lazy. My sexual nature had taken over, and I hadn't been careful.

I was usually careful.

I should have known there was a chance she would show up at my place, especially because we had class that morning. Sarah ran out of there half-naked while Ember watched. She wasn't even that good a lay. But I'd been horny, and Sarah was putting out. She made it easy. *Too easy.* Ember was never easy.

Those first few years fucking sucked. After she broke up with me, she transferred to Cornell to finish her degree. That was my first dilemma: *New York.* How could I keep an eye on her when she lived so far away? I didn't think she had it in her to leave her mom behind. But she did. My girl is strong.

I finished my own degree through an online program. My family and friends were under the assumption that I lived near campus, but I took advantage of the remote learning aspect and spent most of my time at Cornell watching *her*.

Ember and I had scouted out apartments right before she left me, which was where I first met Tony, who served as the perfect cover. I recognized him from one of my classes the previous semester. Tony was the kind of student who was undoubtedly stoned ninety-five percent of the time, yet somehow made great grades and never missed a class. He was laid-back in his own way and always wore relaxed, dingy clothing. I could tell he'd do just about anything to get his hands on some cash, which I had a decent amount of.

I couldn't stay in New York with Ember longer than a few weeks at a time. I had to keep up appearances for my parents, my brothers, my teammates from high school. If people knew what I was doing, they wouldn't understand. It was better to keep them in the dark, to keep *her* in the dark. As much as I hated to be away from Ember, it was necessary for me to keep some semblance of a normal life. Ember would never take me back if she thought I was alone and desperate. She had always thought very highly of me, like I was the best she could ever have. And that's exactly what I wanted her to think. No one else could have her. No one else *would* have her.

I made an agreement with Tony to let me stay with him on the weekends that I had visitors, and in return, I would pay him. My family was wealthy enough from the success of The Plant that I could pay that guy chump change, and he'd be able to get high another day. All he had to do was occasionally pretend to be my roommate. I'd leave some of my belongings in the second bedroom of his apartment, friends and family would visit, and no one would ever suspect a thing. That arrangement only lasted the two years it took for Ember to finish school.

Lucky for me, I didn't have to scare away too many guys who tried to get in her pants in New York. She hardly seemed interested in anyone anyway. She was probably still heartbroken over our breakup, as she should be. The only real threat I ever faced was during her last semester. I noticed that she'd been spending extra time before and after lectures with a guy who I later figured out was from one of her classes. They spent way more time together than I would have liked. I could have put an end to it sooner, but Ember never looked interested in the loser.

One Saturday night, as I was parked outside her apartment, I recognized that same guy walking to her door. He was dressed in jeans and a button-up shirt, not the casual attire he wore when they hung out during the week. Did that low life actually have the balls to ask her out on a date? Ember never did anything that would suggest she wanted him to take her out. They never touched, they never kissed. I knew her body language better than anyone, and he did *nothing* for her.

I watched as Ember opened the door, dressed beautifully in light jeans and a pink sweater that hung loosely off her shoulder. She *always* looked beautiful. He escorted her to an old beat-up Ford, and I scoffed when I followed them into the parking lot of a cheap buffet in town. Ember was worth more than that shitty place had to offer.

I had the perfect view of their table through one of the windows in the restaurant and was pleased when I saw her disinterest. Ember's eyes didn't sparkle as he spoke. Her lips didn't curl into that adorable smile of hers when she looked at him. She hadn't even picked her nails, which was her telltale sign of being nervous. He didn't make her anxious because they had no chemistry. My girl and I *never* lacked sexual chemistry. Once the dinner was over, I was sure she would tell him to get lost.

He drove her back to her apartment complex, walked her to the door, and tried to invite himself in. Lucky for me, Ember didn't take the bait. You'd have to be blind not to see how uninterested she was. But *hell*, he must have been blind, because before he walked away that stupid fucking asshole kissed her.

Livid, I stood back watching. I watched him kiss her perfect fucking lips. Those were *my* perfect fucking lips. It took everything in me not to pummel him right in front of her, but that would have defeated the purpose of my being there. I couldn't let her know that I had never truly let her go, that I would *never* let her go. One day she would understand why I followed her there, why I watched her, but it wasn't that day.

After their short-lived kiss, he finally walked back to his truck with a smug grin on his face, leaving Ember to escape back into her apartment alone. With my fists clenched, I couldn't hold back anymore. I met him at his truck and threw him against the door, his shirt balled up in my fist. I threatened that fucker's life. I told him if he ever even *looked* in Ember's direction again, I would beat his ass.

It really was that easy. Ember stopped spending extra time with him, and he never showed up to her place again. I knew she didn't want to be with a lowlife like him, but I never wanted to give him the opportunity to touch her again. He didn't try to argue. He hadn't even put up a fight. Maybe he didn't think she was worth it. What a fucking idiot.

That girl is worth it all.

I didn't have to get rid of many others while in New York, only the occasional guy here and there. It was much easier to keep an eye on her in Chicago, though it got a little more difficult to keep the men away. They were vultures, but who could blame them? Ember was sexy as hell. She had no idea how attractive she was, which only made her more appealing.

She sought out a few men herself, but they never saw a second date, thanks to me. I hired some much scarier people to threaten whoever tried to get close to her, and it worked. For that reason, she never loved another man.

Only me.

She lived with Taylor those few years in Chicago. I used to watch her through the window of my apartment. I had the perfect view of her bedroom across the way. I, of course, had followed her there, to the city, as I had followed her over the last several years. Directly in my line of vision was the most beautiful woman I would ever lay eyes on. She had a body that I couldn't resist. I watched her every night. I couldn't even count the amount of times I got off just by eyeing her. Watching Ember undress herself was almost as good as the real thing. *Almost.*

I've worked for my father's company since I graduated college. He took over the marshmallow factory after my grandfather passed away. I oversee operations and business dealings with the various markets we sell our product to. It is my family business that allows me the freedom to be anywhere I want at any time, and it is convenient as hell.

I have known about her move back to Haven Springs for some time now. I never stopped watching her, after all. I've visited her new house a few times, though she doesn't know. I have to do whatever I can to be closer to her. Sometimes I sneak in while she sleeps, and other times I enjoy the coziness of her living room while she is at work.

Ember has chosen a picturesque neighborhood to live in, only a few minutes from my parents' house. Once we get back together, we'll get our own place, or she will move in with me for the time being. I won't have it any other way.

I had been so close to getting to spend my life with her before I fucked it all up. There is no way I will do that again. Nothing is going to get in my way this time.

Before I show up on Ember's doorstep, I have to ensure some sort of explanation as to how I know where she lives. Obviously, I don't *actually* need to find out where she lives, but I need a paper trail, per se, that leads to someone else in case she questions how I found her.

Mallory is one of our mutual friends. She is just another high-pitched, high-strung, annoying slut from high school. Yeah, I've slept with her. And Ember doesn't know. Mallory annoys the shit out of me, but she's always been a decent fuck. I've called her occasionally over the last few years if I ever needed to bust my load into someone, especially after Lisa and Beth didn't work out. My hand can only do so much.

I make a vow to myself that once I win Ember back, I will remain faithful to her. She is worth as much. But in the meantime, a man still has needs. Mallory is always more than willing to accommodate.

It's easy getting Mallory to tell me where Ember lives. I tell her that my mom wants to surprise Ember with a housewarming gift and needs her address. Still high on the orgasm I gave her, she relents. It is a believable lie. Mallory doesn't even hesitate when she texts me the address.

I decide to show up on a beautiful Friday afternoon in May, because it's been exactly *five years* since Ember left me on my driveway. Five years to the day when the most magnificent woman I had ever met left me. She has no idea how heartbroken I was. How heartbroken I *am*.

I always knew Ember had to be mine. It didn't matter how many times we broke up, or if she was the one who had ultimately broken up with me. We would end up together. Ember belongs to me. Deep down, she knows it too.

I knew the first time I laid eyes on Ember that she would be my wife. Hell, I told her that much at the homecoming parade. She was so shy and innocent. Her incorruptibility was attractive to me. She looked damn sexy in everything she ever wore, showing off her perfectly curvy yet petite figure. I have always been attracted to platinum blondes, but Ember's hair fell in waves and was a mixture of dark and light colors. It was beautiful. *She* was beautiful. I knew I had to have her.

Ember fell in love with me quickly. It only took a few dates and a hell of a lot of wooing before I had her wrapped around my finger. She was easy to love back. I never loved anyone before, not the way I loved her.

It took nearly a year before she finally allowed me to have sex with her. Of course, I had been fucking other girls the entire time, but none of them had my devotion. I would have done anything for Ember, anything but stay faithful.

That's changed now. I saw the hurt on her face when she walked in on me and Sarah. It killed me to see what I had done to her.

I will never let her leave again. I will never give her a reason to leave again. I was an idiot back then. No fuck was worth the woman I love.

The first time I made love to Ember was the most warm and intimate moment I had ever experienced in my life. Sex with her was unlike sex with anyone else. When my hands glided over her perfectly smooth skin and her incredible curves, it was enough to nearly send me over the edge, but I was determined to make it special for her. I had to hold it together, make it last as long as I could. Her moans and the way she gripped my hair tightly when I sent her into her first orgasm was enough to send me into a spiral of my own. I knew it was different with her after that.

No one could drive me quite as crazy as she could. My body needs her, *I* need her. I was hardly fifteen years old when I took her virginity, and I had already slept with half the girls at our school, but something about Ember left me wanting more and more.

After we slept together, it only solidified my intentions. I wanted to be with her for the rest of my life. Unfortunately, that wasn't enough to stop me from fucking my way through high school. Sure, I had broken up with her a few times after word got out of my infidelity. I had to stay in control of our relationship. I had to keep the power.

Ember felt lucky to call me hers, and I knew that. I took advantage of that. Whenever she'd find out that I had been with another girl, I used our relationship as an excuse. I blamed something she had done that drove me away. I made her take the blame. Truth is, it was never her fault. She didn't drive me away. I was just a fucking idiot. But I don't regret making her think it was. I needed to stay in control, and it worked. She always took me back. She knew I could have anyone, but I wanted *her,* and that made her feel damn special. My only regret is that she caught me with Sarah on my couch. That was the first and last time Ember would ever leave me.

She probably won't remember that it has been exactly five years, but there is no way I can ever forget. I plan on spending the five-year anniversary of our breakup by showing up on her driveway and winning her back.

I know getting her back this time is going to be difficult. For the first time, Ember has control.

This time is going to be different. Not only am I going to convince Ember to fall in love with me again, this time I am going to make her my wife. This time, I won't fail.

chapter nine

Sawyer

I know she'll get home from work around four today. I show up about a half hour early so that I'll already be here when she gets home.

I see her car as it turns into the cul-de-sac.

I watch as she pulls into her driveway. She steps out of the car, and my gaze falls over her.

Damn, is she beautiful.

Ember never fails to take my breath away. Her beauty is unmatched. No one will ever measure up.

I slowly step out of my car that is parked on the street. I stand with my door open as she grabs her things from the back seat. When she stands up, we make eye contact. She sees me for the first time. Her beautiful emerald-colored eyes look into mine. They are wide. She is surprised to see me, as I expect. After all this time, I am standing in front of her house, in front of her.

There were only a few instances over the years that I have been this close to her. Each time, I wanted to get closer, to reach out and touch her, but I couldn't. It is easiest to be near her when she goes out to crowded bars and gets too drunk for her own good.

If for some reason Ember did see me out, I would have played it off as a coincidence or maybe even twist it around and blame it on fate. I had to have a lot of self-control and wait for the perfect moment to enter her life again. I had to make the moment unforgettable for her. When I woke up this morning, I knew it was time.

All I can do as I stand here, with this beautiful woman staring back at me, is take all of her in. She has the most enthralling body. I have her perfect curves memorized, but they never cease to amaze me. I want more than anything to touch her, place my hands on her tiny waist and pull her close. And in time, I will. She is so beautiful. I can't help but picture her naked.

My groin tightens.

I try to think of anything else. Ponies. Pigs. Grandmas in thongs. I have to pull it together. Now is not the time to let my dick do the talking.

After I gain some semblance of control, thanks to imagining a very unattractive ninety-year-old in a thong, I walk up the driveway toward the lovely creature before me. She stands still.

"Hey, Ember," I say.

She doesn't speak, and she still hasn't moved a muscle. Her eyes never leave mine. Frankly, I am not sure if they even blink.

I continue, "Mallory said you moved back. I tried calling, but I figured my number is probably still blocked. I was hoping we could talk."

Thank you, Mallory.

She still hasn't responded. Instead, she turns around, her back toward me as she walks to the front door.

This is going to be harder than I thought.

I quickly follow and call out for her again. "Wait, Ember! *Please.* I just want to talk."

"What could we possibly have to talk about, Sawyer?"

"*Please,*" I plead.

85

She relents. "Fine. Come in."

I glance around her house, acting as though it is my first time inside. The foyer has tall ceilings, the space very open and spacious. It attaches to the living room and eventually the kitchen. She has a spiral staircase near the kitchen that leads to her bedroom.

I glance at the stairs, picturing the moment I finally whisk her away and make love to her again. I have imagined it so many times before. There won't be a surface of this house that I won't cover. Ember and I will make love everywhere. We will need to, to make up for all the time apart.

I take a seat at the kitchen table while she brews a pot of coffee. She hands me a cup with cream and sugar.

She remembers how I like my coffee.

She sits across the table from me, staring at her own cup of coffee before she finally meets my gaze.

She is so fucking perfect.

Her beautiful porcelain skin looks soft and smooth. I want so badly to graze my hand over her cheek, to feel her skin beneath mine again. I long to touch her. Her eyes are heavy, but they are still beautiful. The perfect hue of green.

"Why are you here, Sawyer?" she asks.

I take a deep breath before I begin to win back my girl.

"I was a really shitty boyfriend to you."

"You can say that again."

I try not to take offense. She is right. "I took advantage of how much you loved me because I never thought you would be the one to leave me. I was such a fucking idiot for thinking my immature behavior could last. I never thought I would lose you, Ember."

"And yet, you did."

Not exactly. I have never truly lost her, though she can believe what she wants. She will know the truth one day.

I nod. "You know, I was going to propose to you that year. How could I have been so stupid to think I even deserved to marry you? I know we were happy together, but I was so dishonest with you. I lied. I cheated. I was an awful boyfriend. And even after all that, I thought you would *still* want to marry me."

I know she wanted to marry me. She had been in love with me. She still is, she just needs more time to realize it. If she hadn't walked in on Sarah and me, there would already be a giant rock on her finger.

"Ember, I am so sorry. I have been wanting to say this to you for a long fucking time. You are the most amazing, kind, and beautiful woman I have ever laid eyes on. You're even more beautiful today than you were the first time I saw you, and I don't even know how that's possible. My life has been miserable since the day you left me on my driveway. I have to try, Ember. I have to try and win you back."

That is fucking convincing.

Not that it isn't the truth. I mean every word.

"I've changed, Ember. I came here today because I was hoping you might give me another chance," I say, making sure to get my point across.

She looks surprised at my words, that I would want her back.

Why would that surprise her?

What man on this earth is crazy enough not to want her? Though I suppose it's my fault she might feel that way. She hasn't met a man yet that is willing to fight for her. They all walked away willingly after I got involved. But I will fight for her. She is worth it.

"I have a boyfriend," she lies.

Is she playing hard to get?

I play along. "How serious is it?"

"Pretty serious," she lies again.

I sense her fear. She's afraid I'll hurt her again. Why else would she lie?

I won't do that again, baby. Never again.

"Ember."

She doesn't speak.

"Ember, I have been spending every day of the last *five years* trying to better myself. Trying to better myself for *you*. I never stopped loving you."

"Sawyer, this is ridiculous."

"Please, hear me out. I dated a few women over the years, and I compared them all to you. No one came even remotely close. I used those relationships to improve the kind of partner I could be. The kind of man I could be. I want to be that man for you, Ember. I love you. I *still* love you. I've always loved you."

I know she wants this. My words mean something to her. Hell, they mean something to *me*. They are the truth. I will make Ember the happiest woman in the world. Nothing will stop me.

She takes a deep breath. I expect her to make this challenging. I know how this works. She can't take me back after my first plea, though I have no doubt she wants to. Ember can't resist me. She may be stronger now, more independent, but deep down, she craves me. She wants this as much as I do. She will take me back. She always does.

"I stopped loving you. I have *not* spent the last five years bettering myself for a relationship with you. I broke up with you, *remember?* I did that because I was ready to be done with you, with *us*. Breaking up and getting back together was so easy for you. It wasn't easy for me. I took back more and more of my heart after each breakup. By the time I had enough of your shit, I had my entire heart back. I didn't even cry when I left your house that day, Sawyer. I was *relieved*."

It had not been easy for me. How can she think it was easy for me? It has been hard fucking work making sure she never got away while we'd been broken up. It's been anything but easy. I would have done anything I had to do to keep her, even back then.

Her words sting, mostly because she has no fucking clue what she is talking about. I continue to play along. If Ember wants to be in control, then so be it. I let her think she got away from me, but she never did. She has always been mine. She will *always* be mine.

"But we are supposed to be together…"

"No, Sawyer. We aren't supposed to be together. We dated a long time ago. We are different people now. I'm sorry, but I can't do this. Not again."

She walks toward the front door.

Does she want me to leave already?

I watch this captivating human walk away from me. I have never looked at another woman like I look at Ember. She must know that I love her, that I am in love with her and always have been.

My eyes speak the truth no matter the lies I've told. I can't lie about my feelings. I fucking love her.

I stand up slowly. I will continue to plead with her and do whatever I need to until she takes me back. "Please, just give me a chance. Let me prove to you that I'm a different man. I'll do better this time. You have to believe me."

She picks at her nails. "I will unblock your number. I can't promise you that I will respond to your texts or calls, but it's a start, okay? I'm not agreeing to date you. I'm not even agreeing *to go* on a date with you. Right now, all I am willing to do is unblock your phone number."

Fuck. Yes. I can work with that.

I smile.

I can't resist her another moment longer. I have to touch her. I have to feel her soft skin against mine. I have to feel her breath on me.

I walk toward her slowly. I can feel my breathing becoming more shallow. She still has the same effect on me. My body always reacts to hers.

I wrap my arms around her petite frame and embrace her. I feel her as she breathes into my chest. It is warm and comforting. She doesn't hug me back, but I don't care. I have her where I want her.

After a few moments, I can finally feel her relax against my chest. I know she can feel what I'm feeling. It feels right. We belong together.

I place a soft kiss on the top of her head. Her hair smells of vanilla and cucumbers.

"Thank you," I whisper.

As much as it pains me, I have to let her go for now. I walk toward the front door, but right before I step out, I look back at her and smile.

"I'll talk to you soon, Ember."

I wink just before I close the door.

She watches me through the window as I step into my car. As my car pulls away, I glance in the rearview mirror. I can still see her. She pulls out her phone. She finally unblocks me.

Happy Anniversary, baby.

chapter ten

Sawyer

I park around the block and wait to see what she'll do, as I do most nights. Shortly after I leave, I watch as she drives away.

Where are you going, Ember?

I follow her.

She pulls into a bar known as the Bungalow. Maybe she's meeting someone there. But who? It isn't normal for her to go to a bar alone. Ember hardly drinks unless Taylor drags her out. Could this have anything to do with me?

I watch her through the glass windows from my car. She saunters up to the bar and takes a seat by herself, but she isn't alone for long. I watch as multiple men approach her, offering to buy her drinks, I assume. She is a beautiful woman sitting at a bar alone. However, she never lets any of them stay. She happily takes the drinks they offer, and after a few moments, they leave.

That's my girl.

It's late, but I don't leave. The bar is supposed to close in five minutes. It is nearly three in the morning, and Ember still sits inside drinking alone.

She must be inebriated by now. There is no fucking way that girl can drive home tonight. Maybe she'll call and ask me for a ride. I hope she will.

She suddenly stands up unsteadily from her seat. I've never seen her drink as much as she has tonight. I'll stay until she has a safe ride home. I can't risk something bad happening to her.

Just when I think she might be calling for a ride, I hear her yell at someone right as the door opens to the bar and an old man hurries out. I have no idea what happened, but I can't help but laugh. That girl never fails to make me smile.

After watching the old man rush to his car, I glance back to the small window in the door that gives me the perfect view of her just as she collapses. I almost jump out of my car to help her. I have the door open, with one foot outside, but the bartender moves from behind the bar and attends to her quickly. She isn't responding to him as her limp body lies on the floor of the bar.

I rush out of my car. I have to get closer to make sure she is okay. The bartender picks her up, and the sight of his hands on her body is enough to make me green with envy. I don't like seeing another man's hands on my woman.

I peek through another one of the windows as I watch him carry her through the back. I notice that the door opens to a staircase that leads upstairs. I watch his hand placement carefully as he carries her over his shoulders. If that motherfucker tries to take advantage of an unconscious woman, I will fucking kill him myself. *Especially* because that woman is Ember.

I know I have to do something. I have to make sure he won't touch her, take advantage of her. I have to make sure she is okay. I can't help the jealousy that runs through my veins. I want to rescue her. I want to be the one who saves her.

He'd better not fucking touch her.

I have to get inside, but how? I check the entrance to the Bungalow.

Damn.

It's locked. The bartender must have locked up from the inside before that old man left. I look around the building and find an old fire escape. The bar is in the historic district of town, so the buildings are quite old. Lucky for me, the fire escape is an easy way to access the second level.

I pull down the old rusted retractable ladder and climb to the first landing. One more set of stairs stand between me and the top floor of the building. I climb hurriedly as if her life depends on it, because it might. The landing at the top is long, extending between four windows evenly spaced across the building.

I rush to the farthest window that allows me to peek into a bedroom. She isn't there, so I move to the next. That one looks into a hallway, but again, I can't see her. The third and fourth window exposes the open living room and kitchen, as well as the door that I assume leads back downstairs to the bar.

Finally, I eye her sitting on the gray cushioned sofa. I have the perfect view of her through the fourth window. She is awake now, which comes as a relief. She won't let this man take advantage of her, not while she is conscious. I peer to the other side of the room where I see the bartender stand. I can hear their muffled voices through the window, making out only a few of their words. And then, I hear my name. Her sweet voice and those beautiful lips speak my name.

Sawyer.

I long for her to repeat it.

Say my name again.

And she does.

Sawyer.

She fucking says it again.

She is talking about me. It only confirms that I am the reason she has to drink tonight. Ember needs to get me off her mind. I *like* that I am on her mind. She finally has a taste of how I've felt for the last decade. I can never get her off my mind. *Never.* Even when I was inside someone else, I pictured Ember. She is all I think about, all I *want* to think about.

I wear a huge fucking grin on my face the entire time as I try to listen to their conversation. I want to hear what she has to say about me. I want to know what she thought about today, about my coming back for her. But the words are too inaudible through the old brick and glass-sealed windows that pose as an unwelcome barrier. Either way, I am thrilled that she is even thinking about me.

He eventually shows her to the bedroom. I watch closely and wait until he closes the door behind him, leaving her alone. I follow him through the windows back to the room with the couch.

Good.

If he had tried to sleep in the same bed as her, I would have choked him out in front of her.

I switch back to the window that looks into the bedroom. She doesn't undress for bed as I hoped. I am slightly disappointed. Ember drank a lot tonight, and she will be sound asleep soon. I can sneak in through the—*dammit.* It's locked. That won't work.

I wait until Ember falls asleep before I move back to the living room window and see that the bartender is sound asleep on the couch.

I climb down the ladder to the first landing, then back down to the ground. I lift the retractable ladder until it is safely stowed the way I found it and walk back to my car. I can sleep there for a few hours while I wait for her to wake up. Once inside, I lean my seat back and picture Ember and that glorious body of hers, naked.

Fuck.

I wake up and check the time. It is nearly ten in the morning. I look to the left, where her car is still parked in the lot. She hasn't left yet. My car is the only other car in the parking lot. I contemplate moving it, though I don't think Ember would recognize it. As long as I stay out of sight, she won't know it is me.

I rub my hands over my face and sigh. "Ember, what are you doing?" I say to myself.

It is broad daylight out. I can't very well climb back up the fire escape and peek inside. Someone will see me.

I wait impatiently, tapping my foot to the floorboard. Another hour passes before she finally walks out the entrance of the Bungalow. I recline in my seat again, making sure I can still see her through my front window as I lie back.

She doesn't walk out alone. She is accompanied by the bartender, who clearly hasn't bothered to put on a shirt this morning. I give him the once over. Dark hair. Blue eyes. Chiseled jaw line. Definitive abs. The guy is ripped, I'll give him that. I am in shape myself, but my muscles aren't as defined as his.

Should I be worried? Is he Ember's type?

No one compares to me, and I know that. Ember knows it too. I am the best there is in this town. I have a laundry list of ladies who will gladly fall into bed with me. Too bad I only desire one.

Ember.

The bartender accompanies her to the car.

What a fucking gentleman.

I wish he would have put a goddamn shirt on. But I have to remember, the only reason Ember is here is because of me. She can't get me out of her head, that's how big of an impact I made yesterday. She isn't here for the bartender.

She is here for me, I think to myself, repeating those five words over and over in my head.

"It was very nice to meet you, Ember," I hear him say.

I don't like the tone of his voice. He is sweet-talking her. I would know, I always know the right thing to say. No one else should talk to my Ember that way. He'd better watch his back.

"It was nice meeting you too," her sweet voice says.

I love her innocence. Problem is, he probably loves it too.

"I know I already said this, but I *really* want to see you again."

Oh, hell no.

He won't be seeing her again if I have anything to say about it, and I do. I'll have to keep an eye on him. That asshole better watch his back.

"Come back soon, please. Bye, Ember," he says.

Ember's honied voice replies. "Bye, Ace. Thanks for looking out for me last night."

Ace? What the fuck kind of name is that?

I watch as her car veers out of the parking lot. I sit tight for a few minutes as I watch Ace stand still in the parking lot. I don't like the look on his face. He is smitten. I can read that guy's face like a fucking book. I know exactly what he is thinking, exactly why he wants to see her again.

I have to talk to him. I need to know more.

After he walks back inside the bar, I step out of my car. It is now or never. I have to get back to Ember and soon, before this guy fucks it up.

I walk toward the entrance. The '*Closed*' sign hangs visibly, but I don't give a shit. I know he is inside.

I knock on the door.

I can see a now-clothed Ace walk toward the door through the window. He's still wearing the sweats he had on earlier, but thankfully he has finally decided to put on a shirt.

"Can I help you?" he asks, the door partly open.

"What time do you open?"

His head turns to the hours that are blatantly displayed on the door. I don't care. I want him to talk. I need to get inside.

He points to the bar hours. "Says right here. Today we open at noon."

I look at my watch. Another forty-five minutes.

"Damn," I say, grabbing the back of my head with my hand. "My car just started acting funny. I pulled into your lot not too long ago when I realized I left my phone at home. Mind if I borrow yours?"

He looks over my shoulder at my car. "Yeah, man. No problem. Come on in."

I step into the Bungalow and take a seat on one of the barstools. Ace walks behind the bar and hands me his cell phone.

"Here you go, er…"

"Tom," I say. "You can call me Tom."

"Nice to meet you, Tom. Name's Ace."

I force a smile. I discreetly scroll through his phone searching for Ember's name. She isn't there.

Good. She didn't give him her number. *That's my girl.*

I still needed to keep an eye on this guy. Something tells me he won't back off as easily as the others had.

I type in my home phone number that is no longer in service and pretend to speak with my mom. "All right, thanks. I'll do that. See you soon. Love you too. Bye," I say into the phone.

I hand Ace back his phone. "Thanks. I appreciate it. I'm going to meet someone down the street and get the problem taken care of. You have a good rest of your day."

"You as well, Tom."

I walk outside, sit inside my perfectly running vehicle, and drive away.

I drive past Ember's street to make sure she got home safe before I return to the house I grew up in. I've been staying with my parents several nights a week since Ember moved back into the suburbs. There isn't a need for my apartment in the city anymore, not since she moved out of her place with Taylor. I'll get rid of it soon and find a way to break my lease.

Thoughts of Ace still flood my head.

She was there for me. She was there for me. She was there for me.

I repeat it over and over. If I can't get him out of my head, what has he done to hers?

I need to get that fucking bartender off her mind, and mine too, and focus her thoughts back on me.

I pull out my phone and send her a text message.

Me: Hey, beautiful. I hope you had some time to think about what I said yesterday. I meant it, Ember. All of it. I hope you'll give me the chance to prove it to you.

I click send. That should do it.
It takes a few minutes before she finally answers.

Ember: Hey. I've been persuaded to at least text you back. Nothing more, yet.
Me: Yet? So, there's hope. I'll take it.
Ember: You can't see me, but I'm rolling my eyes.
Me: You have the prettiest eyes.

If there is anything I am good at, *other than fucking*, it's complimenting a lady.

She never answers my last text, but it's okay. I needed her to think of me again, and that will do it. And thankfully, I know she isn't texting Ace.

I am slowly making my way back into her heart, and I love every fucking second of it.

I spend the day with my brothers shooting the shit. They are younger than me, but they are still a good time. I love those guys a lot, but I'd never love anyone as much as I love Ember. She will always come first, no matter what.

I feel the need to stop by Ember's again. It has only been a few hours since I've driven by. She'll most likely still be at home, and if she wasn't, I'd find her.

As I drive by her street, I notice Taylor's red Volkswagen Beetle parked in the driveway. No wonder she hasn't texted me back all day, she has company.

Her front window expands across the front of her house, and I see them sitting on her tan-colored sectional in the living room. I also notice the empty wine bottles on the coffee table. So long as Taylor goes home at the end of the night, I'll have another opportunity to get close to Ember. A movie plays in the background. I can't tell what it is, but that is hardly the point of my watching. I've only come to watch her.

Ember and Taylor's movie nights started back in high school, and there is a pattern to them. After the first time I told Ember I loved her, they had a movie night. After the first time we had sex, they had a movie night. After we had our first pregnancy scare, they had a movie night. They only have movie nights after something significant happens, and something significant had happened this time.

Me.

A couple of hours pass before I watch Taylor get picked up. Her red Bug remains in the driveway.

I leave my car parked down the street and walk stealthily toward the house and around the back until I am in her backyard. I want to get closer to Ember.

I need to.

My craving for her has only grown stronger since last night. I held her for the first time in so long, and I want to do it more. But for now, just being near her will have to do.

I love to watch her sleep. That's what I'll do tonight. She always looks beautiful, but when she's asleep, she's alluring, *peaceful*. I can't wait to sleep next to her again, to be the one lying next to her when she lets go of the world. The time will come soon enough, and I'll never let her leave my bed again. I smile, knowing she hasn't slept next to any other man besides me. I am the only man that will ever be lucky enough to see her at her most vulnerable.

Ember keeps a spare key to her garage door under a planter in the backyard. Her mom had done the same thing when they lived together, so it is easy to figure out where she keeps hers. I sneak in often, whenever I can, but I have to be cautious and only do so on nights when she drinks enough wine. Wine makes her sleep heavily, and I know she won't wake until the morning.

I walk inside the back door that leads into the garage, then inside another door until I am standing inside her family room. Her bedroom is up the spiral staircase near the kitchen. I step quietly up the steps until I stand inside the doorframe of her bedroom.

The covers hang slightly off her, just enough to see her bare leg peeking out. She lies there placidly, sound asleep, in nothing but a giant T-shirt.

She used to sleep in my T-shirts.

I remain in her doorway for a few extra moments, taking in the sight of her.

Fuck, she is gorgeous. Even more so than I remember. How is that even possible?

I step closer to the bed, thanks to my need to see more. I have to get closer to her. It's going to be so hard not to touch her when she looks so heavenly, but I can't risk her waking up. I don't want to scare her. My being here is harmless, and soon she will welcome me into her bedroom. But for now, she can't know I am here.

She breathes heavily as I carefully move the blanket to uncover her, exposing her tranquil body before me.

Dammit. I still need to see more. I cautiously place my hand on the hem of her T-shirt, lifting it over her stomach until her panties show. She's wearing a dark purple laced thong, and I am instantly hard.

I back away a few feet, taking in the sight of her. I have to have her, and soon. I reach into my jeans, the effect she has on me restrained tightly in the denim. I am so hard. The sight of her always does that to me.

I stroke my dick as I watch her. I imagine what it would feel like to have her warm mouth on me again. I picture fucking her right here on the bed.

I can't wait to fuck her again.

I stroke faster. Faster. It doesn't take long before I come in my pants.

"Fuck," I whisper, trying to hold back my groans.

I take one last look at her before I walk out.

chapter eleven

Sawyer

I wake up the next morning feeling rejuvenated, something I feel after most nights I'm able to see her. I was able to release the pent-up tension building inside of me, just waiting to be free with the sight of Ember. She has a hold on me that I will never deny. I crave her body, her touch, and if I can't fuck her yet, what happened last night is the next best thing.

The words, *she was there for me,* continue to repeat in my head. I still can't shake the thought of the possible threat of the bartender. I have to do something about Ace, but what? What can I do? She hasn't tried to see him again, and I have to believe that she won't, not with me in the picture.

Regardless, I find myself driving to the Bungalow yet again. I sit in the parking lot, watching through the window as he bartends again. Luckily, there is no sign of Ember.

I watch his every move and his facial expressions. I watch to see if he will hit on any girls. Maybe that is his personality. I can't fault the guy for that. If I see a pretty girl, it is nearly impossible for me to ignore her. But that has to change. It already has. Ember is the only girl I will be interested in from here on out. This guy, on the other hand? He can have anyone he wants, so long as it isn't my girl.

I stay in the parking lot for a few hours. It is uneventful for the most part. Sunday is clearly not their busiest day. Ember hasn't shown up, and that makes me too fucking pleased.

I leave and drive past Ember's house. Taylor's Beetle is gone, the light is on in the kitchen, and I can see Ember working feverously at the kitchen table.

She doesn't leave the house at all this evening, so I eventually return to my parents to make some phone calls to the new vendors for work. I still have to make some money despite the funds I have stored away in a separate account. I am prepared for my future with Ember, and money will never be an issue for us. Ember will have anything she ever wants, and I will have her. She is all I want.

Monday morning didn't come soon enough. It has been three days since the anniversary of our breakup. Three days since I surprised Ember and pleaded with her to take me back. I have already confessed my love for her, planted the seed. Now, I need to spend time with her, allow her to get to know me again so she can remember all the reasons she fell in love with me in the first place. I can't expect her to understand me the way I did her.

I plan on stopping over at her place this afternoon. This time, I won't remain in my car and watch from afar. I will breeze up her driveway as I did last Friday and insist on spending time together. Perhaps I'll even stay the night. But if I have any intentions of being there to say goodnight, I need to start the day out strong. I need to be on her mind. I pull out my cell phone and send her a good morning text.

Me: Good morning, beautiful. I hope you have a great day at work.
Ember: Good morning. Thanks, hope you have a great day at...wait, do you work? I don't even know what you do.

She is showing interest.

Me: You can't see me, but I'm smiling. I work for my dad's company. Can't escape the family business...But at least I mostly get to work from home.

Ember: No kidding, you decided to work at The Plant after all. I bet your dad was happy about that. I'm an instructor now at Haven Springs University.

Me: I can't say he wasn't thrilled. An instructor, huh? You never cease to amaze me.

Anyone who can put up with horny college kids daily should be given an award. Ember deserves all the praise I can give her.

Once our text conversation is over, I drive to the local flower shop in town. I already knew where she works, but now that she has told me that piece of information personally, I can send her gifts. I want to shower her with rose petals and water lilies. But knowing her, she'll be embarrassed. I'll keep it simple, like Ember. She is simple, and beautiful, and elegant. She is *perfect*.

I order a small elegant arrangement filled with white and red roses, with baby's breath sprinkled throughout. They have the option for delivery, but I want to ensure their safe arrival myself.

I look at my watch. The flowers will be ready in two hours, just in time for Ember's lunch break. She won't see me as I deliver them, and that is the point. I want to surprise her with a beautiful gift, something I didn't do when we were younger. I won't make that mistake again.

I deliver the flowers without a hitch during her lunch break and write a personal note to leave inside the display. Afterward, I drop by the bar again to watch over Ace for a bit. He is bartending again. Things seem fine over here, so I am not as concerned as I was the last few days.

A few hours later, as I drive into her neighborhood, I think of the smile that likely spread across her features when she walked into her classroom and saw the arrangement of flowers. I want to witness that smile in person.

I wait a few extra moments before I turn into her cul-de-sac, expecting her to be home any minute. I expect her to be excited to see me again. I know I am excited as fuck to see her.

When I arrive, she is already inside. I pull into her driveway and sit for a few moments before I step out of the car. I can see her watching me through the window. Her face doesn't look happy, but it doesn't look angry either. Maybe she didn't see the flowers? I know I left them in the right lecture hall. If she got them, why isn't she happier to see me? Does it have anything to do with Ace?

I tense at the thought of him. Pacing back and forth, I anticipate what my plan of action is going to be.

After a few moments though I know it can't be Ace. As far as I know, she hasn't so much as spoken to the man since she left that morning. Maybe she is still playing hard to get.

Fuck, Ember.

It's working. I have never wanted her more in my life. She isn't making it easy on me this time.

"Chill the fuck out," I whisper to myself.

I need to get my shit together. I contemplate my decision to knock on her front door, though it is pointless. I have every intention of knocking on her fucking door.

I walk the rest of the way up her driveway and knock. She doesn't answer, so I knock again.

Finally, she opens the door.

She looks sexy as hell.

She is still wearing her clothes from work and is by far the sexiest teacher I've ever laid eyes on. If I had a professor like her in college, there is no doubt I would have bent her over and fucked her on top of her desk.

See? Horny kids.

I smile at her.

"Hi," she says.

"I'm sorry to show up unannounced again. I wanted to make sure you got your flowers," I say apologetically.

"You could've made sure of that through texts, Sawyer."

"You're right. I just…wanted to see you again."

After a few moments, she opens the door and invites me in. "Would you like something to drink?"

I don't answer. I'm not some random guest that she needs to be hospitable for. I am Sawyer. She is Ember. Why is she acting like this? Is she mad that I'm here?

As if she can read my thoughts she says, "It's fine that you're here, Sawyer, I'm not mad."

She isn't mad.

I walk closer to the beautiful woman standing before me, wearing tan heels and a tight black dress.

Damn. I can't resist. I pull her into my arms, into my embrace, as I wrap her small body in mine like I have so many times before. She fits perfectly in my arms. I smell the familiar vanilla and cucumber scent in her hair. It is captivating.

And then, she does something she hadn't before. She hugs me back. Her small arms reach around my back and cling to me as I hold her.

We stand like this for several minutes. It takes everything in me not to kiss her right there. Holding her feels so right, and I know she feels it too.

"I've missed this so much, Ember. I could hold you for the rest of my life and never grow tired of it."

After we hold onto each other for a little while longer, we separate. The loss is unbearable. I want to pull her back immediately, but I settle for a soft kiss on the top of her head.

She leads me into the kitchen. It is dinner time, but she hasn't prepared anything yet.

"Are you hungry?" I ask.

"Yes, but I don't feel like cooking. I was thinking of ordering pizza. Would you like to stay for dinner?"

Hell. Yes. No shit I want to stay for fucking dinner.

"I'd love to," I say instead. "My treat."

We sit at her kitchen table, eating her favorite pizza from a family-owned pizzeria in town.

"How are your parents?" she asks. "And Eric, Cole, and Katie? I think about them a lot."

"They're all doing well. Really well. Mom and Dad are the same. Eric is a senior in high school now. Cole is a freshman. It's pretty nuts how fast those two have grown. And Katie is trying to get pregnant now. She got married two years ago."

Ember's mouth drops open. "Holy shit. That's awesome. I'm so happy for her!"

I smile. "Yeah, it's pretty great." I take another bite of pizza. "How's your Mom been?"

"Mom's been good. I get to see her every few days now that I've moved back to the suburbs. It was hard living so far away from her in New York, and even Chicago was almost an hour drive with traffic."

"Tell me more about college."

I already know all about her college experience. I was there, but she doesn't know that. I want to hear about it from her.

"Cornell was great. It opened the door to a lot of opportunities for me. Not many people here have a New York university on their resume. Then I got my master's at a private university in downtown Chicago."

"And look at you now." I smirk. "Look at this house you've got. The life you've built for yourself. It's amazing what you've accomplished, Ember."

She grins, maybe even blushes a bit as she finishes the last of the pizza on her plate. "Where do you live now?" she asks.

"I have a place in the city. You'll have to come by soon. I have an insane view."

A view that used to allow me to watch you.

Her eyes grow wide. "You live in Chicago?"

"I do."

"And you drove all the way out here to make sure I got my flowers?"

I smile. "I did."

"You really didn't have to do that, Sawyer."

"I know."

"Do you need to head home soon?"

"Not unless you want me to." *Please don't want me to.*

"You've got a bit of a drive ahead of you. I don't want you to be tired for work tomorrow."

I glance at my watch. It is almost seven, but I'm not ready to leave. Besides, I basically work for myself. My dad has given me a lot of freedom within the company, and my hours are as flexible as I need them to be.

"I appreciate the concern, but I work for my dad, remember? I make my own hours."

"That must be nice."

"I can't complain." I change the subject. "Want to watch TV? There has to be something good on tonight."

She nods. "There is, actually. Monday night television is my favorite."

"Is that right?"

"You know my obsession with *The Bachelorette*."

I laugh. I do know her obsession. She never misses an episode.

"I do know. It's cute." I wink.

She rolls her eyes and walks over to the couch. I follow suit. As much as it pains me, I leave a little space between us when we sit. If I sit too close, I won't be able to keep my hands off her.

Truth be told, *The Bachelorette* bores the shit out of me, but I have spent five years following Ember, keeping up with her every move, and I am finally sitting beside the beautiful woman I love so much, the woman I will undoubtably love for the rest of my life. I never want to leave her side. This is where I belong, wherever she is.

At some point I doze off. In my dreams, I can hear her sweet voice. It's soft and calming. Why is everything about her so damn perfect? Her voice seems so real, and then I feel her touch. Her soft and gentle touch is warm as her smooth skin presses into mine. How is this possible?

Then, my eyes flutter. I can still hear her soft whisper, but I can't make out what she is saying. I wake up and soon realize I haven't been dreaming. That beautiful voice is here, in real life, as is her tender touch.

She puts her hand on mine and gives it a gentle squeeze. I quickly snap back to reality from the contact our skin makes. It is real, and the sensation sends shivers up my arms.

"Sawyer, you fell asleep," she says.

I open my eyes completely, and the first thing I see is her. Her emerald green eyes stare into mine. Her perfect, flawless skin looks so smooth that I long to touch it. Her beautiful blonde hair hangs over her shoulders.

I smile. "I want to wake up to you for the rest of my life."

She smiles back.

She likes that. This is my chance. "Do you think I could crash on your couch?"

She doesn't answer right away. Our eyes remain fixed on one another.

I continue, "I really wanted to spend time with you, Ember. I didn't mean for it to get so late. I promise, it won't happen again. I'm just too exhausted to drive home. I'll stay put on the couch. You won't even know I'm here."

Eventually she stands before she shuffles to a closet around the corner. When she reappears, she is carrying a clean blanket and pillow. She sets them next to me on the couch before she ascends the stairs to her bedroom.

"Goodnight, Sawyer."

She doesn't say no. She doesn't kick me out. She relents.

Fuck, yes. "Goodnight, beautiful," I say back.

chapter twelve

Sawyer

I wake up early so I can watch her sleep again. She looks sexy as hell, just as she did the other night. Soon, I will be sleeping next to her and feel everything that is beneath the sheets.

I want so badly to touch her, to see everything that she has to offer. I've seen it before, but she is a woman now. Her breasts are larger, her ass is perkier. I feel my groin tighten. Just the thought of this woman drives me crazy. I imagine being inside of her and almost lose it, but I have to be careful. She can wake up any minute.

Get it together, Sawyer.

As much as it pains me, I leave her room. I walk down the stairs and into the kitchen. I want to have breakfast made for her when she wakes up.

I rummage through the refrigerator to find something I can cook. I spot bacon in the lower left drawer and grab the carton of eggs off the shelf. It isn't anything special, but it is more than I have done for her in the past.

I have just about finished frying the bacon when I hear her walking down the stairs. She stops at the bottom of her spiral staircase, eyeing me.

"Good morning," I say. "I hope you don't mind that I made breakfast. I usually—"

My gaze falls to her legs, her toned and sexy legs. I notice that she is still only wearing an oversized T-shirt that falls right above her knees. Does she want me to check her out? If that is her intention, it's worked.

I can feel my dick strain in my pants.

Dammit.

I can't control my urges around this woman.

I walk to the refrigerator and open it, the cold air hitting me exactly where I need it to. I have to cool down. She has me so worked up just by not wearing pants.

I act as though I am looking for something while I calm myself down. When I close the door, her head is slightly tilted, and she is looking at me as if waiting on me to finish my thoughts.

"You usually, what?" she asks.

"Sorry." I dare to look down at her legs again. "You're not wearing any pants. I just realized that you're not wearing any pants and now, I'm very distracted." I meet her gaze with a smirk.

She blushes, then rolls her eyes, no doubt in an effort to act unfazed. She loves it. She has me wrapped around her finger, and she absolutely *loves* it.

She grabs a cup of coffee that I'd brewed earlier. "Thanks for making coffee," she says before walking toward the table.

"What time do you have to be into work?" I ask, finishing the bacon.

"I need to leave in about twenty minutes. I teach an early morning lecture."

Of course, I already knew that. Just as I know what time she wakes up every morning. I already know everything, and I use it to my advantage.

I walk to where she is sitting and take a seat beside her at the table. I reach for her hand and turn to face her. And then, she smiles.

My heart sinks.

I fucking love that smile.

When Ember smiles, I automatically smile. I can't fucking help it.

She lifts her mug and tries to hide behind it.

"Please…Please don't hide that beautiful smile of yours."

She puts the coffee down.

"I was thinking…" I start. "Would you like to get dinner with me this weekend?"

Her smile falls. I instantly regret being so forward.

I try to recover. "Ember, it's just dinner. Please, let me buy you something to eat. It's the least I can do after you let me crash on your couch."

After what feels like the longest fifteen seconds of my life, she finally agrees, saying, "Sure."

Before we can discuss the plans further, she stands and walks back toward the staircase. "I have to get ready for work," she says with her back toward me. Then, "Thanks for making breakfast, but I don't have time to eat."

She practically yells the last few words from the top of the stairs. She sounds annoyed.

Yikes.

But she has already agreed to dinner with me. That is a win in my book.

Hell. Yes.

She disappears somewhere upstairs while she dresses for work. I put the breakfast I made in a plastic container for her to take with her. A small gesture goes a long way with Ember. She has to see that I am trying. Packing her breakfast is about the easiest thing I can do. If she only knew the lengths I would go to, just to prove to her that I love her.

When she returns to the kitchen, it takes everything in me to keep my jaw from falling to the floor. Ember takes my breath away.

She is effortlessly beautiful. She has only been upstairs ten minutes or so, but dammit, when she comes back down she looks sexy as fuck.

She's wearing a tight skirt that shows off her petite legs just as the T-shirt had. Her top shows off her perfectly plump breasts. And those heels. *Damn.* They make her legs even longer, sexier. With the way she looks right now, there is no way I can keep my hands off her.

I watch as she grabs something off the island. Her perfect ass teases me in her tight skirt. I can't hold back anymore.

Approaching her slowly, I place both of my hands on her tiny waist. I feel her body tense beneath my touch. I pull her closer, until her back is against my chest.

I lean into her vanilla cucumber hair. She always smells so good.

My arms wrap around her shoulders as I hug her from behind. My mouth finds her ear. I want to nibble it, just a tiny bit. But I refrain from doing so.

Instead I whisper, "You look amazing."

I move around her until we are face to face. It takes everything in me not to kiss her. Not to take her up to her bedroom right now.

I have to get my mind off having sex with her. I won't be able to resist my urge forever.

Moving my gaze away from hers, I find the food I had put together.

That'll do.

I can't scare her off. I can't try to fuck her right now. I have already made her breakfast. I will give it to her, and then I will walk away. I've waited five years to make love to this woman again, what's a few more days?

"Breakfast," I say, handing her the container. "I hope your day is as good as you've just made mine."

Before I do something I will regret, I grab my keys and make my way to the front door. My dick is hard and squeezing in my waistband. I have to get out of here, or else I won't be able to control myself much longer.

Just when I am about to be safe from my desires, she calls out my name. Her sweet voice saying my name is all it takes for me to stop in place.

"Sawyer, wait."

I look back at the perfect woman who is internally driving me insane. Her green eyes are heavy-lidded.

"Thanks for breakfast," is all she says.

I know that isn't what she wants to say. I can tell by the way her eyes glaze over that she wants to give into her desires. I want to run back to her and press my lips to hers. I want to carry her up the stairs, rip off all her clothes, and finally make love to her. But I do none of those things. Instead, I nod and leave.

I keep tabs on both Ace and Ember daily, though I don't feel that Ace is much of a threat anymore. Ember still hasn't been back to the bar, and they never exchanged numbers. She obviously isn't as into him as he would have liked.

Ember keeps busy with work and grades papers most nights. I haven't been back inside her house since Monday, but I watch. I *always* watch.

I have the perfect view of her from my car right now. She sits on her couch and eats a pint of ice cream. I wonder how she keeps her perfectly slim figure. She hardly follows any sort of healthy diet. It doesn't matter what that girl does, I've always thought she was the hottest thing to ever walk the planet.

We still need to talk about our plans for dinner Saturday night. It is the perfect excuse to talk with her again, and since we haven't done much texting this week, I jump at the idea.

I take my cell phone out of my pocket as I stay parked down the street and pull her name up on my phone.

Me: How was your day, sweetheart?

Ember: Busy. Relaxing now. Much needed.

Me: You deserve some relaxation.

Ember: How was your day?

Me: I kept busy as well. I wanted to talk to you about our dinner Saturday. I'm going to surprise you with the place, but what time can I pick you up?

Ember: 7?

Me: 7 is perfect. Dress up. I'm going to spoil you.

Ember: That's not necessary.

Me: Nonsense. It's the least I can do. A pretty girl deserves to be spoiled every once in a while.

It has been a several days since Ember agreed to have dinner with me. I've spent most of those nights sitting in my car and watching her in her house. She never leaves after she returns home from work, until Friday.

I follow her when I see her leaving.

I trail behind her car onto the expressway, then into the city, toward her old apartment. I figure she must be visiting with Taylor. That isn't a big deal since I still have a semi-clear view of Taylor's apartment from my own down the block. She switched apartments after Ember moved, but lucky for me, it is still on the west side of the building facing mine.

I am hoping to keep an eye on her there, but no sooner than she enters the building, she leaves again with Taylor. They are dressed to impress, which means they are probably heading out for a night of drinking.

Taylor's wild red hair makes it easy not to lose sight of them. I follow them from bar to bar, sometimes stepping inside and keeping myself hidden in the crowd, sometimes camping out in my car.

Taylor picks up several guys, which isn't unusual. Ember plays the innocent wing woman, as always.

They eventually make their way into a country bar. I try to wait it out, but after nearly three hours, I'm losing my patience and am about to storm inside and see what the fuck is going on. I need to know that Ember is all right, but more importantly, I have to know what's keeping her.

I give them another ten minutes, and right as I am about to enter, I see them walk out with a small group of people. Initially, I can only pick Taylor out of the crowd with her fiery red hair. I peek over Taylor's shoulder, my body instantly filling with rage as I watch Ember walk out holding hands with a man.

Fucking hell.

I completely lose my shit when I realize that man is Ace. That damn bartender is a pain in my ass. He wasn't with them earlier. How did I let this happen? How did he know she was here? There is no way they planned this; at least, I don't think so.

I try my best to keep my emotions under control. I follow them all the way back to Taylor's apartment without causing a scene. Ember sits with Ace on a nearby bench while Taylor ferociously makes out with another guy she picked up. She's a whore. Thankfully, Ember isn't. She'd never do that to me, not after everything we've gone through.

It is pitch-black out, so I park down the street, far enough away that they can't see me. They are illuminated under the streetlamp. I can't hear what they are saying, but I can see their body language and the way she looks at him. I don't like it one fucking bit. Then, I watch as he kisses her. His fucking lips touch her, *taints* her.

My blood boils. How can she let him do this?

He wraps his arm around her, and all I can think is, *What the fuck is happening?* Have I read her wrong?

I saw it in her eyes when I left the other night. She wants me. She wants me just as much as I want her. We belong together. How can she be getting involved with another man while we are in the process of getting back together? Ember is not a fucking whore, so why the fuck is she acting like one?

I am ready to pound his face in. I can't take it any longer. Thankfully, Taylor finally yells for her.

I am relieved when Ace walks away with the guy Taylor has been mauling. I have witnessed Ember kiss other men in the past, but that was when she didn't think I would ever be a part of her life again. She didn't know there was still a chance. But now I am *here*. I am *back*.

Fuck this shit.

My tires screeching, I veer my car out of the parking spot. I drive to my apartment complex only a block away.

I couldn't stand watching that man touch her like that. I don't know why she let him do it. It makes me sick to think of Ember with anyone else other than me. He isn't right for her. *I am.*

Storming into my apartment building and slamming the door shut behind me, I quickly take out my phone. I have to text her. I want, no *need*, her to go to bed tonight thinking of me, not that fucking loser.

Me: I miss you.

I hit send.

I wait a few moments, expecting a reply. It never comes.

I stay up the whole fucking night waiting for her to answer me, and she never does.

"Fuck, Ember. Come on," I say to myself.

I am going to have to come up with something quick. *A plan.* We are having dinner together in less than fifteen hours. I need to do something that will guarantee she will be mine.

I could try to pay off someone to scare Ace away like I had all the others in the past, but something tells me he won't go without a fight. No, I have to make her *choose* me. Ember needs to want to be with me and not him.

But, how?

What can I do to make sure the woman I fucking love will stand by my side and choose me? I need her to want me over everyone else. I need our night together to be so larger-than-life that she has no other option but to choose me.

It has to be larger than life. Or literally *life* itself.

And that's when it hits me.

I know what I have to do.

chapter thirteen

Sawyer

I leave my apartment before the sun comes up. I haven't slept, but it doesn't matter. My body is running strictly on adrenaline.

Forty-five minutes later, I pull into my parents' driveway. The neighborhood is silent. The day hasn't quite started for most, but it has for me.

I walk quietly into the garage, hoping not to wake up anyone in the house. I eye my mother's car and walk toward the front. Popping open the hood, I notice the engine and the power-steering pump located in front of it. I stare at it, but only for a few moments. I don't have time to second-guess my decision. I gash a giant hole through it with a knife, and power-steering fluid floods out and empties beneath the car.

In my haste to figure out how the fuck I can make Ember choose me, I figure I have to somehow leave her with no other choice. If Ember doesn't have a choice, then there is no problem.

Ember has the biggest heart of anyone I know. I realize with complete certainty that if something happens to someone close to me, to someone I love, she will stand by me. She will do whatever it takes to help me through it. There is no fucking way she will choose that fucker over me while I am going through a difficult time with my family. It will work. It *has* to work.

Without power-steering fluid, whoever drives this car will lose control. I understand the risk I am taking, but I can't live my life without Ember. I will risk it all for her. No one on this earth means more to me than her, and I will always do whatever it takes to keep her. One of these days she'll realize that everything I have done is for her, but I need to take this risk to ensure that I have a future with her.

My parents always go out every Saturday night. *Every* Saturday. It doesn't matter what is going on in our lives, Saturday night is saved for them. They'll probably leave sometime during my dinner with Ember. It is better that way.

The second part of my plan isn't necessary but will simply be for my own pleasure. I have to eliminate Ace. Not literally, though if it comes to that I won't be afraid of the task. I'll have to eliminate him *figuratively*. I need Ace to know that Ember is mine. She will *always* be mine. I don't share. No man will ever touch her again. I can tell by the way they acted together last night that he won't give up so easily. I need him to know he has no chance with her. *None.* And he never will.

It is easy to find out everything I need to know about him on the internet. After a quick Google search, I discover that he owns that bar Ember went to the night I originally showed up at her house, along with several other restaurants in town. He happens to have an event scheduled tonight at the Lux, where I've made dinner reservations. He will see me there with Ember and know she is off limits.

My plan has come together quite nicely, but I can't wait for it to come to life.

Ember still hasn't responded to my text from last night. I texted her again a few hours ago, right after I'd drained the power-steering fluid from my mother's car. She hasn't responded to that one either.

I am supposed to pick her up in a few hours. I contemplate driving back to my apartment in the city to see what the hell is going on. Maybe she is still asleep. She and Taylor had been up late, as had I, but I am still running on adrenaline.

She can't bail on dinner, not after everything I am risking for her. Tonight has to go perfectly. I need her to respond. I need to take her to dinner. I need Ace to see us and for there to be a car accident. This all has to go according to plan, and the plan does not include her bailing.

I text her again. I hate the uneasiness I feel. I love this girl too damn much for my own good.

Me: Please don't tell me you've changed your mind about dinner?

My muscles relax when I see the ellipsis appear. She's typing.

Ember: Sorry. Late night with Taylor. Just woke up. I'll see you at 7.
Me: Can't wait.

We are still on.

I jump in the shower and prepare myself for the night that is going to change both of our lives forever.

chapter fourteen

Sawyer

They say if you don't go after what you want in life, you'll never have it. I have never wanted something so fucking bad in my life. Or rather, *someone*.

Ember looks stunning tonight. She dresses up for me, as I requested. She's beautiful. Elegant. She's wearing a satin green dress that falls just above her knees. It shows off enough of her legs that I can't help but admire them. Her chest is exposed. I have to work damn hard to keep my eyes from falling to her cleavage during dinner.

But her breasts…*damn*.

I want to run my tongue over her hard nipples and feel everything that is beneath the satin, the place no other man has ever been. During dinner, Ember confirms that I am the only man she has ever slept with. I fucking *love* that.

I can't wait much longer. I haven't even kissed her yet. Ace is the last man she's kissed. I have to change that. This dinner will change that.

We just finish our desserts when my phone rings. Looking at the screen, it reads, "Unknown number."

It's probably the call I'm expecting.

I look up at Ember as I answer. "One sec, I have to take this. I'll be right back."

I walk toward the bathroom in the back of the restaurant and put the phone to my ear. "Hello?"

I hear a woman's voice on the other end of the call. "Hi. Is this Sawyer Christensen?"

"Yes."

"Hi. My name is Allison, I'm one of the nurses at Oakbrook Memorial. There's been an accident. Your parents are in surgery." There is a brief pause as she clears her throat. "Mr. Christensen, they're in critical condition."

I have expected this call. I'm the one who caused the accident. I knew there would be a wreck, but one causing them to be in critical condition? That wasn't my intention.

"Oh," I croak.

I pace back and forth, still on the phone with Allison. She remains quiet as I process the information.

I'd intended for there to be an accident, but maybe I hadn't fully considered the possibilities of the situation. Both of my parents could die. Did I subconsciously know that could happen? Did I care?

"Fuck," I finally say. "All right. I'm on my way. I'll be there as fast as I can."

I hang up.

I turn back toward the table where Ember waits and smile. Ace is there.

That is all it takes for me to accept whatever has happened to my parents. This is going to be worth it. *She* is going to be worth it.

Ace and I have met once before, when I pretended to have car trouble. I had told him my name is Tom. The truth will come out now. He'd know I lied, but I don't care. Ember is going to choose me.

He stands next to our table, talking with Ember. I can't stop grinning. My plan is working. He's already heard all about me from her drunken night at his bar, and now it is time to lay claim to my woman. I will whisk her away, and there won't be any time for her to explain. There is no way she will stay here with him over leaving with me after she hears the news of my parents.

I no longer care about the phone call I received or the outcome, though I'll need to act as if I do. Ember is all that matters, and she needs to see hurt and fear in my eyes.

Wiping the smile off my face, I walk toward Ember. It is time to play my part. Ember has to feel for me, to feel *with* me.

As I approach, I make eye contact with Ace.

I reach out and grab Ember by the arm. "Em, we've got to go. There's been an accident. I don't know what happened, but we have to get to the hospital. It's my family. We have to go."

Ace's face drops.

Ember's eyes widen. "Oh, my God, Sawyer."

"Sawyer," Ace mumbles under his breath.

Surprise. My name isn't Tom. But there is no time to explain. He knows now. Ember is mine.

I don't look back. I know what his expression likely holds. It is probably similar to mine the day Ember broke up with me. I'd given her time. I had given her more time than I wanted. But it is time for us to be together now.

I place my hand on the small of her back as I lead her toward the door. When she looks back at Ace, I feel a punch in my gut. Why is she looking back? Still, she leaves with me. She doesn't hesitate. That has to count for something.

We walk out of the restaurant and directly toward the valet. There is an urgency in our step. Once we are outside and waiting for the car, she squeezes my hand in a comforting gesture. She doesn't look back again. She is there with me, present in the moment. She's confirming what I have believed all along without even meaning to. She loves me and I need her.

I am glad that son of a bitch finally realizes the truth.

Ember is and always will be *mine*.

chapter fifteen

Sawyer

So, my parents died. Both of them. *Dead.* Cause of death: *Blunt force trauma.* Their airbags didn't deploy. Because of that and the damage I had done, they died, but I don't feel guilty.

Eric and Cole are devastated, but I know they'll eventually be okay without our parents. Ember and I will be sure of it.

Ember is upset. I try to comfort her, but she is too busy comforting me. I haven't cried. I'm not *that* good at acting. Maybe I'll form actual tears eventually, but right now, I'm just happy she is here with me.

I called her my fiancée at the hospital. I couldn't see her reaction to the words because I was speaking with the doctor, but she didn't run. She accepted them. I liked the way the words rolled off my tongue. She deserves a proper proposal, though, and I'll give it to her, along with a giant rock on her finger.

She is still wearing that satin dress that matches her beautiful emerald eyes. Even after spending most of the night at the hospital, she is gorgeous.

She follows me up the stairs to my bedroom, no doubt in another effort to try and console me. And I let her. Just maybe not in the way she expects.

I can't wait any longer. She sits beside me on the bed, and I instantly harden between my legs. I have to kiss her, and when I do, I can't stop.

I finally make love to her. I have waited five years to do this again. Five fucking years. She welcomes me with open arms, literally. She pulls me on top of her and I fall inside of her.

I am so in love with her.

"That was mind-blowing," I whisper into her ear.

Fuck. Yes.

My plan has worked. It fucking worked.

The last twelve hours have been insane. My parents are dead, but I've finally had sex with Ember. I would do it all again just to be inside her.

We lie on the bed, naked. I have already made her come once, her moans music to my ears. She is magnificent. I can't begin to describe what I am feeling, but fulfillment is one word that comes to mind. Ember is all I will ever need in this life. If I have her, I have it all.

"You're so amazing," I say, kissing her cheek.

She smiles. "You're pretty incredible yourself."

Fuck. I am already hard again. I love this girl. I love her so damn much.

"I love you, Ember. I know you might not be ready to say that yet, but I never stopped loving you, you know that."

She nods.

I don't need to hear her say it back. I know how she feels.

I can't stop looking at her slim figure. This incredibly perfect human is lying in my bed. I've just had her, but I'm ready to have her again.

Pressing my lips to her skin, I place several tiny kisses down her neck and onto her chest. My groin tightens even further. I don't think I've ever been this hard.

I can't keep my hands off her. It has been way too long and being inside her only once in the last several years isn't nearly enough.

I lower my head until it meets her breasts. I run my tongue over her erect nipples. She whimpers.

Fuck.

My tongue presses firmly against her skin as I lick down her flat stomach and stop between her legs. She opens them, allowing me access. I slide my tongue along her slit until I find that sensitive spot, the one I know so well. No one can make this girl come like me. And after today, no one will have the chance.

I grip the outside of her waist and steady myself between her thighs. I move my tongue, nibbling and sucking on her. She arches her back and moans in response to me. I don't stop until she reaches her climax. Her entire body shudders as I squeeze her thighs tighter, making sure my tongue does exactly what it needs to make her lose herself. And she does.

"Fuck, baby," I say breathlessly. "I'm ready to be inside you again."

She doesn't look at me as she recovers. Her eyes are closed as she comes back down from another earth-shattering orgasm.

I second-guess a condom this time. What is the worst thing that can happen? She gets pregnant? But I don't want to risk her stopping me. I have to be inside her again. I used a condom before, so I will again. This time at least.

Placing the rubber over my hard shaft, I slide myself inside of her. It is warm and tight. This time somehow feels even better than the last.

I thrust into her, each time a little deeper. She moans beneath me as I kiss her neck, her lips, anywhere I can reach.

Her walls clamp around me. She is about to come again, so I stop her. I change my rhythm, pushing in and out of her slowly. I pause her climax and build up the tension. I want her to beg for it. Beg for *me*.

I savor every moment of being inside her. She squirms underneath me, frustrated with my change of pace. She is so close to her release, but I want to tease her just a bit longer. All she'll have to do is ask. I can't say no to her, but I want her to want this as bad as I do.

I ignore her silent plea as I continue moving myself in and out of her slowly.

"Sawyer," she moans.

Finally.

"Yes?"

"Faster, please."

I laugh. She sounds so cute and desperate. "What's the matter, baby?"

She pulls at my shoulders until our chests press against each other. Holding me tightly, she silently begs for me to make her come until she can't stay silent any longer.

"Sawyer, please."

"Please, what?"

"Please," she whines again.

"Tell me what you want, Ember."

She finally relents. "I want to come. I want you to make me come."

And with that, I slam myself back inside of her. She moans as I fill her.

Her walls clamp around me again. Her grip on my shoulders tightens as her nails dig into my back. She is about to come again. This time, so am I. I am ready. More ready than I've ever been.

Fuck, she is so hot.

"Come for me, baby," I demand. "I want to come with you."

Her head tilts back, and her spine arches. Her body stiffens beneath me as she orgasms around me.

"Shit," I groan, releasing myself into her.

Nothing has ever felt more perfect than the two of us coming together. I love her so much.

Once we are both finished, I roll onto the bed next to her.

My hair is stuck to my forehead from the perspiration. I rub my face with one hand as I try to catch my breath. I never imagined that things would work out this well. Everything has gone according to plan, and I fucked the shit out of her, *twice*.

There is no way she will ever leave me now. We are in this together. Sawyer and Ember are officially back together, and there isn't a damn thing anyone can do about it.

chapter sixteen

Ember

It's been four weeks since Sawyer's parents died. The days are emotionally draining, to say the least. They had a nice funeral. Everyone in town stopped by to pay their respects.

The last few weeks have been hard on me, though I am sure it pales in comparison to the difficulty Sawyer faces. I am sad for Sawyer and his siblings. I can't begin to imagine the pain they feel. They didn't only lose one parent, they lost two. And it was so sudden. No one has had time to process anything. I'm not even sure if I've truly processed it yet.

Sawyer says the wreck was ruled an accident. Officials don't know what caused them to swerve off the road into oncoming traffic, but they suspect some type of malfunction with the car. The toxicology report came back clean, so drugs and alcohol were ruled out right away.

Sawyer moved all his belongings into his parents' house. He easily broke his lease to his apartment downtown because of the extenuating circumstances. His sister came to town for the funeral and stayed a few extra days but is back in Michigan now.

Sawyer has taken an extended leave of absence from work. Now that his dad is gone, there will be some major changes to the company—the biggest being that Sawyer is now in charge.

I've been staying with him several nights during the week, helping where I can with dinner and laundry. I know Sawyer appreciates my help. It comforts me to know that I am making a difference in their lives, albeit a small one.

Sawyer was given guardianship of his brothers until they turn eighteen. They missed school for a few days but have returned in time for finals.

Today is Eric's high school graduation. His plan is to move to Iowa and begin college in the fall. Luckily, their parents have college funds already set aside for both boys, so tuition isn't something Sawyer needs to worry about. Their life insurance policy also leaves Sawyer and his siblings with a nice cushion to move forward. Money has never been an issue for Sawyer's family, and now it certainly never will be.

I stand in the kitchen, waiting for the boys to finish getting dressed. Eric has already left. He had to be at the high school an hour ago so he can line up for the procession.

I'm wearing a light blue floral sundress with tan espadrilles. The summer months are brutally hot, so I have my hair in a long flowy ponytail. Cole walks down wearing jeans and a polo. He is a handsome young man. It still surprises me how grown he is, but in my eyes, he will always be the same sweet little boy that I remember.

"Sawyer!" I yell. "We're going to be late!"

Sawyer rushes down the stairs. "I know, I know. Sorry. I'm ready." At the bottom of the stairs, he buttons the last few buttons on his charcoal slim-fit poplin shirt.

Damn. He looks good. His facial hair has grown out over the last few weeks, and his chin is lined with scruff. He looks edgier, and if it is possible, more attractive.

"You look beautiful, babe," he says as he walks toward me. He places a soft peck on my cheek.

"Thanks. You don't look so bad yourself."

"Gross," Cole interjects. "Can you guys save your pillow talk for when I'm not standing right here?"

We both laugh.

"Come on, time to go," Sawyer says. He grabs the car keys and leads us out the door.

The graduation is lovely. When they call Eric's name, we all stand and cheer. Noticeably absent are his parents. He doesn't have the two most important people there, the ones who raised him into the young man he's become. We do our best to yell loudly, to try and fill the void that is undoubtedly there, but we all feel that missing piece.

Afterward, Eric poses for pictures with his friends in his cap and gown. He looks happy, despite the recent events that have taken place. I am happy for him, but most of me feels the pain he is hiding beneath that smile. I know it is there. We all do. Liz and Rod should be here to witness their son's graduation.

"Ready to go?" Sawyer asks Eric.

"I'm going out with a few of the guys. I'll meet you guys back home tonight," Eric replies.

"All right, be careful."

I walk over to Eric and hug him. I hold him tightly, hoping he understands what it means. It isn't just a hug goodbye. It's a hug letting him know I am here. That I know what he feels and that it is okay to feel it. I will be here for him. He doesn't have to worry about losing me as he lost his parents because I'm not going anywhere. I'll always be here for him, no matter what.

"I'm really proud of you, you know," I whisper as I hold him.

"Thanks."

I let go, hoping I didn't embarrass him in front of his friends. It takes everything in me to hold back the tears that want to fall. I hurt so much for him. So damn much.

"Can I go with?" Cole asks Eric.

Eric turns to Cole and smiles. He loves his brother. "Hell, yeah. Come on," he says cheerfully.

Cole is hurting too, but Eric is such a great big brother. He is always there for Cole, so I don't have to worry as much for him. There is such a big age gap between Eric and Sawyer, I worry that Eric doesn't have that same protection he provides for Cole. And Eric is going to be leaving for college soon. How can I help protect him when he is so far away? And will his leaving hurt Cole?

The more I think about the future, the more my heart breaks. A small tear escapes, but I quickly wipe it away. If Eric's friends see me crying, they will definitely think I am insane. This is supposed to be a happy moment. Eric just graduated high school!

Cole turns to look at me before he walks away with Eric. Did he see the tear? But his face is seeking approval. He would have asked his parents if it was okay to go out with friends, but now he is looking at me. He is asking *me*.

I quickly glance at Sawyer, wide-eyed. He gives me a slight head nod.

I look back at Cole and smile, trying to hide my heartbreak for these boys. "Have fun."

His face lights up as he runs to meet Eric and his friends.

Sawyer grabs my hand and leads me back toward the car.

"This is all so crazy," I say. "I'm not ready to be a parent, but I can't help but feel a sort of responsibility for them."

"I know what you mean," Sawyer says. "I feel it too."

"But you're their brother, Sawyer. Of course, you feel that way. And now you're their legal guardian. You technically are their parent. But why do I feel like that? I haven't been part of their lives in so long, and now I'm suddenly being thrown back into the mix at the most devastating time of their life."

"I think it was perfect timing, babe. None of us could get through this without you. You're holding this family together."

His words stab at my already broken heart.

I am holding this family together.

I'm technically not even a part of this family, yet I am somehow holding it together.

Too many emotions. My head is a fog. Life is just too dark sometimes. Too much. I need a break.

"I think I'm going to stay at my house tonight, if you don't mind."

Sawyer looks at me concerned. "Is everything okay?"

"Yeah. I've been staying at your place a lot lately, and I think I just need to sleep in my own bed tonight."

"I can stay with you if you want," he offers.

So much for my break.

"Okay."

I don't bother to argue. He would probably end up at my house anyway if I had turned down his offer. Sawyer has had a lot of trouble sleeping since the accident. I suggested he see a doctor or therapist. He was prescribed Ambien, which seems to be helping, at least on the nights he sleeps with me.

But that is the thing, he says he always sleeps better with me. He has called me a few times in the middle of the night asking if he can come over because he can't fall asleep. I always relent. He hasn't started seeing a therapist yet, but he didn't seem opposed to the idea, especially for the boys, who would benefit from talking to someone about the unimaginable loss.

Tonight, I need to be alone, but I can tell Sawyer doesn't want to be alone himself. He is the one who lost his family, not me. I have to stop feeling sorry for myself. My feelings are dismissible, but Sawyer's aren't.

It has been easy to fall for Sawyer again. He treats me well. Really well. Fortunately, we've adjusted to our new normal and have easily become part of one another's lives all over again.

It is different this time for obvious reasons. We are much older, smarter, wiser, and incredibly more mature than we were in high school. We also have had to unexpectedly step into the role of parenting. I can't leave Sawyer alone in that. He has a responsibility to those boys, but I have it too, whether I have asked for it or not. They need a mother figure in their lives. Someone nurturing. They deserve their own mother, but instead they have me.

My relationship with Sawyer feels different this time. I can't pinpoint the right word to describe it, but if I have to choose, I suppose I can say it is easy. Right now, being together is *easy*. But despite its simplicity, my heart is exhausted.

I've been consumed with thoughts of Ace every single day since I ran into him at the restaurant. Since the night of the accident. Just because I am with Sawyer now doesn't mean I can simply forget about Ace. It had hurt him when he realized I was there with Sawyer.

I didn't even *want* to be there with Sawyer that day. Not after the amazing night I'd had with Ace. Unfortunately, one thing has led to another, and I've had to push aside the feelings I feel for Ace out of respect for Sawyer.

As hard as I try, it is nearly impossible to forget about Ace. Sometimes, I dream about him at night while in bed with Sawyer. When I wake up and see Sawyer next to me, I'm burdened with so much guilt it weighs me down. I'm trying so hard to get that man out of my head. I don't know why it's so hard.

Sawyer is treating me so damn good, so I shouldn't be having thoughts of anyone else. I am happy, as happy as I can be after the death of two amazing people. Sawyer makes me happy. And my sex life. Oh, my sex life. It hasn't been this good in a long time. *That* makes me happy, too.

chapter seventeen

Ember

I signed up earlier in the school year to teach a few summer courses, most of them online. I still teach one lecture in person on Tuesdays and Thursdays, but other than that, I practically get to work from wherever I want.

Today, I'm grading papers in a quaint little coffee shop in town. The atmosphere in these types of places makes it nearly impossible to be anything but blissful.

The overhead bell above the entrance chimes frequently, signaling when someone walks in. After about an hour, I am zoned in on my work and have become less and less aware of it as time goes on. But for some reason, the last chime catches my attention. When I look toward the door, I realize why.

Ace.

He walks in with another guy, about the same age, maybe a few years younger. I don't recognize him from the night out in Chicago, so I am pretty sure I haven't met him.

Ace doesn't notice me right away, but when he does, he freezes. He whispers something to the guy before he walks over to where I'm sitting.

My heart thumps against my chest, speeding up as he gets closer. I haven't seen him in a month. An entire month since I've looked into those crystal blue eyes. The last time I saw them, I'd been walking away from them. Now, they are coming toward me.

He takes a seat across from me at the tiny table. He doesn't say a word. Neither do I. What is there to say?

We sit in silence for what feels like an eternity. Ace doesn't understand the circumstances of the situation I'm in, so I'm not even sure where I should begin this conversation.

"Hey," I finally say, breaking the silence.

He nods his head, inaudibly saying hello back.

What does he want? He is obviously waiting for me to speak. Maybe he wants an explanation of what I was doing with Sawyer that night and why I hadn't stopped by to see him since. He probably wonders why I haven't answered the text he sent me the night we had our first kiss.

"I said I would go to dinner with Sawyer before we kissed," I blurt out. "I had already agreed to it, so I had to go. I didn't want to. Believe me, I didn't want to."

It takes a few seconds before he finally answers. "Then why did you leave with him?"

His raspy voice sends shivers down my spine. "His parents got into a car accident. It all happened so fast. I left, and the next thing I knew, his mom and dad were dead."

He seems visibly taken aback by my response. I can tell he hadn't expected it.

I study his face and try to gauge what he is feeling, but he is closed off to me. His facial expression gives nothing away, but his body language is not so easily hidden. He is sad. Maybe even still hurting.

"Do you love him?" he asks.

"I don't really know how to answer that, Ace."

"When you kiss him, do you feel the same things as when you kissed me?"

I shake my head. Nothing feels the same as kissing Ace. *Nothing.*

"Does it feel better with him?"

I answer right away. "No."

He reaches across the table for my hand. I slowly place my tiny palm in his. His gaze never wavers from mine.

"Then why are you still with him, Ember?"

I look down, breaking our stare.

"You are still with him, *right*? That's why I haven't heard from you?"

I know that I feel things for Sawyer. It's hard not to. He's been so good to me, and we have so much history. He is going through so much, and there is no way I can abandon him. But if I am being honest, I feel like I don't have a choice but to stay with him.

But now that Ace is sitting in front of me, I'm positive that I still feel things for him too. So many things. Things beyond just recurring dreams.

It's different with Ace. I have always known there was something different. His presence alone makes me feel more emotions than sex ever did with Sawyer. Don't get me wrong, sex with Sawyer is damn good. I have no idea what sex would be like with Ace, but I have a feeling that it would be fucking amazing.

"He needs me," I finally say.

"Do you need him?"

"I don't need anyone."

That is a lie. A lie I have been telling myself since I met Ace. I need him, but I can't have him. Not now. Not ever.

"Then I'll ask you again, Ember. Why are you still with him?"

When I look back into his beautiful blue eyes, I can finally see the emotion in them. He's confused. He doesn't understand anymore.

"Ace," I whisper.

"*Why*, Ember?" he asks again.

I take a deep breath. "I'd feel too guilty if I leave him now, okay? Is that what you want me to say?"

He says nothing.

I continue, "He keeps telling me he doesn't know how he would get through this without me. The loss of his parents. Having to take care of his brothers. He's said that every damn day since the accident. I'm not the kind of person who is going to leave someone high and dry. He needed me. He *needs* me. He's the only man I've ever been with, Ace, and although we broke up five years ago, he came back into my life right before his turned upside down."

Ace never takes his eyes off me.

I can see his friend grabbing their coffees before he walks to the opposite end of the coffee shop and takes a seat. His friend is cute, but not *Ace* cute.

"Ember," he says, refocusing my attention. "What do you need? Is this what you need? Is this even what you *want*?"

"No," I say. "It's not what I need. I don't know what I want. But I know it's what he needs, and I care about him, so it is what it is."

"I'm not giving up on this, Ember. I told you already, you're the girl I want, and I think I know what you want too. I'm not giving up."

My eyes begin to swell, and everything turns blurry. His words and the emotion behind them are all too much. The weight of everything I have been carrying is too much. I can't hold back anymore. I begin to cry. The tears are unmanageable, and I can't prevent them from pouring down my face.

Fuck if I know what I am supposed to do now. It's supposed to be Ace. It was *always* supposed to be Ace. I think I know that subconsciously, but Sawyer has found his way back into my life like he always did. And now, it is too late. I can't fault him for his parents' death, but it *is* his fault for making me feel trapped.

I feel trapped.

Sawyer had never asked if this is what I want. He had always just assumed. It takes Ace all of five minutes to ask that one simple question.

He continues to hold my hand and when he notices the tears spilling out, he squeezes tighter while his thumb moves in tiny, soothing circles.

"Ember," he says, softly.

I can't look at him. I try to wipe the tears from my eyes. *God, this is so embarrassing.*

"Ember," he says again, this time with more force.

I glance up at him.

"What do you want, Ember?" he asks again.

I drop my shoulders. I need to admit to him what I want. What I've wanted all along.

"*You*," I whisper.

His eyes squeeze shut. He releases my hand and stands up.

I look at him, confused. Isn't that what he'd wanted me to say? Why is he walking away after I finally admitted to him that he is what I want?

"Where are you going?" I ask.

He stands tall across the table from me, both hands on the back of the chair as he pushes it in. Leaning slightly forward, he says, "You know where to find me."

I watch as he walks away. His friend hands him his coffee then nudges his head in my direction as though to ask, "Who's that girl?" Ace turns to look at me, our eyes locking immediately before he turns his head again. I still can't look away.

I wonder what he told his friend. *Just a friend,* or maybe*, just a girl that I met at the bar.*

What am I to him? What does he think of me now? Am I a terrible person for being with Sawyer?

It's not that I don't truly care about Sawyer, because I do. I would probably go as far as saying that I love him. I wouldn't be sleeping with him if there weren't real feelings there, but I don't think I'm in love with him. Maybe that's the problem. Could I ever be in love with him again? After everything he's been through, what am I supposed to do?

I finally look away from Ace. I lay my head in both of my hands and sigh.

What the fuck am I going to do?

chapter eighteen

Ember

When I get home later that afternoon, Sawyer is already there. He is at my house more frequently lately, waiting for me to get home. It is summer, and the boys are gone a lot. Maybe he doesn't want to be alone. I don't know. He is always around. I wish he wasn't. Maybe he'll start working again soon.

"Hey, babe," he says as I walk through the front door.

"Hey."

"How was your day today?"

"It was fine. I had a lot of grading to do and then answered some emails."

"Sounds like you were busy."

"I found another coffee shop that I liked, so the time went by quickly."

He meets me at the front door and kisses me on the lips.

"That's nice," he says as he pulls away.

I walk around him and place my things on the counter before I head upstairs to change.

Sawyer follows me up the spiral staircase. I walk into my bedroom and pull out a gray pair of sweatpants and a white tank top. I take the clothes and walk into the bathroom. Sawyer stands in the hallway.

"I'm just going to change, okay? I'll be right down."

I shut the door and hear his footsteps disappear.

Sometimes I feel like he is smothering me. I don't bring it up because of what he's going through, but why does he feel the need to follow me up the stairs like a lost puppy?

I take my time in the bathroom. I know I said I was only going to change, but I decide to shower first. It has been a long day, and I need time to decompress, which is a little hard to do these days with Sawyer breathing down my neck.

The hot water splashes against the back of my neck. The steam surrounds me in a comforting mist. Is the shower the only place I can truly be alone? If I invited him, he'd follow me in here too.

A half hour later I step out, get dressed and head back downstairs to where Sawyer waits.

He is sitting on the couch watching TV. I take a seat next to him as he simultaneously lifts his arm to welcome me, pulling me in close. He places a soft kiss on the top of my head.

"I'm thinking about working again," he says.

"Really? I think that's a great idea."

"What, you don't like having me as a housewife?"

I laugh. "Will you be taking over your dad's position?"

"Yes. Someone has to. I already know what he managed at The Plant for the most part, but I'll probably have to meet with his assistant to go over all the logistics. Of course, then I'll have to hire someone into my old position."

"I think it will be good for you. Keep your mind busy." I try not to sound too eager.

"I think so, too."

Sawyer makes us dinner. I like to cook, but he insists on cooking most of the time. I don't argue. Maybe it's like therapy for him.

After we finish eating, I wash the dishes as Sawyer puts them away.

"Are you heading home tonight?" I ask him, hoping for some space.

"I was thinking about it. The boys will both be home later. I don't want them thinking they suddenly have an open house all the time for parties."

"Yeah."

"Will you stay at my place tonight?"

I sigh. I need a break from him, now more than ever.

"I had a pretty long day," I say. "I'm going to head up to bed now. I just think it's one of those nights I need my own bed."

"Okay," he says, disappointed. He puts away the last of the dishes. "I'll stay if you want?"

"It's okay. You're right, those boys will turn into party animals if they're left alone too often."

He can't hide the displeasure from his features. "Well, I guess I'll get out of here then. I'll see you tomorrow?"

"Yeah. See you tomorrow."

He pulls me into his embrace, and I feel myself sinking into him as we say goodbye. His body is warm and leaves me feeling conflicted. Do I want him to leave, or do I want to stay in his arms all night?

I try to remember how it felt sitting across from Ace today. Did it feel as good as this? As hugging Sawyer? *No.* It was better.

He places another soft peck on my lips. "I love you, Ember."

I force a smile.

His words are soothing. He has said them several times before, but each time they go unanswered. I am not ready to say it back to him, even though I know I love him. He probably knows it too. He just doesn't know it's not the same way he loves me.

I walk him to the front door and shut it behind him when he leaves.

Finally, some alone time.

I lie in bed for the next two hours, tossing and turning, staring at my ceiling. Sawyer texted me goodnight over an hour ago, but I can't stop thinking about Ace. He's been on my mind since he ran into me at the coffee shop. Oh, hell. He's been on my mind for longer than that; I've just tried to suppress it. I can't anymore.

He said, *You know where to find me,* but what am I supposed to do, show up to his bar and confess my feelings for him? I don't think so.

I'm contemplating if I should text him. I don't even know what to say. I should text him though. Maybe we can talk more about the conversation we had. I roll my eyes at my inner dialogue.

"*Fine, Ember.* I'll text him," I say to myself, reaching for my phone.

Me: Hey.

He doesn't text back right away. Maybe I've made a mistake. Maybe he doesn't want to talk to me again.

It's the middle of the week, so I doubt the bar is very busy. Is he ignoring me? He could be working at one of his restaurants. I still don't even know what other restaurants he owns besides the Lux. He could be snubbing me. Or maybe he expects me to show up at his bar, and now he's pissed off and ignoring me.

While I continue to come up with reasons why he hasn't responded yet, my phone vibrates.

It's him. Shit.

I nervously open my messages to see his response.

Ace: Hey, stranger.

Now that he's answered, I don't know what I want to say to him. I haven't thought that far. *I have feelings for you* crosses my mind. *I want to be with you* is also an idea. But instead, I settle for something less extreme, but still honest.

Me: I was really happy to see you today. I haven't been able to stop thinking about our conversation.
Ace: Which part?
Me: All of it.

I wait another few minutes for him to respond, but he doesn't. Maybe he is working.

Me: Are you working?

He answers right away.

Ace: I was. I just closed the bar for the night.

Before I can text back, he sends me another message.

Ace: I'm glad you texted me.
Me: You are? Why's that?

I watch the ellipsis for what feels like an eternity before his texts finally come through, one right after another.

Ace: Because I met the most beautiful girl a little over a month ago. She passed out on my bar floor because she was so drunk. In the little time I got to spend with her the next morning, I felt something I couldn't quite figure out. Then I ran into her again at a bar downtown. I thought, there was no way this woman was put in front of me twice by accident. Well, she was.

Ace: I kissed that beautiful girl that night. I couldn't stop thinking about it. I still can't stop thinking about it. Then I ran into that woman again the next day at my restaurant. How could I be so lucky that she's been placed right there for me a third time? But I wasn't that lucky, not this time, because she was there with someone else. He was the lucky one.

Ace: The last four weeks have been hell. I know it was just one kiss, but it was one hell of a kiss. Then, I walked into a coffee shop today, and my eyes instantly fell on that same beautiful woman. I don't know if I've ever believed in fate before this, but I believe that something is pulling me toward you, Ember. I still can't figure out the feeling that overcomes me when I'm with you, but it's something damn special. So that's why I'm glad you decided to text me, because I think that you might be feeling things too.

Wow.

I read over each word a second time before I can figure out what to say next.

Me: I'm feeling things too, Ace.

Ace: So, what are we going to do about it?

Isn't that the million-dollar question?

Me: I don't know.

Ace: You can't stay with a man you're not in love with forever, Ember.

Me: How do you know I'm not in love with him?

Ace: Are you?

Me: No.

Ace: Then that's settled.

Me: I don't know what to do. That kiss was just as amazing for me as it was for you. I didn't even know I could feel the things I feel for you. Especially this quickly.

I continue to type.

Me: All I've ever known was Sawyer, and he somehow made his way back into my life and he's holding on for dear life. I'm suffocating. He's constantly here or needing my help at his house. Now he's raising his two brothers, and I just feel so much responsibility to help them. I know he would do the same for me. I can't just abandon them.
Ace: Is he there right now?
Me: No.
Ace: Come over.
Me: What? I can't come over.
Ace: Why not?
Me: I can't do that to Sawyer.
Ace: I just want to see you.

I don't argue. I want to see him again too, more than anything. And who knows how long it'll be before I get a break from Sawyer again.

My fingers type the word before I make my final decision.

Me: Okay.

I press send.
I'm going to see Ace tonight.

chapter nineteen

Ember

I have to see Ace. It didn't take much convincing. He asked me to come over, and even though it is almost midnight, I am on my way to his apartment.

I don't know what to expect.

Is this wrong? Sure, I've spent every day with Sawyer since the accident. Yes, he says he loves me every day. But I still have never verbally agreed to be in a relationship with him. That hardly matters anymore. I already know what he would think. In Sawyer's eyes, we are already back together and what I am doing would hurt him if he ever found out.

Guilt consumes me as I pull into the parking lot of the bar. However, it is replaced with comfort and excitement when I see Ace's muscular build waiting for me at the entrance.

I step out of my car and walk toward him, holding back the giant smile that wants to escape. He doesn't hide his though. He is grinning from ear to ear.

"Hi there," he says as I approach the door.

"Hi."

Ace ushers me inside and locks the door behind us before he leads me up the stairs and into his apartment. I haven't been here since the morning I woke up with a hangover in a stranger's bed. Ace takes a seat on the couch. I follow closely behind and sit next to him.

I am still wearing the sweatpants and tank top that I dressed in for bed. I haven't changed. I don't want to make a big fuss about this visit, and really, I was just in a hurry to see Ace. Ace has on black basketball shorts and a gray cutoff, showing off his tanned skin and toned arms. He looks so sexy.

I lean back on the couch and sigh. I want him, and I want him *bad*. But that isn't what I am here for. It feels good just to be back in Ace's company, but the guilt still lingers.

"Are you okay?" Ace asks.

"I don't know. I feel guilty."

"You haven't done anything, Ember."

"I'm here, aren't I?" I argue.

Ace stands and paces behind the couch. His back muscles are so defined. I want to run my fingers along them, across his entire body. I want to feel every part of him.

He brushes his fingers through his hair. He remains silent for longer than I would like, but I am too busy checking him out to be overly concerned about the silence. But eventually, the silence becomes deafening. Maybe he is second-guessing why he even asked me to come over in the first place. Does he regret it?

He finally breaks the silence. "Ember, did either of you ever talk about this? What your relationship is? Did he even give you a fucking option?"

"No."

He finally stops pacing but stays behind the couch. "Then how have you done anything wrong by being here?"

"I don't know," I admit. "I can't help but feel like I'm doing something wrong. But at the same time, I *want* to be here, Ace. I wanted to see you again."

He treads back around the couch and takes a seat next to me, this time closer. Our thighs are touching when he places his hand on my knee. "I know," he says, his voice gruff. "I wanted to see you too."

I find his blue eyes again. "Why did you ask me to come over tonight?"

He takes a deep breath before answering. "I really just wanted to be near you again."

I nod.

He continues, "But I think I also wanted to be able to look you in the eyes, to see how you're truly feeling. I could tell at the coffee shop something wasn't right."

"What do you mean?"

"You seemed off. And honestly, it just doesn't make sense, Ember."

"What doesn't make sense?"

"I don't know. Everything. You. Him. Your relationship with him." He stands and begins pacing again. He walks toward the window and freezes, his body turning rigid.

"What's wrong?" I ask.

He doesn't answer.

Worried, I ask again, "Ace, what's wrong?"

I meet him at the window. When I look outside, I can't see what has made him so tense. "Ace?"

"What kind of car does Sawyer drive?"

"I don't know. Why?"

"Ember, try to think. What kind of car does he drive you around in?" he asks again.

"Um…it's white. It's some type of four-door car. It's slightly bigger than my car but isn't an SUV or anything."

"Yeah. That sounds about right."

"What?" I ask, worried. "What sounds about right?"

Ace backs away from the window and grabs my arm as he pulls me with him. He forces me into the bathroom and shuts the door behind us.

"Ace, what the hell?"

"Listen, Ember. When you got here, you were the only car in the parking lot. There's another car out there now, and I'm pretty sure it's Sawyer."

"What? That's impossible. He went home and went to bed hours ago. How would he even know I'm here?"

"Do you know that for sure? That he went home?" he asks.

I look around as I think. Do I know that for sure? I don't have his location on my phone. All I have is his word. I suppose I have no real way of knowing if he is at home other than his telling me so.

"No. I guess I don't."

He places both his hands on my shoulders and looks at me intently. His brows furrow with concern as he tilts his head.

"Does Sawyer know I live here?" he asks.

I shake my head. "He doesn't even know who you are, Ace."

"Yes, he does. He told me his name was Tom."

"What?" I pick at my nails as I wait for an explanation. *Damn nervous habit.*

"Sawyer. He showed up saying he had car trouble a little over a month ago. Asked to use my phone. Except he said his name was Tom."

"Are you sure it was him?"

"Yes. Same guy you were at the restaurant with. That car that's sitting out there, that's the car he was having trouble with."

"That makes no sense. Why would he say his name was Tom?"

"I don't know." His hand moves to his chin, and he bites his lip. *Is that his nervous habit?*

"Okay. Maybe it's not him, but the car you described is sitting in the parking lot right now. I think we should go, see if it follows us somewhere else."

"Where will we go?" I ask.

"I don't know yet."

It doesn't matter. For whatever reason, I know I can trust Ace. If he thinks we should go, then I'll go wherever he wants.

"Okay."

"Okay?" he repeats.

I nod.

Ace opens the bathroom door and walks out, bringing me with him. He holds my hand as we walk down the hall and into the living room. He grabs his keys off the coffee table and a sweatshirt off a hook as he leads me out the door and down the stairs into the bar. Instead of walking outside the front entrance, Ace takes me through a side door that leads to a garage where his truck is parked.

He opens the passenger side door and helps me in before walking around and getting in himself. He presses a button, and the sound of the garage door echoes as it opens behind us.

With his keys in the ignition, he backs out in a hurry. Ace looks worried, but for whatever reason, I remain calm.

Ace thinks Sawyer has followed me here, but I find that hard to believe. He's never given me any reason to believe he's stalking me. I mean, I've never caught him stalking me. What would the point have been? I'm with him all the time anyway. But why did he tell Ace his name is Tom? That doesn't make any sense other than he didn't want Ace to know who he really is.

Ace rests his right hand on my knee as he drives. I like it there. I like knowing he is there.

"Where are we going?" I ask.

"Somewhere Sawyer would never think to go."

We stop at a red light. He turns his head and looks at me as if he wants to say something important. His mouth opens then closes. Whatever he wants to say, he's hesitating.

"What is it, Ace?"

He takes a deep breath. "If his car shows up to where we're going, then we're going to have bigger problems than just a man who's forced himself into a relationship with you."

"Bigger problems? You really think Sawyer is stalking me?"

"I've seen that car before, Ember. I've seen it a whole fucking lot the last few weeks."

"Like where?"

"For starters, it was sitting in the coffee shop parking lot earlier today. I watched it drive away not too long before you left. Did Sawyer know when you would be heading home?"

Blood drains from my face. Of course he'd known when I would be heading home. We talk constantly, and I'd told him I would be home by four. I guess he always sort of knows where I am and when.

So, what's the point of following me there? Does he think I'm lying? I have never given him any reason not to trust me. But that still doesn't explain why he would be at Ace's tonight. He didn't know that I'd be there. I hadn't even known.

"Yes. He knew what time I would be home."

He squeezes my leg. "It's okay," he says. "We'll figure this out together."

chapter twenty

Ember

Ace and I sit in his truck in silence. I am feeling very unsettled at the possibility of Sawyer stalking me. Everything Ace has said worries me.

If Sawyer is stalking me, how have I not noticed? How long has this been going on? A million different thoughts race through my mind. I pick at my nail beds until they're horrid and bloody.

We've been driving for nearly thirty minutes with no destination in sight. I have no idea where Ace is taking us, but if Sawyer shows up, I will officially lose it.

I remember the comment Ace made when we first left his apartment, that he'd seen a white car a lot over the last few weeks. Maybe Ace has a stalker and it has nothing to do with me, although he really seems to think it does.

"Ace." I say, quietly.

He turns his head to look in my direction for a moment, letting me know he's listening.

"Where else have you seen that white car?" I ask.

He grips the steering wheel tighter. "I saw it that night I ran into you at my restaurant. It was parked in my valet lot. Then I watched you get into it with Sawyer and leave."

My mouth goes dry. "Where else?" I ask, hesitantly.

Ace sighs. "Besides when he said his name was Tom, I've watched it pull into my parking lot a few times. No one ever gets out. It just sits there. Then, when I saw it at the coffee shop today, my gut told me something wasn't right. So, when I saw it, yet again, after you showed up at my place…" He takes a deep breath. "Ember, it has to be him. There's no other explanation. One thing I don't understand is why he sits in my lot when you're not even there. If he's stalking you, what would bring him there? Why did he lie to me about his name? And why the hell does he follow you around in the first place? Have you really never felt like you were being watched?"

I look down at my lap. "No. I don't know. I've never noticed."

"I'm taking us to my brother's house. We're almost there."

Why is this happening to me?

I look out the window into the dark night, feeling scared and uncertain.

We pull into the driveway of what I assume is his brother's house. I see a light switch on, and the front door opens. It's the same guy I saw at the coffee shop earlier with Ace. I guess that's his brother. I didn't even know he had a brother.

Ace steps out of the truck and walks around to the passenger side to help me out. Both of his hands find my waist as he gently lifts me until my feet find the ground.

When we reach the front door, his brother opens it wide, inviting us in. It is the middle of the night, nearly two o'clock in the morning. I wonder why he is even awake. Ace must have texted him to let him know we were on our way.

We stand in the foyer as his brother closes the door. The cold air remains on my skin, and I shiver as I fold my arms over my chest, trying to cover my erect nipples that protrude through the thin cotton.

Ace notices and immediately takes off his hoodie, handing it to me. "Here."

I smile and put it on. *It smells like him.*

"Brennon," Ace says. "This is Ember. Ember, this is my brother, Brennon."

"Nice to meet you, Ember," Brennon says.

"You, too. Thanks for letting us come here."

Brennon smiles. He has the same smile as Ace. His eyes are blue, too. I can tell they are brothers now.

"Follow me, you can relax in here for a bit," Ace says as he grabs my hand, taking me into a huge guest bedroom before he closes the door.

"Does Brennon live here alone?" I ask.

He nods. "Yeah. Sometimes I stay here with him, but most of the time it's just him. We grew up here. He bought it from our parents when they moved to Florida last year. This was my old room."

I sit down on the bed and Ace follows.

"Are you scared?" he asks.

"I guess I should be, but being with you makes me feel better for some reason."

He kisses my forehead and the second his lips reach my skin my entire body melts. I want so much more from him.

"I hope I'm wrong about all of this," he says.

"Me too."

"I'm not going to let anything happen to you though, Ember. You know that, right?"

I smile. "Thank you."

"You don't have to thank me."

I lean my head on his shoulder. I love the way he smells, like lemon and wood.

He rubs my leg. When his hand reaches the top of my thigh, I feel an ache between my legs.

"I'm sorry I didn't come to see you after that night at your restaurant," I say.

"I understand why you didn't."

"I should've at least called."

"You had a lot going on."

"You know, I've dreamt about you almost every night since."

He smirks. "What kind of dreams?"

I blush at what I'm about to confess. "I sometimes dream about what sex with you would be like. I've only ever slept with one man, so it's hard to imagine what it would be like with anyone else. But, *wow*. You thought our kiss was good? You should feel how incredible our sex is."

He laughs. "I'd be lying if I said I haven't already imagined what sex would be like with you, Ember."

A tear rolls down my cheek. What is wrong with me? Why am I being so emotional? He hasn't said anything to upset me.

I quickly wipe it away, but not before Ace sees it.

"What's wrong?" he asks.

"Nothing." I say.

"Ember…"

"I don't know how I let things get to this point. I'm frustrated, annoyed, sad, mad. I don't think those words even really describe what I feel. If Sawyer really is stalking me, then the only man I've ever loved, the only man I've ever given my heart to, is a man who quite literally might be a psychopath."

More tears fall. They are uncontrollable. As much as I want to make them stop, I can't.

Ace pulls me in tighter. He scoots us back further onto the bed until he is leaning against the headboard while I lay my head in his lap. He wipes my tears away as they fall.

"Only giving your heart to one man isn't a bad thing, Ember. You're loyal. You're honest. I love that about you."

He loves something about me.

"No one else has even tried to be with me since Sawyer. Something must be wrong with me. Five years, Ace. I was single for five fucking years."

"Ember. Nothing is wrong with you." He strokes my arm gently, in a soothing manner.

I love his touch. "Ace," I whisper.

"Yeah?"

"I don't know if this makes sense. I know we hardly know each other, but I really like you. I'm afraid to lose whatever this is. You're not even mine to lose, but I don't want to think of my life without you anymore."

"You won't have to," he says softly. "I'm not going anywhere."

I sit up until we are at eye level. He uses his thumb to wipe the remaining tears away. He grabs my cheek with his other hand, and I press my face into his palm. I watch as his eyes fall to my lips. I look at his.

"Is it okay if I kiss you?" he whispers.

I nod, silently pleading for him to kiss me.

His lips gently press into mine. His tongue slips into my mouth as my lips part to make way. This kiss is everything I remember it to be and more. The way he kisses me is far more careful than before, like he is trying to protect me from the world. He is keeping me safe. His lips on mine feel natural. It feels right. My body responds to the passion of the moment and aches for more.

We shift on the bed until my back is flat and Ace is on top of me. He never takes his mouth off mine, never breaks the kiss.

His hands explore my curves that are hidden beneath his sweatshirt while our kisses become more frantic and hurried. For a moment I worry about Sawyer finding me here, that he might see what I'm doing with Ace.

"Maybe we should close the curtains. Just in case."

Ace nods before standing to shut all the curtains, leaving us in our own private safe place.

Thoughts of Sawyer quickly vanish as I get lost in the way Ace touches me, and all I want is to feel our bare skin touch. My hands find the bottom of his shirt and tug. His shirt has to come off. I need to feel what is beneath. I pull it up, exposing his muscular core. His lips only leave mine as he removes his shirt the rest of the way.

Holy shit.

My eyes grow wide. I have seen him once without a shirt, on the morning I woke up in his apartment. The defined muscle is difficult *not* to notice, but I have never seen his body this close. I've never *touched* his body. I brush my hand over his abs. His body is a rock; hard, firm, and so sexy.

He laughs under his breath at my undeniable response to him before his mouth returns to mine.

I can't wait any longer to feel his skin against mine. The baggy sweatshirt creates a thick barrier that leaves me longing for more. I need the sweatshirt off, now.

Tilting my head, I break our kiss. "I need this off," I pant.

He grabs the bottom of the sweatshirt and quickly pulls it over my head in one swift motion.

His mouth falls to my chest, to the areas my tank top doesn't cover. He kisses every spot on my body that is exposed to him. His tongue explores my neck, sporadically leaving small kisses in areas it discovers.

It still isn't enough. There is a layer of cotton between us, my hard nipples suffocating beneath.

"Ember," Ace says, breathless.

I look up at him.

"Can I take this off?" he asks, pointing to my tank top.

He must be reading my mind. "Yes."

He slowly lifts the tank top over my head. He looks down at my sweatpants, inaudibly requesting to take them off as well. I slide both of my hands into my waistband and push them down my legs. Ace takes over at my knees and pulls them the rest of the way down. He throws my clothes to the floor, where they lay in a puddle, and I am left in nothing but my panties.

Ace stares at me, taking in my body. It is the first time he has seen this much of me. The first time anyone, other than Sawyer, has been privy to my curves.

"Wow, Ember." His voice is raspy, and damn, is it sexy. "You're perfect."

His mouth moves to my stomach and leaves soft, subtle kisses there before he finds my mouth again, our bodies pressing together at last. I can feel his hardness push against me.

Our bodies move against one another, naturally. Our lips clash together, even more desperate than before. His hardness rubs between my legs, creating the friction that I desire. It feels so good. I can feel myself nearing the edge.

"Ace," I let out.

He doesn't stop. He keeps grinding himself against me.

"Ace," I say a little louder.

I am going to come. He hasn't even taken his pants off yet. He hasn't even physically touched me there, yet I am already on the brink.

"It's okay," he says.

He knows my climax is near. He pushes against me harder, rocking his hips into me faster. He kisses me everywhere, my cheek, nose, neck, anywhere he can reach until my body tremors beneath his.

His lips find mine, and he absorbs my moans into his mouth. This orgasm feels electric. He doesn't stop moving, doesn't stop kissing me, not until my tremors subside.

Damn.

I lie on the bed, breathless.

Ace moves from my mouth to my stomach, placing kisses along my body until he reaches my panties. He places his thumb between my thighs, the area still sensitive from the orgasm I just came down from. He rubs his thumb over the sensitive nerves while he kisses the inside of my thighs. When he thrusts a finger inside of me, I whimper.

My body feels weak to his touch. Every small trace of him on my skin sends shivers down my spine.

He gradually takes off my panties. He looks up at me, watching my response to his actions. I look back at him with more longing than I've ever felt in my entire life. I want him so bad. I want all of him.

He throws my panties to the floor and kisses along my legs, up to my inner thighs, until his mouth returns to the space between my legs. He kisses me there softly. I feel as his tongue moves along my divide, and my spine arches in response.

I feel his finger inside of me. Then two. Then three. His tongue continues to work as his fingers work. He is going to push me over the edge a second time. I can feel it. It won't take long. I am already sensitive from the first orgasm, and now his tongue is licking me in all the right places as his fingers find those other sensitive spots.

My hands find his hair and grip tightly as I move my body in motion with his tongue. "Oh, my God," I moan.

He removes his fingers, and his hands find my waist, pulling me closer to his mouth. I let out an even louder moan. It is all too much. His touch. His lips. His tongue. The motion. It is all pushing me to the brink, farther than I've ever been before.

When I reach my climax, my legs shake. It feels like I am soaring. It is the most intense orgasm I've ever had. I feel it in every part of my body, from my head to my toes. The orgasm makes my body tremble as if an earthquake has just struck.

His mouth never moves. He continues to work his magic between my legs until I am sent into yet another climax. And another. I am weak. How has he done this to me? I feel every single part of each release throughout my entire body. It leaves me panting and out of breath. I need him to be inside me, and I need it now.

"Ace," I moan.

He slowly stands and removes his pants and boxers, impossibly ready. I can't help but stare between his legs. He is large. The biggest I have ever seen. He's ready, and I feel a wave of pleasure knowing that being here with me has done that to him.

"Wow," I whisper.

He smiles, walks back toward the bed, and kisses my neck. Then my nipples. He hasn't paid them much attention, but the wait is worth it. He sucks and nibbles on them, but I can't wait any longer. I need to feel him.

Lying next to me on the bed, his fingers move delicately over my stomach. I love his touch, but my body aches for him to be inside me.

"What are you doing?" I ask.

"I shouldn't have taken all our clothes off."

His words leave an empty feeling in my stomach. "Why?" I ask, timidly.

"I don't have any condoms."

"It's okay," I say, relieved. "I'm on the pill. And I'm clean. I've never had sex without one before."

I pull his face back to mine and kiss him. I want this. He needs to know that.

He kisses me back with more force than before. I can feel how much he wants this too.

Easing himself on top of me, he gently slides his length inside of me, keeping his eyes glued on mine. He is so big. I feel so full of *him*. It is the closest I have ever been to someone, without the restriction of a condom.

He grunts into my mouth as he kisses me. I tilt my head back, and his lips move to my neck. I whimper. Every touch is heightened. Everything feels so much better with him inside me.

"Fuck," Ace groans into my ear as he continues to thrust himself in and out of me, quickening his pace. He rolls himself off me and onto his back, bringing me with until I am on top, without ever leaving me empty.

I move myself above him. He places his hands on my waist and guides me. He watches me intimately. His eyes never waver. If it is possible, this position makes me feel even more full of him. The way he moves inside of me, thrusting up to meet me, I can feel myself nearing the end once again.

"Ace," I whimper.

He pushes inside of me more hurriedly. I am so close to my climax, it is hard to hold on. I want him to come, I want him to come with me, but it is getting harder and harder to keep myself from falling over the edge.

"Ace, I'm going to come again," I say frantically.

He continues to thrust desperately inside of me. "It's okay, baby."

I tilt my head back and let myself fall. My entire world comes to a complete stop as I soar through a space that is incredibly freeing and secure. My body feels light as the tremors take over. Ace completely consumes me as his body tenses beneath me. I feel the pulsing between my legs as he soars with me.

I move my gaze so I can watch him. His eyes are full of lust and pleasure. He hasn't taken his off me. He watches everything he does to me. *Everything*. And I watch the effect I have on him.

I lean on top of his chest, trying to catch my breath. We are both layered with a small mist of perspiration. He caresses my back with one hand, the other gently resting on the back of my head.

"That was even better than I imagined," he whispers.

I smile against his chest, still breathless and completely speechless.

"That good, huh?" he asks.

"Good doesn't even begin to describe it."

We stay like this for a few minutes before reality sets in, and I remember why we are here in the first place. I stiffen as I roll off him.

Ace stands as he gathers our clothes from the floor. He kisses me tenderly on the lips and hands me my clothes. "Here."

He dresses and sits at the edge of the bed. Once I am clothed, he pulls me to him until I'm sitting on his lap.

"You're remarkable, Ember," he says as he tucks a piece of hair behind my ear.

I smile and kiss him, stroking my fingers through his hair.

He places both of his hands on either side of my face, turning my head until I look at him. He leans in, our foreheads pressed together.

Letting out a sigh, he says, "I have to go back out there. I'm going to see if he's shown up."

I nod, but internally, I am disappointed. I don't want him to go. I want to stay like this forever. But I know that isn't realistic. The only reason we are here is because Sawyer might be stalking me. The thought makes me quiver. I hope Ace is wrong. If Sawyer is stalking me, what does that mean? What will happen?

He picks me up and places me back down on the bed.

"I'm in this now, okay? I won't let anything happen to you," he says before he kisses my forehead.

I smile. "I'm in this now, too."

He stands and walks toward the bedroom door. "I'll be right back, okay?"

"Okay."

I move under the covers and lay my head onto the pillow as I try to relax. My body still feels weak. I lose track of time but know it has to be nearing morning. I am exhausted, and I know Ace is too.

I can't help but feel like I am inconveniencing him and his brother. I have to remind myself that this is Ace's idea. He was adamant about taking me somewhere, and he evidently feels his brother's house is the best option.

All we can do is wait. In the meantime, I get to lie comfortably in a bed we just made love in.

This changes everything.

Ace makes me feel safe, incredible. He makes me feel like I am on top of the world. That was without a doubt the best sex I've ever had. It is so different with Ace. He made me forget about everything else when we were together. The accident. Sawyer's insistent need to be with me. His potential stalking. Ace has allowed me to escape reality for a while.

I know I can't be with Sawyer anymore. Even if this is all a misunderstanding, it's over between us.

I wonder how long we will be here. If Sawyer doesn't show up, will we leave in the morning?

I yawn. What time is it, anyway? Surely, they won't mind if I get some rest.

I close my eyes and drift into a deep sleep.

chapter twenty-one

Ember

I hear yelling. And banging.

I open my eyes and look around. It takes me a moment before I remember where I am.

Brennon's house.

I am still alone in the now dark bedroom.

I hear another loud bang. Glass shatters. A door slams.

My hands are shaking. I don't know what is going on, but my body recognizes that something isn't right.

The door suddenly bursts open. Ace stands in the doorway, out of breath.

"Let's go. We have to leave. Now," he says, his voice in a panic.

I jump off the bed. "What's going on?"

He doesn't answer. Instead, he grabs my hand as we run out of the bedroom and toward the front door. The house is in disarray: broken furniture, overturned tables, a shattered lamp.

Outside, Brennon already sits in the truck. Ace opens the door and helps me into the back seat before following behind and slamming the door shut.

"Go!" Ace yells.

I look out the window as we drive off and notice a white car parked on the street. Is that the same car that Ace saw at the bar? Is it Sawyer's? Has he found us?

"Did he show up?" I ask.

He looks at me, concerned, but doesn't answer the question.

"Ace?"

He ignores me again and leans into the front seat, saying something to Brennon.

"Ace!" I yell, frustrated. "Did he fucking show up or not?"

He leans back in the seat and meets my gaze. "Yes. He showed up."

"What happened?"

"Ember," Ace says quietly.

"Tell me what happened."

Ace wraps his arms around me and kisses the top of my head. "I'm sorry. I'm so sorry I didn't realize this sooner."

"Didn't realize what sooner?"

I back away, pushing him away from me so I can see his face when he finally gives me some answers.

"Ember, he's been watching you. He's been watching you for a long fucking time."

"What? What do you mean? How do you know that?"

"Because he just tried to get rid of me like he's gotten rid of every other guy that ever tried to get close to you."

Every guy that has ever tried to get close to me? What is he talking about? Guys hardly notice me. I've made out with a few here and there, but then they lose interest. Was that because of Sawyer? How had Sawyer kept them away?

I have so many questions, but now isn't the time. Ace looks afraid, and if he's afraid, then I must be in danger. I wish I hadn't fallen asleep. If I had stayed awake, then maybe I would have the slightest clue of what is going on. I need to know what happened back there.

"Where is he?" I ask.

"He's locked in Brennon's basement. We got him down there long enough to get you out of there. I'm sure he's broken down the door by now, but at least we got a head start."

My mouth drops open. Is this really happening?

I can't stop the tears from welling in my eyes. How many times would I cry tonight? This is all too much.

Ace pulls me back into his arms and gives me a squeeze. I rest my head on his chest as I soak his shirt with my tears. He holds me like this as he moves his hand up and down my back in a soothing motion. He is so good at comforting me, but unfortunately, it isn't enough.

The realization hits me like a ton of bricks. Sawyer is stalking me, and I have been blind to it. How long has he been doing this? Since high school?

I cry harder. Ace repeatedly whispers comforting words into my hair, letting me know that everything is going to be okay, that he is there for me, that he will protect me. But I'm not so sure.

"Why don't we go to the police?" I whisper between sobs.

"We don't have any proof right now. As soon as we can prove that he is stalking you, then we will go to the police."

I back away again, so my voice is clear. "*Proof?* Didn't he just break into Brennon's house? Isn't that proof enough?"

"No. He didn't break in. He was acting like a normal worried boyfriend when I opened the door. Everything that has happened between the two of you has been consensual, Ember. If anything, I'm the one who looks bad in this situation. Driving you to a stranger's house in the middle of the night, locking you in a bedroom…He just asked where you were, and I wouldn't tell him. He could say he thought you were in danger, being held against your will. Of course, he was going to lose his shit. I would have too."

"How do you know what he's done? Did he tell you?"

"Kind of."

"Ace, you're not making any sense."

"I know, Ember. I know. It doesn't make any sense. None of this makes sense. But he is stalking you, I'm sure of that. I could see it in his eyes. He's dangerous. There's no telling what he would do to get to you. I can't let him get to you. *I can't.*"

Ace is so sure that I am in danger. In turn, it only makes me more afraid. It hurts to see the fear instilled in his eyes. He is worried for me. He is doing everything he can right now to protect me, but it is still hard to fully comprehend what's happening.

"Where are we going?" I ask.

"I don't know yet." Ace holds my hand tightly, his knee twitching anxiously.

"Are you okay, Ace?"

A slight grin emerges on his face, and he kisses my lips softly. "You just found out you're being stalked, and you're worried about me?" He chuckles. "Don't worry about me. I just want to make sure you're okay."

Ace pulls out his phone and starts to scroll through something. I don't want to pry, so I keep my gaze fixed on the road ahead. He turns his head and looks at me again with an expression I can't read.

"Hey," he says softly. "I have a question. It might seem kind of strange, but I need to know."

"All right."

"Did they finish the investigation?"

"What investigation?"

"Sawyer's parents. Do they know what caused the wreck?"

"Sawyer told me it was ruled an accident. The car was totaled, so there wasn't much they could look at. I think he said it was some kind of malfunction."

He looks out the window.

"Why?" I ask.

He turns his attention back to me. "Something he said back there. It just made me think maybe he had something to do with it. I just looked up the police report." He hands me his phone. "It says the accident could have been due to a leak. Apparently, the power-steering pump had a giant gash in it, so by the time his parents got on the highway, it was completely out of fluid, so they lost control."

"What?" I scroll frantically through the report. "What are you trying to say?"

He stays quiet.

"You think he did it? You think he caused the leak? Why would he intentionally cause his parents to wreck? They *died*, Ace. You think he's capable of killing his own flesh and blood?"

"I don't know."

Liz and Rod had been two of the best people I'd ever known. They'd loved their kids more than anything on this earth. They had given them an amazing home, an amazing *life*, and I knew Sawyer loved them. He'd been devastated when they died.

Sure, I never actually saw him cry, but that didn't mean he isn't hurting. I helped make their deaths easier for him. I'd done everything I could for him. He'd been damn lucky to come back into my life when he did. If he hadn't shown up at my house, then we wouldn't have ended up at dinner that night, and I wouldn't have been at the hospital with him, at the funeral with him, at the house helping him. He would've had to do it all *alone*.

Holy shit.

I gasp for air. I suddenly can't breathe.

Ace's eyes grow big. "Ember? Ember, it's okay. You're okay."

I know I'm hyperventilating, but there is little I can do to stop it. As panic instills, the world around me grows fuzzy. Ace's face becomes impossible to focus on. He keeps repeating for me to breathe, over and over again, but I can't breathe.

He opens the window. The fresh air and wind snap me back into reality.

"Breathe," he says again. "Breathe, Ember. Breathe."

Eventually, I catch my breath, though my breathing remains labored. I finally feel the air as it moves throughout my lungs once again.

But then, the tears. The sobs. Just as some of them dissipate, I somehow have more to spare. It is embarrassing, really. This time it is an uncontrollable, ugly cry. I would hate to look at myself in a mirror right now.

I start to yell and scream, like a two-year-old having a temper tantrum. I know I am being ridiculous. What good will screaming like a child do? But I have to let it out. This is all too much.

The tears fall rapidly down my face. I kick the seat in front of me. Ace tries to grab me, but I push him away. I am in a complete downward spiral, and I don't know if I'm about to hit rock bottom or if I am already there.

Ace is eventually able to throw his arms around me. He squeezes tightly until I can't move anymore. He holds my legs down with his until I relent. He is too strong to fight. I give up, and my body falls limp.

"It's okay," he whispers. "I've got you."

Eventually, my tears dry. I don't have any left. I have cried more in the last twenty-four hours than I have my entire life.

Ace has no idea what caused my sudden panic attack. I have to tell him what happened. What I am so *sure* of.

"He murdered his parents," I whisper.

He only nods.

He already knows.

chapter twenty-two

Ember

We have been driving for hours, and I have no idea where we are.
The sun is rising, which means Ace and Brennon have been up the
entire night. Hopefully we are going to find somewhere for us to
sleep soon.

Another hour or so passes before Brennon pulls into a janky
motel. We passed a sign that said *Ohio Welcomes You* earlier, so I
guess we've crossed a couple state lines. Brennon pulls up to the
front door and walks into the motel while Ace stays with me inside
the truck.

He'd suggested I get rid of my phone in case that had been how
Sawyer kept track of me. We threw it out the window an hour ago.
Before getting rid of it, I called my mom to let her know I was okay.
I told her I was going out of town for a few days with a friend and
gave her Ace's contact info.

My mom hardly questions my actions anymore, but she wanted
to know a few details about Ace. It is hardly like me to keep my
mother in the dark about my life, but it is neither the time or place to
go into detail about anything. I'd also emailed a substitute instructor

to fill in for me. I told her I have a family emergency, so she made plans to take over my lecture and online classes for the next week or so.

Brennon returns from the motel lobby and hops back into the driver's seat. He drives us around back. Once we are parked, he turns to us in the backseat and hands Ace one of two room keys.

"Thank you, Brennon," I say. "For everything."

He doesn't know me. He doesn't have to be involved in any of this, but he is. And he'd done it without question.

He smiles at me. "Of course."

Ace steps out of the truck and turns to help me out.

I don't have any luggage with me. None of this is planned. I hadn't been expecting a road trip. *Or a stalker.*

Ace grabs a duffle bag out of the bed of the truck before we walk toward our room.

"You packed a bag?" I ask.

"I grabbed a few things from Brennon's. My mom left some clothes there. I didn't know how long we'd be gone, so I took some stuff for you. They should fit."

I kiss him. "Thank you."

He smiles, grabs my hand, and leads me toward the door labeled 12C. Brennon had rented himself a separate room right next door.

When we walk in, my eyes immediately find the lone bed centered in the room. I remember what happened the last time he and I were in a bed together. I am excited to be alone with Ace, though I can't help but feel like an inconvenience to both him and Brennon.

"Ace," I say. "You and Brennon don't have to do this for me, you know. I can take care of myself."

Ace throws his duffle on the bed and turns to face me. He puts his arms around me and draws me into his chest. "I know you can." He kisses the top of my head. "But, fortunately for you, I protect the people I love."

"The people you love?"

He kisses me softly on the lips. "Yes."

"You love me?"

"I love you."

I don't know how to respond. So much has happened, and it is happening so fast. I know what we have is different than what I have felt in the past. I love Sawyer, but not like this. Whatever I have with Ace is something deeper. Something stronger. But am I ready to admit that I am falling in love with this man?

Maybe his emotions are heightened because we had sex for the first time not too long ago, or because of the situation we are in. He could have a hero complex, a desire to save. Does he love me because I need saving? I won't hold it against him if he doesn't mean it.

"Isn't it a bit soon to be professing your love for me?" I tease. "I mean, I don't even know your last name..."

He laughs. "You're right. It's probably too soon to admit that. But I can't help it. I love the shit out of you, Ember Johnson." He kisses me again. When our lips part, he is grinning. "And my last name is Cooper."

"Ace Cooper." I kiss him again. Then I say, "Wait, how did you know my last name?"

He smirks. "Your bar tab. Which you never paid, by the way, but most of your drinks were covered."

We both burst into laughter. I drank a lot that night. I don't know how many drinks I bought and how many were bought for me, but he is right, I did not spend a single dime.

The laughing leads to kissing, and the kissing leads us to the bed.

"You should get some sleep," I say, pulling his mouth away from mine.

"You should too," he rebuts.

"I'm going to shower first."

"Great idea," he says. "Me too."

I jump off the bed and run toward the bathroom, trying to beat him there. Ace chases me inside and closes the door behind us, even though we are alone in the hotel room.

He spins us around until my back is flat against the door, his strong body pressing into mine. Our lips crash together as we frantically pull off each other's clothes until we are both completely naked.

Ace turns the shower head on and steps inside. His hand reaches out for mine. I take it as I step into the shower. The water falls on us from above. Our lips discover one another again, and I find mine instantly parting, making way for his tongue.

He kisses me more slowly than before. The water glides down our bodies, making the kiss warm and wet.

Ace takes a step back as he reaches for something on the other side of the curtain. He holds a hotel-sized bottle of shampoo and squeezes it into his hand. He motions for me to turn around and gently massages the shampoo into my hair. It is such an intimate gesture that I feel a soothing sensation erupt down my lower back and all along my arms. When he is done, he rubs shampoo into his own hair, though not as delicately as he had mine.

Once he finishes, he pulls me closer to him so we can continue our kiss where we left off as the water rinses the rest of the shampoo from our hair. It glides down our bodies, leaving streaks of white suds as they empty down the drain.

He repeats the gesture with the conditioner and body wash. He takes his time when he washes my body, making sure not to miss an inch. When his palms rub against my breasts, I release a small moan. He notices right away, and his lips return to mine. We stay that way until the soap rinses from our bodies.

He shuts off the shower, never breaking our kiss, before he picks me up at my waist. I wrap my legs around him as he carries me back to the bed. He gently lays me down, then falls on top of me. We are soaked, and now our bed is wet, but neither of us cares.

His lips leave mine for the first time once I am lying down, my back flat against the bed. His mouth explores every inch of my body, leaving nothing untouched. He slides against my skin with his tongue, hovering over my nipples, carefully circling and teasing them one by one.

As he makes his way back to my mouth, I moan. My body is craving his. He moves on top of me, and with one swift motion, he is inside me until I am completely filled with him.

He takes his time, and I savor every moment, our bodies connecting as one. Nothing has ever felt so good.

"God, I love you," he whispers as he kisses me.

I whimper into his mouth, the vibrations from my moans only amplifying the kiss. Will I ever get used to Ace telling me that he loves me?

He changes his pace, moving with more force, thrusting into me with purpose, with *love*. I feel his arm muscles tighten as he nears the edge. But he slows down, not allowing himself to reach it yet.

He pulls himself out and kisses down the length of my body until he is between my legs. I feel the emptiness he leaves behind, but his tongue fills it quickly. It gently presses against me and slides up and down in the place I am most sensitive.

I reach for his hair and grip tightly as he carries me toward the edge, but he retreats yet again.

"Ace," I moan.

He plants kisses back up the length of my body until he finds my mouth again. And before I know it, he is back inside me, giving me what I want. *Him*.

My body moves with his. It doesn't take long before we both completely let go. He comes inside me as I unravel beneath him. My nails dig into his back from the intensity of the orgasm. Making love to this man leaves me breathless. My heart races, and I feel his heartbeat pounding as he lies on top of my chest.

After a few moments, he carefully pulls himself out of me and stretches out beside me. His hand gently skates over my stomach. My arm wraps around him while his head rests on my chest. I can't help but stare at him. He is a beautiful man. A beautiful man that *loves me*. I look into his enchanting blue eyes as I play with his dark, thick hair. I want to savor this moment forever.

We move under the covers, still naked. We haven't said a word since we finished. We recover silently, our bare bodies appreciating one another.

I continue to run my fingers through his hair as I think about all the events that have happened in my life since I met this man. I wonder how Sawyer found out about Ace. How I let him keep Ace and me apart for as long as he did.

"I'm sorry I let Sawyer ruin our first kiss," I say, breaking our silent recovery. His face falls instantly, and I continue, "When I saw you at the restaurant, I wanted so badly to tell you that I wasn't there romantically with him."

"He didn't ruin our first kiss, Ember. Nothing could ruin that."

I smile, twirling a strand of his hair in my fingers.

"After we kissed, I knew there was more to our story. I wanted you so badly. I hadn't even kissed Sawyer yet at that point. It was *you*. It was always supposed to be *you*, Ace."

He sits up and moves his hand to my face as he looks down at me. "You have nothing to be sorry for. He manipulated you into an impossible situation. He took advantage of you. You don't ever have to be sorry, okay?"

He lays his head back down, and this time my cheek presses against his chest. My hand explores him, trailing across his belly button and eventually landing between his legs. I already want him again, and it seems he is ready too. Will we always want each other this much? Here we are, in the middle of a conversation, and my mind has already wandered to having sex with him again.

"I thought about calling you," he says, interrupting my thoughts. "I never would have imagined in a million years that we'd be in the situation we're in now. I thought you wanted to be with him. I thought maybe you didn't feel the same way I did. I wanted to reach out to you so many times, but then I figured you would have let me know in some way if you were interested in me. I tried to give you space. I wish I hadn't."

"I was always interested in you, Ace."

He kisses the top of my head.

"I'm glad I ran into you at that coffee shop," I say.

He smiles. "Me too."

We both scoot until our heads share a pillow, my back against his chest, and I can feel his breath against my neck. He wraps his arms around me and holds me tight. There is no space between us, no indication of where his body ends and mine begins.

I feel his hardness pressing against my backside. I push my ass against him. He reacts by moving his hand over my hip, then my thigh, until it finally stops between my legs. I am already wet for him.

A moment later, I am filled with Ace. He thrusts into me from behind, his fingers paying attention to me exactly where I need. He breathes heavily on my neck as he thrusts into me again and again.

"Oh, my God," he moans.

"Faster," I beg.

He thrusts into me again, quickening his pace. Both of his hands find my breasts. He squeezes my nipples, sending an electric shock of pain and pleasure radiating directly between my legs. A moment later, I am sent into another orgasm.

"Fuck," Ace grunts.

We climax together. Each orgasm is better than the last.

Our soaked bodies are no longer wet from the shower, but from perspiration from making love again. He leaves my body weak and exhausted.

He pulls out once we both finish but never leaves my side. He only pulls me in closer, surrounding my body with his big masculine figure.

It is calming, having Ace hold me. He makes me forget what is going on. I can relax knowing he is here. I will sleep well with him protecting me.

"Goodnight, Ember," he says as he places a gentle kiss on my shoulder.

"Goodnight, Ace."

chapter twenty-three

Ember

When I wake up, it is still light out. I turn over to look at the clock on the nightstand. It reads *5:38 p.m.* I notice Ace isn't in bed. I look around the room and don't see him anywhere.

"Ace?" I call out.

He doesn't answer.

I quickly get out of bed and throw on Ace's T-shirt from earlier. I frantically open the door to the motel room and step outside. Panicked, I search the parking lot, instantly thinking the worst. Did Sawyer find us? Did something happen to Ace? Thankfully, I am filled with relief when I spot Ace standing with Brennon by the truck. They both notice my moment of panic.

Ace runs over to me. "Are you okay?"

"Yeah. You weren't in bed when I woke up, and then I couldn't find you. I thought something had happened."

He kisses my forehead. "I'm sorry. I've been out here talking with Brennon."

I look over in Brennon's direction and smile. He is already smirking.

"What?" I ask Brennon.

He looks over at Ace. "Your girlfriend isn't wearing any pants."

Ace and I both look down at my bare legs. The T-shirt is long enough to cover me, but I'm not wearing any underwear. I look up, embarrassed, but Ace smiles and laughs.

"I put the bag on the dresser," he says. "Why don't you go get dressed before you give my brother a boner."

"Oh, my God, Ace!" I say as I push against his chest.

I turn around and walk back to the motel room, careful not to expose my bare ass. I can hear Ace and Brennon laugh behind me. Although I am completely mortified, I can't help but laugh a little too.

I find a nice sundress that Ace says belonged to his mom inside the duffle. It is light yellow with a beautiful floral pattern. It fits me perfectly and falls just above my knees. My breasts fill it out effortlessly. The dress makes me feel beautiful.

I slip on my sandals and join them back outside. Brennon and Ace both face me as I make my way toward them.

Ace grabs my hand as I get closer. "That dress looks amazing on you."

"I preferred the T-shirt and no pants," Brennon says, sarcastically.

Ace punches him in the arm.

Brennon flinches. "Shit, dude," he says.

I roll my eyes. "So, what's the plan, boys? How are we going to prove that my ex-boyfriend is a psycho stalker killer?"

Ace's face falls flat.

"I was only kidding with that comment," I say to Ace. "I didn't mean to make you upset."

He shakes his head. "No. It's not that."

"Then what is it?"

Brennon steps in. "We think Sawyer spies on you from his car. So, unless you scrutinized every car in your neighborhood, you'd never actually know he was stalking you. Unfortunately, that leaves very little evidence."

Ace chimes in. "The only way we're going to be able to prove anything is if we get him to admit what he's done."

Brennon continues. "A confession will hold up best in court. Or we get pretty damn lucky and find some incriminating evidence about his involvement with the accident, but the chances of that are slim to none. We're also looking into any doorbell cameras in your neighborhood."

"Okay," I say. "Say we don't find any evidence, and there are no cameras that captured him. How do you expect us to get him to admit anything?"

Ace squeezes my hand. "You're going to have to get him to confess to you," he says, softly.

"*Me?*"

Brennon interjects again. "He would never admit anything to me, he doesn't know who the hell I am. Besides, once he does figure it out, there won't be a chance in hell he tells me anything. And there's no fucking way he talks to Ace."

"What do you mean when he figures it out? Who are you?" I ask.

"He's a cop," Ace says,

"*You're a cop!*" I yell. "Why the *hell* didn't you arrest him at your house?"

Ace squeezes my hand again. "I already told you, Ember. He couldn't do anything about that. Sawyer was being a protective boyfriend. I looked worse in that situation, taking you away and bringing you to a random house in the middle of the night. Brennon would've only been able to hold him for twenty-four hours at best. We need to lock him up for good, to make sure he can't get to you."

"Can't I get a restraining order?" I ask.

"I'm working on that." Brennon says. "But I don't want to put it into effect until after we get his confession. If you can get him to confess to the murder, he will be put away for life. You're our best shot at this."

I lean against Ace's truck and slide down until I am sitting on the ground. I thought I would be safe from Sawyer, and I didn't think I would ever have to face him again. The thought of being in the same room with him scares me half to death. I have no idea what else he is capable of.

Ace sits next to me and pulls me into him until my head is leaning against his shoulder. "Babe, we're not going to let anything happen to you. If it comes to that, we'll be there too. He just won't know it. I promise, I'm not going to leave you alone with him, okay?"

"Okay."

He kisses the top of my head. "I'm going to keep you safe," he whispers.

We are back on the road again. They don't tell me where we're going, and I'm too afraid to ask. I haven't said a word since we got in the truck and started driving. I don't know what to say. Or I have too much to say. Either way, I can't speak. I can hardly think. I don't even know *what* to think.

My mind races. I hope they aren't taking me to see Sawyer right now. They'd better warn me before they make me do that.

How the hell did I get myself into this mess? How did I not know Sawyer killed his own fucking parents? The thought scares the hell out of me, and now I am freaking out more than I was two seconds ago.

There's been a constant battle in my head since we left. As each minute passes, I find myself more frightened than the last. I feel my heart beating out of my chest. I hope I'm not having another panic attack, but it is getting harder and harder to catch my breath.

Ace and Brennon are talking in the front seat. I sit in the back this time, alone. Neither of them notice anything is wrong with me.

My hands shake as tears spill out of my eyes.

Not again.

I fucking hate Sawyer. Fuck him.

I pull my feet onto the seat and bring my knees closer to my chest so I can rest my elbows on them. I lay my face in my hands, which proves to be harder than I thought with how bad they are shaking.

There are a lot of tears pouring from my eyes, and my heartbeat speeds up. This can't be normal. Each breath is getting harder and harder to take, and soon I am gasping for air between sobs.

Ace finally notices when he turns his head. "*Jesus*, Ember. Are you okay?" He turns to Brennon. "Pull over." He looks back toward me. "Ember, look at me. Are you okay? What's wrong?"

His hand is on my knee, and he keeps asking if I'm okay, but I can't form words.

Brennon pulls over at a rest stop, and Ace hurries out of the car to open the back door. He carries me out and to a nearby picnic bench. Sitting down, he cradles me in his arms. I bury my head into his chest and cry uncontrollably. My heart rate slows down a bit, but I am still trembling beneath him.

"Ember, you're shaking," he whispers. "It's okay. Everything is going to be okay."

I know he is trying to calm me down, but he doesn't know if everything is going to be okay. We have no idea how far Sawyer is willing to go. He'd killed his own parents, for crying out loud. I have no doubt he will kill Ace without even batting an eye.

Shit. There I go again. I cry even harder as the fear keeps building. I don't want something to happen to Ace. Not because of me. Not because of Sawyer. I want to keep him safe, and I am scared as hell that Sawyer will do something terrible to him like he did his parents. How could he have killed them? His own fucking parents? For what? For *me*?

"I'm scared, Ace," I whisper.

"What's your biggest fear?"

"That something is going to happen to you."

Ace holds me tighter. "Ember, listen to me. Brennon isn't going to let anything happen to me. He's already made a few calls, and some buddies of his are going to help us out. There's only one of him, Ember. We're all going to watch out for each other. I'm going to keep you safe, and they're going to keep me safe. I promise. Nothing is going to happen to me."

"Are we going to Sawyer's now?" I ask.

"No, Ember. *No.* Is that why you're so worked up?" He places his hand under my chin and lifts my head until I am looking up at him. "You and I are going to spend a few days at another hotel. Brennon is taking us there now. No one will know where we are. Sawyer won't be able to find us." He kisses my forehead and wipes away my tears. "In the meantime, Brennon is going to find out what he can about the accident. He thinks he can find evidence that proves it was a homicide. We both want to keep you as far away from him as possible. So, believe me, babe, everything is going to be okay. Your having to face him is our last option."

Relief.

There is an overwhelming sense of relief that comes with his words. I'm not ready to see Sawyer. I hope I will never have to see him again, but if, in the end, I am our only hope of putting him away, then so be it. At least I have some time to build up the courage to be near him again.

The tears subside, and I relax, thanks to this amazing man.

I stay cradled in his arms, never wanting to leave. He is so muscular. I sink into his body. There is no place I'd rather be than in his arms.

"Thank you, Ace." I gently kiss his lips.

After I assure him that I'm okay, he stands up and carries me back to the truck. This time, he gets in the back seat with me. He gives Brennon a head nod, signaling that we can leave.

I have Ace's full attention now. He doesn't take his eyes off me.

"You don't have to watch me," I say. "I'm fine. Really."

He smiles. "It's hard not to stare. Your boobs look fantastic in that dress."

Brennon chimes in from the front seat. "That's why I preferred the T-shirt!"

We all laugh. It feels good to laugh, even if it is at my expense.

I pull the top of the dress up, trying to cover my chest. But he is right, there is no hiding my breasts. They look fucking awesome.

"So, now that we've all established that Ember is hot as fuck, what are we going to eat for dinner?" Ace asks.

I shake my head, blushing, and look out the window. I don't have much of an appetite, so I let them decide where we'll eat.

The sun has set, and it is pitch black outside. We drive for what feels like several more hours. Brennon said a couple of miles back that we are almost there. Wherever *"there"* is, I still have no idea. I've been staring out the window trying to figure out where he is taking us, but I only see corn fields and mile markers indicating we are somewhere in the middle of nowhere.

The car begins to slow down as Brennon turns off the highway. We drive for several more minutes before he pulls into a driveway. An old Victorian home with a wraparound porch and numerous windows shed small inklings of light around the perimeter of the house.

"I thought we were staying at a hotel," I say.

"We are...kind of," Ace answers. "It's a bed and breakfast. Fewer people stay at these types of places, and they're usually more private and secluded."

Brennon and Ace step out of the truck at the same time. I see Brennon hand Ace a cell phone. It is small and black and looks like an old flip phone.

"Burner," Ace says as he holds up the phone to show me.

I nod.

Ace helps me out of the back seat. I stand on the gravel driveway while Brennon takes our duffle bag out from the bed of the truck.

"All right, man," Ace says, grabbing the duffle from Brennon. "Thanks for everything. Call me in the morning."

I walk over to Brennon and give him a hug. "Thank you so much, Brennon. I owe you."

"Hey, you two just stay safe out here. I'll be in touch."

He gets back into the truck and looks at me. "Do me a favor and never wear that dress again." He winks before he closes the door.

I roll my eyes and wave to him as he backs out of the driveway.

I turn to Ace. "Can we go check in? I need to change out of this damn dress." I walk ahead of Ace and up the stairs to the front door.

He catches up quickly. "You're not changing. Not if I have anything to say about it."

Ace opens the old wooden door and signals for me to enter first. I step inside and walk toward the desk where a tiny white-haired woman is standing.

Ace checks us into our room, which is apparently the most demanded room in the place. The sweet lady informs us there is only one other couple staying here tonight before she escorts us up a deep-rooted staircase lined with dark red carpeting. Once we are up the stairs, we find our room tucked away on the opposite end of the hall. We are left alone once the white-haired woman descends the stairs.

Ace unlocks the door.

When I walk into our suite, I view a breathtaking bedroom filled with antique furniture. The carpet is a baby blue that matches the curtains over the windows. There is a small kitchenette and a fireplace with a seating area. The king-size bed has draperies on its bedposts similar to the curtains.

"Wow," I say in awe.

Ace and I sit in front of the fireplace, the flames lighting up the room in an orange and red hue. There is a tiny bar cart in our room with a few different spirits and mixers. Ace pours us a cocktail.

"So, what are we going to do for the next few days?" I ask.

Ace smirks. "I can think of a few things."

He's flirting, I think with a grin as I take a drink of my martini. "Yeah? Like what?"

"I could probably show you better than I could tell you."

"No. I want you to tell me what we're going to do, Ace."

He laughs. "First, I'm going to kiss you. I'm going to kiss you a lot."

"I like kissing you."

"Not as much as I like kissing you," he argues back.

"Then what?"

"Well, the kissing will start slowly. Then I'll eventually make my way down to your neck. But I won't be able to stop there, so I'll keep moving down until I reach…there," he says, eyeing my breasts.

"Here?" I say seductively as I rub my breasts with one hand.

He nods and takes a sip.

"What happens next?"

"I still won't be able to stop there. As much as it'll pain me, I'll eventually have to take that dress off you. I'll lower your straps one by one. My hand will reach for your back as I unzip it slowly. The dress will fall to the floor and you'll be standing there in your bra and panties."

"What if I'm not wearing a bra or panties?"

His eyes widen. "Ember," he says deeply.

"Yes, Ace?"

"Are you naked underneath that dress?"

I grin. "Maybe."

Ace groans. He wipes his hand over his face, and I watch as he adjusts himself in his pants.

"Something wrong, Ace?" I ask promiscuously.

I know what's wrong. He can't hide the bulge in his pants.

"Fuck, Ember," he groans again.

I laugh at his attempt to hide what I am doing to him.

"Tell me what happens next," I demand.

"Well, that all depends on if you're actually naked or not."

"Why don't you come find out?" I challenge.

Ace sets his drink down and paces toward me. His lips crash into mine as he pulls me up from my seat. Our bodies press against each other, his hardness pushing into my stomach.

We stay like this for a while, until he does exactly what he said he would. Once my dress reaches the floor, he shows me what is next instead of telling me.

chapter twenty-four

Ace

The last four weeks have been hell. It started as I watched Ember walk out of my own damn restaurant with him, and all I could mumble was that fucking guy's name.

Sawyer.

From what she had told me about him during her drunken night at the Bungalow, he seems like a complete asshole. The guy had his chance with her, and he'd blown it. Now, he shows up years later, and she just takes him back?

My fucking luck.

I haven't heard from her. I've wanted to call her so many times, but my pride gets in the way. She chose *him*. If I had misunderstood what was going on the night I ran into her at the Lux, then she would've showed up at the bar and told me. Or at least called.

I am meeting my brother Brennon at the coffee shop around the corner from my apartment. It is something we like to do weekly since our jobs keep us both pretty busy. He occasionally stops by the bar on his days off, but those days have become few and far between.

I pull into the parking lot and park my truck. I step out and walk toward the entrance where Brennon is waiting. The overhead bell dings as I open the door.

Brennon and I walk into the coffee shop and head toward the counter to order our usual. Brennon is talking my ear off about an arrest he'd made earlier that week. I am only half listening because something makes me glance at the table across the room. That's when I see her. I completely freeze.

Being in the same room as her nearly takes my breath away. She is so beautiful. Her perfectly wavy hair falls over her shoulders, so blonde and so pretty. She looks like an angel as she sits at the small table alone.

This is the first time I've seen her in weeks. Her green eyes lock with mine, and time stands still.

I turn to Brennon. "I'll take my usual. I'll meet you at the table, okay?"

I can't ignore her. I don't want to.

I walk to her table, not paying attention to Brennon's response, and take a seat directly across from her. It has been so long since I've looked into her hypnotic emerald eyes. I stay silent because I don't know what to say.

She finally breaks the silence. "Hey."

I nod.

I guess she can't take the quiet any longer as she suddenly blurts out what I have been wondering since the moment she left me for him in my restaurant.

"I said I would go to dinner with Sawyer before we kissed. I had already agreed to it, so I had to go. I didn't want to. Believe me, I didn't want to."

She didn't want to go to dinner with him.

I finally speak. "Then why did you leave with him?"

"His parents got into a car accident. It all happened so fast. I left, and the next thing I knew, his mom and dad were dead."

Shit.

That explains their hasty exit that night, but it doesn't explain why I haven't heard from her in a month.

"Do you love him?"

"I don't really know how to answer that, Ace."

What does she mean? She either loves him or she doesn't.

"When you kiss him, do you feel the same things as when you kissed me?"

She shakes her head.

"Does it feel better with him?"

"No."

I reach for her hand across the table. She hesitates before she places her delicate palm into mine.

When our skin touches, it makes the hairs on the back of my neck stand, and I feel this overwhelming desire to never let go. This girl has a power over me, a power I'm not quite sure she knows exists. No one has ever affected me like her. I don't understand it, but I'm being pulled to her. I need more than just this simple touch.

"Then why are you still with him, Ember?" I ask.

She looks away.

"You are still with him, *right*? That's why I haven't heard from you?"

After a long pause she finally answers, "He needs me."

"Do you need him?"

"I don't need anyone."

She might not need anyone, but I need her. And I realize that now more than ever.

"Then I'll ask you again, Ember. Why are you still with him?"

"Ace," she whispers.

"*Why*, Ember?"

"I'd feel too guilty if I leave him now, okay? Is that what you want me to say?"

No. That's not what I want her to say. It isn't what I want to hear. She is with him because she feels too guilty to leave. She's with him out of pity.

"He keeps telling me he doesn't know how he would get through this without me. The loss of his parents. Having to take care of his brothers. He's said that every damn day since the accident. I'm not the kind of person who is going to leave someone high and dry. He needed me. He *needs* me. He's the only man I've ever been with, Ace, and although we broke up five years ago, he came back into my life right before his turned upside down."

This poor girl.

I try to reason with her again. This isn't about him. She has to put her wants, her *needs*, first.

"Ember, what do you need? Is this what you need?" I ask again. "Is this even what you *want*?"

"No. It's not what I need. I don't know what I want. But I know it's what he needs, and I care about him, so it is what it is."

No.

She doesn't need him. I'm positive she doesn't even want him. But he loves her. He needs her. He wants her.

"I'm not giving up on this, Ember. I told you already, you're the girl I want, and I think I know what you want too. I'm not giving up."

She starts to cry. I don't like seeing her sad, but she is still so beautiful, so delicate. I feel a wave of guilt take over as the tears roll down her face. I don't want to upset her. It is the last thing I want to do. She may think she is doing the right thing, but it isn't the right thing for her. It isn't fair to her. Doesn't she understand that?

"Ember."

She tries to wipe away the tears with her free hand.

"Ember," I say again.

She looks at me. Her emerald eyes are bloodshot and puffy from crying. Still, she is gorgeous.

"What do you want, Ember?" I ask, softly.

"*You*," she whispers.

Me.

I shut my eyes as I absorb her words. *Me.* She wants *me.*

I know I'm not alone in this. She clearly has things that she needs to work through on her own, things with Sawyer. I can't help her with that. But she wants me, and I need her. So, I will wait. No matter how long it takes.

I let go of her hand and stand.

She looks up at me, concerned, confused. "Where are you going?"

I push my chair in and lean forward. "You know where to find me."

Then, I walk away. I walk away from her, and it is the hardest thing I have ever done. I want to stay longer, spend the rest of the day with her, never be without her again, but she already knows I want to be with her, and now I know she wants to be with me. She has to take care of her situation with Sawyer, and when she is done, she knows where to find me.

I walk back to where my brother is now sitting with our coffees near the window.

"Who was that?" he asks.

I smile when I turn to look back at her. She is watching me. I don't want to look away, but I force my eyes back to Brennon. Then I watch as a familiar white car pulls out of the parking lot behind him. I ignore the uneasiness in my stomach.

Something isn't right. I quickly shake the thought.

"I think that girl is the love of my life."

chapter twenty-five

Ace

Work is slow. A few of the regulars sit at the bar top, beers in hand. I'm working the night shift at the Bungalow. The hours seem to drag. My mind isn't with me tonight, it is somewhere else. On someone else. I try to keep myself busy tending to the bar, but it is no use.

I have never let my personal life affect my working life before. I am a businessman with several successful operations under my belt, and it is because I keep business and pleasure separate. But tonight, I can't get her off my mind. Even more so than normal.

Since the night she stepped into my bar and passed out on the floor, she is all I can think about. When I saw her with her damn ex that night at the Lux, it nearly crushed me. I'd tried damn hard to brush it off. After all, I hardly knew her. How could I be so broken over a woman that I'd only just met? But I had been. I *still* am.

When I saw her at the coffee shop earlier, I couldn't resist walking up to her. Everything in me wanted to touch her, to hold her. Hell, I wanted to kiss her again like I did that night in the city. But I knew I wouldn't be able to just kiss her. The next time my lips touch hers, it won't end there. And there *will* be a next time. There has to be. But I have no idea when.

How long does it take to break up with someone? Days? Months? *Fuck.* If it takes more than a few weeks, I think I might lose my mind.

I've just grabbed a bottle of Bud Light from the mini-fridge and popped off the cap to ease my mind when my phone vibrates in my jeans.

It's Ember.

She's finally texted me. It's late, but I'm just about to close the bar. I yell for last call as I clean off the bar and high tops.

When the last customer leaves, I walk upstairs to my apartment and lie in my bed, the bed she slept in all those weeks ago. It had been so hard not to lie next to her tiny body and take in her fresh vanilla scent that night, but I'd resisted the urge. She was drunk, after all. She didn't know who I was, and I didn't want to scare her.

We text back and forth for a while. Eventually, I can't take it anymore. She is home alone and so am I. I need to see her again. I think about it for a second more before my fingers move across my phone screen.

Me: Come over.
Ember: What? I can't come over.
Me: Why not?
Ember: I can't do that to Sawyer.
Me: I just want to see you.

A few moments later she responds.

Ember: Okay.

I don't know what I'm thinking. It will be so hard not to touch her, not to kiss her. In her eyes, she's together with Sawyer, whether she wants to be or not. And I will have to respect that.

On the bright side, I've convinced her to come over. I have no idea what to expect, but I can't wait to see her again.

I wait at the entrance of the bar for her and watch as a car pulls into the parking lot. When Ember steps out, I can't help but smile. I probably look so tasteless holding the door open for the girl I just convinced to come over in the middle of the night. If I were watching us right now, I would think my booty call has just arrived. But that isn't what this is. I won't do anything she doesn't want to do. Ember deserves more than a late-night hookup.

"Hi there," I say.

"Hi."

She looks amazing, even though I'm pretty sure she just rolled out of bed. But then again, she always looks amazing. She's wearing sweatpants and a tight tank top that hardly hides her breasts. I try not to stare. She's so fucking hot.

We walk up the stairs, and I open the old wooden door to let her into my apartment. She sighs as we relax against my sofa.

"Are you okay?" I ask.

"I don't know. I feel guilty."

"You haven't done anything, Ember."

"I'm here, aren't I?"

I stand quickly, immediately frustrated. What am I thinking asking her to come here so soon? She has things she needs to deal with, and I've hardly given her a few hours to do so.

"Ember, did either of you ever talk about this? What your relationship is? Did he even give you a fucking option?"

I can't hide the anger in my voice. It's not directed at Ember, but rather Sawyer, or *Tom*, whatever the fuck his name is. Something doesn't feel right about him. I need to tell her about that, but right now I need to focus on her.

"No."

"Then how have you done anything wrong by being here?"

"I don't know. I can't help but feel like I'm doing something wrong. But at the same time, I *want* to be here, Ace. I wanted to see you again."

She wants to be here. She wants to see me.

I sit next to her on the couch again and place my hand on her knee. I instantly feel the surge of electricity that runs through my veins. Her sweatpants create a barrier between her skin and mine, but it is still enough to leave me wanting more.

"I know," I say. "I wanted to see you too."

"Why did you ask me to come over tonight?"

"I really just wanted to be near you again."

She nods like she understands.

I continue, "But I think I also wanted to be able to look you in the eyes, to see how you're truly feeling. I could tell at the coffee shop something wasn't right."

"What do you mean?"

"You seemed off. And honestly, it just doesn't make sense, Ember."

"What doesn't make sense?"

"I don't know. Everything. You. Him. Your relationship with him."

The annoyance is evident on my face. I'm frustrated that the woman I want to be with so fucking badly is stuck in a situation she doesn't want to be in. What kind of man would do that to her?

I stand again, this time pacing toward the window. I look into the parking lot of the bar, and my entire body stiffens at what I see.

The white car.

"What's wrong?" she asks.

That is Sawyer's car. I'm sure of it. What the fuck is he doing here in the middle of the night?

"Ace, what's wrong?" she asks again, standing to join me near the window. She looks out but doesn't notice it. "Ace?"

"What kind of car does Sawyer drive?" I ask.

"I don't know. Why?"

"Ember, try to think. What kind of car does he drive you around in?"

"Um…it's white. It's some type of four-door car. It's slightly bigger than my car but isn't an SUV or anything."

She's describing the car that is sitting in my parking lot right now. I no longer have any doubts. This is the car I've been seeing in my lot, that I saw at the coffee shop earlier, the same car Ember left in the night I ran into her at my restaurant. And it is the same damn car that 'Tom' said broke down when he asked to use my phone. Tom is Sawyer. Sawyer is Tom. Why the fuck did he lie about his name?

"Yeah. That sounds about right."

"What? What sounds about right?"

She has no idea.

I grab Ember's hand and pull her as far away from the window as I can. Of course, the only room in this damn place without a window is the bathroom. I take her inside and shut the door behind us.

"Ace, what the hell?" she yells.

"Listen, Ember. When you got here, you were the only car in the parking lot. There's another car out there now, and I'm pretty sure it's Sawyer."

"What? That's impossible. He went home and went to bed hours ago. How would he even know I'm here?"

"Do you know that for sure? That he went home?"

"No. I guess I don't."

"Does Sawyer know I live here?"

"He doesn't even know who you are, Ace."

Yes, he does.

"Yes, he does," I say out loud. "He told me his name was Tom."

"What?" she asks, her eyebrows creasing.

"Sawyer. He showed up saying he had car trouble a little over a month ago. Asked to use my phone. Except he said his name was Tom."

"Are you sure it was him?"

"Yes. Same guy you were at the restaurant with. That car that's sitting out there, that's the car he was having trouble with."

"That makes no sense. Why would he say his name was Tom?"

"I don't know."

How can I voice my concern to her? Something isn't right, and I am certain of that now more than ever.

"Okay. Maybe it's not him," I say. "But the car you described is sitting in the parking lot right now. I think we should go, see if it follows us somewhere else."

"Where will we go?"

"I don't know yet."

"Okay."

"Okay?" She surprises me when she agrees so quickly. She trusts me. No matter what happens, I'm going to protect her.

I take her to my brother's house. He is a cop, and it is the safest place I can think of to take her in the middle of the night. If Sawyer really is stalking her, Brennon will know what to do.

We sit together on the bed in my childhood bedroom. It is one of the many guest bedrooms in the house now.

"Are you scared?" I ask her.

"I guess I should be, but being with you makes me feel better for some reason."

I kiss her forehead. It is the first time my lips have touched her in nearly a month. "I hope I'm wrong about all of this."

"Me, too."

"I'm not going to let anything happen to you though, Ember. You know that, right?"

"Thank you."

"You don't have to thank me."

"I'm sorry I didn't come to see you after that night at your restaurant."

"I understand why you didn't."

"I should've at least called."

She has a point. "You had a lot going on."

"You know, I've dreamt about you almost every night since."

That makes me smile. I'd always thought about her, awake or asleep. "What kind of dreams?"

She blushes. "I sometimes dream about what sex with you would be like. I've only ever slept with one man, so it's hard to know what it could be like with anyone else. But, *wow*. You thought our kiss was good? You should feel how incredible our sex is."

Damn. She has sex dreams about me. Actual sex dreams. I am instantly hard beneath my shorts. The loose material hardly hides what the thoughts of her and me naked together did to me.

"I'd be lying if I said I haven't already imagined what sex would be like with you, Ember," I confess.

I watch as a tear falls down her face. She wipes it away quickly, trying to keep me from seeing that she is crying.

Dammit, Ace. This is twice now that I've made her cry.

"What's wrong?" I ask.

"Nothing.

"Ember…"

"I don't know how I let things get to this point. I'm frustrated, annoyed, sad, mad. I don't think those words even really describe what I feel. If Sawyer really is stalking me, then the only man I've ever loved, the only man I've ever given my heart to, is a man who quite literally might be a psychopath."

She cries harder, and I pull her in closer to me as I scoot us back on the bed. She lays her head on my lap. I try so hard to calm myself down, but it is no use. Has she noticed yet? I don't want this to be sexual, but I can't help my body's natural response to her. She is so beautiful, even with tears in her eyes. I wipe at the drops as they trickle down her cheek.

"Only giving your heart to one man isn't a bad thing, Ember. You're loyal. You're honest. I love that about you."

I love a lot about her.

"No one else has even tried to be with me since Sawyer. Something must be wrong with me. Five years, Ace. I was single for five fucking years."

"Ember. Nothing is wrong with you."

She is the most beautiful woman I have ever laid eyes on. It makes no sense that men haven't been throwing themselves at her. She'd caught my eye the second she walked into my bar. She hadn't noticed me, but I'd served her every damn drink that night.

"Ace," she whispers.

I love the sound of my name as it leaves her lips.

"Yeah?"

"I don't know if this makes sense. I know we hardly know each other, but I really like you. I'm afraid to lose whatever this is. You're not even mine to lose, but I don't want to think of my life without you anymore."

It makes perfect sense.

"You won't have to. I'm not going anywhere," I assure her, and I mean it.

She lifts herself off my lap. Her swollen eyes look deeply into mine. I try to wipe away the wetness that surrounds them. Despite the redness, they are still a striking green.

I lift my hand onto her smooth cheek. She rests her head into my palm. Her skin is warm and soft, and I can smell the vanilla scent in her hair that flows over her shoulders.

I look at her perfect lips. Pink and plump. *Very* kissable. I can never forget the feel of her lips on mine. Our first kiss had been unexpected, in the underground room of a downtown bar. It is hardly the place she deserved to have our first kiss, but for selfish reasons, I couldn't wait any longer. And again tonight, I have selfish reasons for wanting to kiss her.

My groin tightens further as I imagine my lips on hers. I can't handle being this close to her anymore without kissing her. She's just found out that Sawyer is likely stalking her, and my thoughts are hardly appropriate, but I can't resist her any longer. I know if I kiss her, I won't want to stop. It won't just stop at our lips pressed together. It will go farther. Does she want that? Does she want that *right now*?

"Is it okay if I kiss you?" I ask.

She silently gives me permission with a slight nod of her head. My lips immediately fall to hers.

The kiss is even more captivating than her touch. I know she feels it too, because she is moaning into my mouth and pulling me toward her until our bodies can't possibly get any closer.

Our clothes make their way to the floor. Her body is seamless. She has a petite yet curvy figure and the perfect sized breasts. I have never seen a more beautiful woman.

I had no intentions of taking it this far tonight, though I know it will be hard to resist her. Being with her feels so good, so *right*.

I continue to kiss her until my lips touch every single inch of her body, and when I am done, I make love to her. It's not just sex with Ember, as it has been with other women in the past. I've had my fair share of sex, but this is unlike *anything*. She is unlike *anyone*. It is two humans coming together and becoming one.

Ember is everything I ever wanted. She is the first woman I've ever made love to. In this moment, I realize that I love her more than I've ever loved another human being.

I check on her again a half hour later. She fell asleep after I left the room to talk with Brennon. I don't want to wake her up. It is the middle of the night, and she needs to rest.

Brennon and I sit on the sectional in his living room, expecting Sawyer to show up at any moment. I keep glancing outside. I feel paranoid, and I can't sit still for long. I'm sure he is going to show up, it is just a matter of when. There is no doubt in my mind that the white car is his.

Another hour passes before there is a knock at the door. Brennon and I turn to face one another. It's him, it has to be. Who else would be knocking on Brennon's door in the middle of the night?

I hurry toward the door. Brennon lingers behind me, blocking off the hallway that leads to Ember.

I don't have any weapons, but I can hold my own well. Brennon has his hand on his holster. If it comes to that, he will take care of things.

I open the door. Sawyer stands in front of me, his face beet red.

Here we go.

"Where is she?" he asks through clenched teeth.

"Where is who?" I play dumb.

"Cut the shit, Ace. I know who you are. Where the fuck is my girlfriend?"

"And what was your name again? Tom? Or wait, do you go by Sawyer now?"

"Where the fuck is she?" he snarls.

"Why would you think she's here?"

He clasps his hands behind his head, his expression desperate. "Come on, man. Just let me talk to her. I know she's inside."

"No," I say, sternly.

"Fuck this," he says, as he pushes his way inside.

Brennon immediately displays the gun in his waistband. Sawyer stops in the middle of the living room, trapped between the two of us with nowhere to go.

"Are you really going to fucking shoot me? I'm only here to take my girlfriend home." He looks back to me. "You brought her to some random fucking stranger's house in the middle of the goddamn night! Where the fuck is she, Ace?" he yells.

He is fuming. There is no way I can let him get to her. Especially when he is in this state.

"How did you know she was here?" I ask. "Are you stalking her, Sawyer?"

"Stalking? I don't need to stalk her anymore, you stupid fuck. She's my girlfriend. She tells me where she is. Except now, because you kidnapped her."

"I didn't kidnap her. She came with me willingly."

"Why would she do that?"

"Because she knows you're stalking her. What the fuck is wrong with you?"

I see the anguish in his features as he glares at me. He turns to look at Brennon. Whatever he is thinking, it won't work. He can't take us both.

I continue to antagonize him, "Do you enjoy watching her from your car, Sawyer? I saw you today, by the way, at the coffee shop. Did you know I was there?"

If it is possible for his face to turn a darker shade of red, it does. He is livid.

"Do you enjoy watching *me*?" I continue. "I've seen your car in my lot. In fact, I saw it there a few hours ago. Then you followed us here. So, I'm going to ask you again, are you fucking stalking her?"

This time, he lunges at me. Bold move when there is a gun only a few feet away from him in Brennon's holster. He could shoot and kill him instantly. Brennon never misses.

I'm bigger than him, but he's strong. Brennon steps in, without his gun, and pulls Sawyer's body off mine. When I have a clear shot, I punch him square in his face. He's lucky I didn't kill him for being a such a fucking creep.

Brennon holds him down on the ground. I step toward them and bend down until my face is a mere inch from his.

"You said you don't need to stalk her anymore, so that means you did. Did you watch her after you two broke up? Is that why she's never been with another man? You wanted to keep her for yourself. Is that what happened? Tell me, were you fucking other girls the entire time you let that poor girl think that something was wrong with her?"

He spit in my face, and it takes everything in me not to kill him.

"Let him go, Brennon."

He looks up at me confused.

"Let him go," I demand.

My brother listens, and Sawyer springs at me again.

He gets a hold of me and pushes me into the wall.

"Did you fuck her?" he shouts, his words so angry I can feel the saliva spray from his mouth.

I shove him off me. That is none of his fucking business. I pin him against the wall this time.

"I'll fucking kill you," he yells again.

As much as I would love to punish this man by telling him I had slept with her, I think better of it. I hadn't fucked her, I'd made love to her. It is special and it is ours. Not his. I won't let him take that moment away from us.

"Why are you following her, Sawyer?"

"Because she's mine."

"She's not an object. Besides, she doesn't want to be *yours*."

"Bullshit. She's always been mine, and she always will be."

"You're stalking her."

"I have every right to know where she is after what I've done to be with her, asshole."

"What have you done?"

"Fuck you."

I look at Brennon. He is ready to jump in at any moment, I can see it in his eyes. He wants to kill him almost as much as I do, but I need to get us out of here. I have to put Ember first and get her away from this psycho.

"Go start the truck," I say to Brennon.

Brennon nods and grabs the keys off the coffee table.

Once he is outside, I return my attention to Sawyer, still pinned against the wall. It is just him and me now.

His demeanor changes, and I can feel him stand up straighter beneath my touch. He thinks he can take me.

Try me.

He pushes against my chest until he is no longer backed against the wall. We stand in the center of the living room in a standoff. He takes a swing, but I duck out of the way just in time, causing him to swipe at air. As he loses his step, I heave my shoulder into his stomach to take him down.

He is flat on his back with my 220-pound frame straddled over him, my fists pounding his face. I pull back and swing at him again. And again. And again. He's a bloody mess. I know I broke his nose, but that doesn't stop me. I want him to be scared. Scared of what I am capable of.

I pick him up by his shirt and throw him against the wall like dead weight. His body bashes into an end table, pushing over a lamp. It shatters.

The fury in his eyes only grows with every move I make. I overpower him, and he knows it. He springs back toward me, pressing firmly against my chest until I am backed into another wall.

"Did you fuck her?" he yells again, blood spewing from his mouth as he speaks.

I force his hands off me and quickly shove him again until we land in the hallway that leads to the basement. I notice the door is already propped open and see my opportunity. I punch him again, the force strong enough to send him tumbling down the stairs into the darkness. I quickly close the door and push a chair in front of it, hoping it will hold long enough for me to get Ember out.

I burst into the room where she's been sleeping, but she is already awake.

I look at her beautiful trembling body as she lies in a fetal position on the bed. She's so scared, and my heart aches for her. I know I have to protect her. I will do anything to keep this woman safe because I love her. I am in love with her, and I will do whatever it takes to protect her.

Right now, it is time to do just that.

"Let's go. We have to leave. Now," I say, breathlessly.

chapter twenty-six

Ace

We sleep for a few hours at a motel before Brennon drops us off at the bed and breakfast, where we will be staying for the next few weeks while he does some investigative work.

I had gotten her out of Brennon's in time to escape Sawyer. We're convinced he killed his parents as part of some sick scheme to win Ember over. What kind of person does that? He couldn't handle that Ember wasn't interested in him anymore, so he pulled at her heartstrings. He manipulated her into an impossible situation until she felt like it was her job to support him and his family.

But Ember has a big heart. I love that about her. She hasn't shared that heart with anyone for a long time because of Sawyer. He kept her at arm's reach, and she hasn't even known it. I will love her enough to make up for all the lost years, her heart deserves it. I love her so much already.

We sit at the fire inside our suite at the bed and breakfast, sipping on the cocktails I made. Ember asks what we'd do while we stayed here, and I can't help but think dirty thoughts. Who can blame me? This girl is one in a million.

She is naked beneath the dress.

Fuck.

It lays on the floor in a puddle of yellow.

My hands cup her perky breasts as I continue to kiss her deeply. She tugs at my shirt and lifts it above my head until it joins her dress on the ground. Her breasts press against my abdomen, and she tugs on my bottom lip. I pull her closer, tangling my hands in her hair.

I break our kiss so I can feel her nipples between my lips. They are so hard. I suck on them as she moans. My hands hold her waist, keeping her close to me.

Then I move my mouth lower until I'm between her legs, in the warmest part of her. I slide my tongue between her thighs, keeping my eyes on her face the entire time as she stands over me. Her eyes squeeze shut. Her fingers grip tightly to the armrest beside her as I taste her, enjoying every moment of it.

It doesn't take long before her moans grow louder. Without moving my mouth or my gaze, I shove two fingers inside her. Her legs give out as she nearly collapses from the pleasure.

I use my free hand to hold her and bring her down gently. I guide her to the chair, though my mouth never quits working her as I kneel, and soon I send her soaring over the edge. My tongue continues to work as her legs tremble around me. Her fingers pull at my hair. I can't take my eyes off her. It is a beautiful sight to see this woman have an orgasm.

Once she catches her breath, she stands, motioning for me to follow. I tower over her petite frame as she bends down to her knees, taking my pants with her. Is this really happening, or am I living a dream?

Her hand finds me as she strokes my length. She teases me with her tongue before she puts her warm mouth around my hardness. I am so ready for her that I'm afraid I won't last long, and I still want to be inside her again.

It takes everything in me not to come as her mouth moves over me. She may not have been with many guys, but she knows exactly what the hell she is doing to me. No blow job has ever felt this good. Her mouth suctions me, and I want to push into her, to finish in her mouth, but not as badly as I want to finish inside of her.

When I know I can't last any longer, I motion for her to stand and pick her up by her waist until she straddles me. I can't even wait to get to the bed. I slide inside her, her tight walls clenching around me as I fill her with all of me. I never want to be with another woman again. No one will ever feel this good.

Soon, we both hit our climax. With our lips pressed against each other, I grunt into her mouth as I release. I feel her trembling body squeeze mine as she comes.

Once we both recover, I lay her next to me on the bed.

"You're so amazing, Ember."

Her eyes are glazed over, a satisfying grin spread across her face. Though being with Ember is incredible, I know there is still a lingering uncertainty in the back of our minds.

"Are you doing okay?" I ask.

"Despite everything that's happening, I've never been more relaxed."

She rests her head on my chest. My fingers brush against her back.

"I love you so much," I whisper into her hair.

I feel her smile against me. She hasn't said it back, but it doesn't bother me in the slightest. I want her to know how I feel. Ember doesn't believe anyone can love her because Sawyer made sure no one ever had. I don't want her to live another minute of her life believing that. I love her, more than she can possibly imagine, and whether I am lucky enough to ever be loved back by her, I still want her to know that she is someone worth loving.

"What happens if he finds us?" she asks.

"He won't."

"You're sure?"

"I promise. Just relax. He can't find us here. Brennon made sure of that."

We'd ditched our phones and driven to the middle of nowhere. We have no car and nothing to trace us here. I even paid cash for the room in case he somehow has access to our bank statements. I doubt it, but I wouldn't put it past him. He'd killed his own parents. It's evident that he'd do *anything* to get to Ember. But he won't find her. Not here.

She falls asleep in my arms, our naked bodies warm together. This is going to be our lives for the next few days, until Brennon figures out our next move. All I have to do is keep this girl safe and happy. Neither should be a problem.

A short time later, I feel her stir against my chest. She is waking up, her sleepy eyes slowly opening before she looks up at me and smiles.

"How long have I been asleep?" she asks.

"Not too long," I say, kissing her blonde hair.

Her arms wrap tightly around me, her head still on my chest. She squeezes me tightly, and her soft lips press a gentle kiss on my abdomen before she giggles.

"What?" I ask.

She puts her hand between my legs, grabbing my length. "That didn't take long."

I tilt my head back and run my fingers through my hair. How can I not be hard when she is lying next to me naked? I think I'll always be ready for her. I'm only a man, and I can't resist the urge I have to be inside her again.

She scoots up on the bed. "It's okay," she says. "I like that I have this effect on you."

"You have no idea what you do to me."

She smiles. I kiss her lips, then pull away before we get carried away.

"We should get some sleep," I say.

"Not yet."

My eyebrows raise.

Her lips smash back into mine. This time, she takes control. She climbs on top of me until she straddles me.

Fuck.

She is so hot. Any willpower I have is gone as she slides herself over me until I am inside of her again. She sits up, parting our lips as she moves over me. My eyes are locked on her beautiful body and the way it fits so perfectly with mine. I have the best damn view of her from this position.

My first instinct is to reach for her breasts. I hold them, playing with her nipples as she rides on top of me. I pump into her as she does a figure-eight over me. The more she moves, the deeper inside of her I feel.

Soon, she yells out. She moans as she climaxes, causing me to come with her. Her legs shudder around me as I pulse inside of her, releasing everything that I am. She has all of me. I am hers. Completely hers.

There are no unexpected visits from Sawyer for the remainder of the week. He hasn't found us, thanks to Brennon. The time we spend in that old Victorian home will go down as some of the best days of my life. All that uninterrupted time with Ember only validates how easy it is to love her. She is selfless, kind, and easily the most beautiful woman I have ever laid eyes on.

Ember checks in with her mom quite a few times during the week. Her mom seems especially interested in the new man in Ember's life, *me*. We speak with her for hours on the burner phone. Ember doesn't tell her all the details of the situation, but she does tell her mom that she believes Sawyer has been following her for the last five years. Her mom understands why Ember might want to go off the grid for a few days.

The investigation into the accident is still ongoing. Brennon says there is evidence of power steering fluid mixed with cleaning solution in the garage where the car was parked. Unfortunately, that doesn't prove the car had been tampered with, it only confirms that the car did have a leak that was cleaned up at some point.

No one has seen or heard from Sawyer since the night he showed up at Brennon's house. When Brennon returned home, he said the basement door had been flung wide open. Sawyer had obviously left, but he never went home.

Sawyer's brothers had shown up at the precinct the next day to file a missing person's report. Brennon gave a statement of the incident at his house after that. The police are aware of the stalking claims and potential murder allegations, but Sawyer isn't considered a person of interest yet in the case because of insubstantial evidence. So, for now, he remains a missing person.

When we got back in town, the police put us in a safe house. Brennon says it's the best option for us while he continues with the investigation. He doesn't like the idea that Sawyer is missing. He'd rather we know exactly where he is than not have a single clue as to where he might be.

It's now been two months since they put us in the safe house. Brennon has been searching for Sawyer while I keep Ember safe. Ember continues to teach her online classes but has a permanent sub placed for her in-person lectures. I hire a few new managers to keep my businesses running, though they are the least of my concerns. There isn't anywhere else I'd rather be than stuck in a tiny one-bedroom, one-bathroom house with the love of my life.

For the first month, we had a squad car parked out front. The police department no longer deems Ember in danger after there has been so sign of Sawyer. *Or* they don't want to waste any more taxpayer dollars on us. Either way, they believe he isn't a threat anymore. Unlikely.

Brennon and a few of his buddies volunteer to keep watch of the tiny house at night since the state allows us to stay in the house so long as we pay rent. Ember insists that it isn't necessary to stay, but I argue that it is.

Ember cooks dinner in the tiny pale-yellow kitchen every night. She looks at home in the little shack, though we both knew it isn't.

But we grow to appreciate our life together behind these four walls. If we have each other, that is all that matters.

I smell spices simmering on the stove as I walk into the kitchen. I place both hands on her waist and plant a soft kiss on the top of her head. "Smells amazing, babe."

"It'll be ready in seven minutes. I hope you're hungry!"

"Starving."

Later, we lie in bed watching tv, as we have every night. She likes to sleep in nothing but a giant T-shirt and panties. She's become accustomed to sleeping in my T-shirts. She says she loves that they smell like me. I love seeing her in them, but I love taking them off her more. She is so sexy. So beautiful. I can't resist her.

Ember curls up to my bare chest as she slowly traces my abs with her pointer finger, something she does often.

"How much longer do you think we're going to be stuck here?" she asks.

I have no clue how long it will be until it is safe to go home. I hope they find Sawyer soon. If we know where he is, we can keep an eye on him and make sure that he stays away from Ember. There is already a restraining order in place. If he violates the terms of the restraining order, that is another way to put him behind bars temporarily.

"I don't know, babe," I answer honestly.

"Do you miss it?

"Miss what?"

"Everything. Life. Your bar. Your restaurants. Your apartment. Your family. Your friends."

I can sense sadness in her voice. I know she misses home. She misses everything that we had to leave behind.

"Ember, none of that matters to me. I only care to keep you safe."

"That's bullshit, Ace. You don't like being stuck here any more than I do."

I sit up in bed, bringing her with me so I can look into her mesmerizing eyes. No, I don't want to be locked in this place. I want to take her out on dates, to the movies, eat at my restaurants. I want to sleep in my own bed with her. There is a lot I want, and while I don't want us to be stuck, I also don't want to risk Sawyer finding her.

"Baby, where is this coming from?"

Her eyes swell with tears. It's been a long time since she's cried. It had taken some adjusting when we first moved into the safe house, but we have gotten into our own routine. Sure, we are secluded and have little contact with the outside world, but we have each other. She is enough for me. She always will be.

She dips her head into her hands as she cries silent tears. I brush her hair out of her face as I do my best to sooth her. Nothing makes a man feel worse than to see his love cry such emotional tears. She cries for what feels like hours but is likely only minutes. There isn't anything I can do. I feel helpless.

"Ember," I whisper.

She lifts her head, exposing her bloodshot eyes.

"What can I do?"

"I'm sorry, Ace. Nothing. There's nothing you can do. You've already given up so much for me. This is all my fault. I'm the reason we're in this mess."

"No."

I kiss her. I kiss her hard. This is not her fault.

When I pull away, her lips are swollen like her eyes. They are beautifully kissed, but her eyes are still full of sadness.

"Ember, listen to me. This is not your fault. It has never been your fault. Don't ever let what he's done define you. You don't deserve this, baby. You never deserved this."

She tries to lower her head again, but I catch her with my fingers, lifting her chin to maintain eye contact with me.

"Don't do that. It's not your fault. Believe that."

215

"How can I, when I'm the reason we're in this place?" She looks around the bedroom that hardly has room for a bed and a dresser.

The accommodations aren't ideal. We are living in an 800-square-foot house, but Ember is safe. That's all I need to tell myself every morning to accept the fate we were given.

"Tell me what's really bothering you, baby."

"I miss my mom."

Of course she misses her mom. Ember has told me so many stories about her, about how close they have always been. She is an only child, and after her dad passed away, it was just the two of them. If I had to guess, Ember's mom probably isn't handling this well either.

"Why don't we go visit her?" I offer.

She cocks her head slightly to the left. "Are you serious?"

Her excitement breaks my heart. Is this my fault? Did my willingness to protect her keep her from her mom? From her *life*?

I kiss her lips. "I'm so sorry, Ember."

"What are you sorry for?"

"I've been so concerned with protecting you, I didn't realize how much you would miss your mom. I'm an asshole. You haven't spent any time with her since I took you away."

She rubs her hand against my cheek, this time trying to comfort me. "Ace, it's not your fault."

I kiss her palm. "Let's go see her tomorrow."

"But what if it's not safe?"

"Then we'll make it safe. I'll call Brennon in the morning. We'll figure it out."

I watch as the wetness builds up again in her already puffy eyes. She quickly wipes at her face as more tears cascade down her cheeks.

"Baby," I say softly.

"They're happy tears. I'm just excited is all. I miss her so much."

I take her hand from my cheek and hold it tight. I kiss away her tears as if I am kissing away the hurt that truly caused them. With each tear that falls, I plant a small peck in its place.

"I love you, Ember."

I don't give her time to respond. I press my lips to hers, and she opens to me instantly.

She still hasn't said that she loves me yet, but I know she does. I can't blame her for her hesitation. She has been through a lot. She's only said those three words to one man, a dangerous man who is stalking her. I'll give her all the time in the world. Time is all we have.

When I pull away for air, I look into her sweet emerald eyes. I rub her soft skin with my hand and place one last soft kiss on her forehead.

"Are you ready for me to meet your mom?" I ask.

She laughs. "I can't wait."

I pull her on top of me, taking my T-shirt off her in the process. I kiss her harder and harder until we can't kiss anymore.

chapter twenty-seven

Ace

We've stayed in the safe house for five months total. Last month, we'd decided that we couldn't keep hiding. Maybe Sawyer will never come back. Maybe he will. Either way, we can't live our lives in fear, and I don't want her to.

Originally, I'd insisted that Ember stay at my apartment so she won't be alone. I am partly being selfish. I have been sleeping next to her every night for months, and I can't stand the thought of having to sleep in my bed alone. I don't want to be apart from her, either, especially when we still have no idea where Sawyer is.

As a result, she stays with me for another few weeks before she is ready to go back home. We change the locks and install a new alarm system at her place, and she no longer has a spare key hiding out back. The only people who have a key to her house are Ember and me.

We talk about moving in with each other often. When the time comes, I will likely move into Ember's place with her rather than have her move into my apartment above the Bungalow. We've spent so much time together at the safe house, I can't imagine us not living together anymore. But that will come with time, and I don't want to rush things or rush her.

I brought her home today. I've just finished carrying in the last of her bags when I walk into Ember's bedroom to find her stuffing drawers full of clothes until they can hardly shut. She has accumulated quite a few things over the last several months.

"That's the last of it," I say as I set down another bag full of clothes.

She looks around the bedroom and circles back toward the doorframe where I stand. "It feels weird being back."

"That tiny shack was starting to grow on you, huh?" I tease.

She laughs. "Thank you, Ace."

"For what?"

"For everything. You completely uprooted your life for me. Thank you."

I pull her into my arms. "I would do anything for you."

The sun shines brightly through the beige curtains in Ember's bedroom. Things quickly got carried away last night. She'd asked me to stay the night amid another passionate round of kissing that led to us naked in her bed in a tangled mess. Afterward, Ember had expressed her nerves about being alone for the first time in months. I understand because I am worried to leave her too.

I roll over her naked body still in the bed beside me and plant soft kisses along her back until I reach her shoulders. She shuffles as she wakes up, rolling onto her back. Her eyes open slowly, adjusting to the light inside the bedroom.

"Good morning," I say.

"Good morning." She smiles and glances around her bedroom. "Did you sleep okay?" she asks.

I kiss her nose. "I always sleep good with you."

After breakfast I can tell that she is well-rested and ready to ease back into her normal routine. She says she is going to run some errands and grab groceries for us. She hasn't asked me to go with her, so I head back to my place.

It has only been twenty minutes since I left her. It is the first time we've been apart since this whole thing started, and I already miss her. I have to fight the urge to call and check in with her every five minutes.

As soon as I walk up the stairs to my apartment, my phone rings. I laugh. It's probably Ember, calling to check in with me.

I pull the phone out of my pocket, expecting to see her name flash across the screen, but it isn't her. It is an unknown number. I answer it, half expecting it to be one of my new managers calling with an issue to report.

"This is Ace."

No one responds. I can hear breathing on the other end of the line, and my heart thumps as an uneasy feeling settles in my core.

"Hello?" I say again.

"Hi there," the voice says.

Fuck. I lose feeling in my face as the blood quickly drains. *Sawyer.*

"Sawyer," I say out loud.

"Ace! Old friend. Glad you can recognize my voice. How've you been? Did you have fun playing house with my girlfriend?"

"You better stay the fuck away from her."

"Oh, it's a little late for that. You kept me from her for months, Ace. I waited *years* to be with her again, and when I finally got her back, you took her away. How could you expect me not to be there the second you finally left?"

"What do you want, Sawyer?" I ask.

"I just want my girl. And I want you to leave us alone."

"That's not going to happen."

"Oh, but it is, Ace. You wouldn't want something to happen to her, now, would you?"

"You wouldn't hurt her."

"You're right," he says. "I'd never hurt her. But I can make sure that she never sees anyone else ever again. Kind of like what you did. I think it's my turn to play house now. Goodbye, Ace."

The line goes dead.

I try to call the number back, but it goes straight to voicemail. After the third attempt, the line is disconnected.

I grab the keys to my truck and immediately drive back to Ember's house. I call Brennon on the way.

"Hey, what's up?" he says.

"Brennon, he's got her. He's got Ember."

"What? What do you mean, he's got Ember?"

"Sawyer. I left her house twenty minutes ago, and he just called me. He's got her," I say, my voice panicked.

"Send me the phone number, let me see if I can trace the call."

I text him the number. "I'm on my way back to her house now. They probably won't be there when I get there. *Fuck*, Brennon! How could I be so fucking stupid to leave her alone?"

"Ace, you haven't left her side in months. You did everything you could. We're going to find her."

"Shit. Shit. *Shit*."

"I'll call it in. Let me know when you get there. And be careful."

I hang up and punch my steering wheel again and again and again.

My heart pounds out of my chest as I pull into her driveway. Her car is still parked outside, and her front door is closed when I unlock it. There is no sign of a break-in. No broken windows. No broken door hinges. The alarm doesn't even sound off. I would have received a notification if it had. None of this makes sense. He hasn't broken in, and she hasn't left, but he has her.

I call Brennon back.

"She's not here. He's not here. The front door was locked. No windows were broken. The back door was shut. Her car is still here. What the fuck happened to her, Brennon?" I yell into the phone.

I pace back and forth in her living room, where I had left her less than an hour ago. *Dammit.* I hate myself for leaving her. I shouldn't have left her side until Sawyer had been found.

I wait for Brennon to give me some positive news.

"I don't know what happened to her, man. We are going to find her though, okay?" he says.

That isn't what I want to hear.

The phone falls to the floor. My vision blurs as my eyes fill with tears. I have no idea when I'd last cried, but I have never been more afraid than I am right now.

I cry because I let her down. I cry because I am scared shitless of what is going to happen to her. I cry because I know she is scared, and I'm not there to protect her.

I'd promised I wouldn't let anything happen to her.

I have completely broken that promise.

chapter twenty-eight

Ace

I drive around all day looking for Sawyer and Ember. She'd gotten a new cell phone a couple of months ago, and I try calling it, but it keeps going straight to voicemail. Brennon has officers at both Sawyer's and Ember's houses in case they show up. Sawyer isn't an idiot, though. Of course he won't take her there.

I look in every car window I pass hoping to see Ember's face inside. It is nearly midnight before I get back home. I feel defeated. Lost. Empty.

I slam the door to my apartment and go straight to my bedroom. I fall flat onto the bed, wiping my hands over my face. I feel so helpless. I don't know what I can do for her. My heart aches, and I feel hollow without her.

How do I get her back?

"Fuck!" I yell out to no one.

I stand, and in one swoop of my hand, I throw everything off my nightstand. The lamp, clock and glass that is half full of water crashes against the wall. As more rage fuels me, I walk through the hall and into the living room to find more things I can break. I kick a glass vase off the coffee table, knock chairs over and rip picture frames off the wall.

I am a fucking mess. I slide down the wall and bury my face in my hands. I have no tears left, only anger at myself for letting this happen to her. Anger at Sawyer for not staying away. She doesn't deserve any of this.

I open my eyes, looking at the mess that is my apartment. It pales in comparison to the chaos that is my life.

Something catches my eye, hanging on the inside of my door. I didn't notice it when I first got home and stormed into my bedroom. I've had tunnel vision since Ember went missing.

I walk toward the old wooden door and rip off the loose-leaf piece of paper that clings by a single piece of tape. It's a letter.

My hands tremble when I see who it's from.

Sawyer.

How had he gotten into my apartment? Brennon and Ember are the only ones with keys, which means Sawyer fucking brought her here while I was driving around like a maniac looking for her. They were here. They were fucking *here*. If I would have stayed home, maybe I could have saved her. But he knew I wouldn't be home. That fucking bastard knew.

I look down at the letter.

Ace,

You're not going to find us, so stop trying. By the time you read this, I'm sure you'll have exhausted all your options for the day trying to find her. Let me say this again, you won't find us. You will never see Ember again. I need you to understand that.

Ember and I are meant to be together. She was made for me, Ace. She never had a hard time seeing that until you came into the picture. I don't know why you couldn't just leave us alone. I'm going to love her, more than you ever could. I won't hurt her. I don't know if that's what you need to hear to be okay with this, but it's true. I would never think of hurting her. I love that woman more than I love myself. She will always come first. I can guarantee her a lifetime of happiness.

I've always made her happy, Ace, don't you see that's why she took me back so many times? There's no one like me. There will never be anyone like me. You can never be to her what I am. I hope you enjoyed the last several months with my wife. That's right, my wife. Well, soon-to-be wife. I'm going to marry her in a few days. And after that, I'm going to make her a mother. God, can you imagine? She's going to be an amazing mother. There shouldn't be any problem getting her pregnant. God knows there will be plenty of sex between the two of us.

Ember's sitting on your couch while I write this. It's unfortunate that you aren't home to say goodbye. Pretty shitty how that happens, huh? Well, I've got some time to make up for. It's been a long fucking time since I've gotten to kiss her perfect lips or touch her in the place that makes her tremble beneath my fingers. Fuck, I can't wait. I'm getting hard just thinking about it. I better get going before I fuck her on your couch. Actually, that sounds like a brilliant idea.

See you never,

Sawyer

I collapse to my knees.

Brennon is at my place in less than fifteen minutes. He calls the precinct and has ten to fifteen officers dusting for prints, questioning my staff, and looking for evidence of where he might have taken her. He plans to get Sawyer's picture out to all courthouses within a 250-mile radius and to all the police stations and major news outlets.

They find Sawyer's fingerprints all over my apartment. There are even fucking fingerprints on my bed.

My fucking bed.

This is all too much. I don't know what he did to her, I don't want to think about it. I know what he is capable of, and I can only imagine what he made her do on my bed.

"Fuck," I say out loud.

A few of the officers look my way, but Brennon shakes his head, and they turn away.

I am a fucking mess. I can't remember the last time I ate.

It was this morning. Breakfast. With Ember.

I have to get out of here. I can't be here without her, not after knowing he brought her here. The only other place I want to be is Ember's. Brennon says they already searched her place and found nothing out of the ordinary. Maybe I will find some comfort sleeping in her bed. Her house is the last place I'd seen her, and it is exactly where I need to be.

I grab my keys and walk out the door.

Brennon yells from the top of the stairs, "Where are you going?"

"Sleeping at Ember's. Call me if you find anything."

I lie in her giant empty bed. Everything smells like her. Sweet vanilla. I miss the warmth of her skin next to mine as we fall asleep. I miss her long hair falling into my face. I miss her soft lips and the way she looks at me while I make love to her.

I toss and turn most of the night. When I'm about ready to give up on sleep altogether, my phone rings. My hand searches the nightstand frantically for my phone. Maybe it is Ember. Or maybe it is Brennon with news. Good news, I hope.

When I finally find my phone, the screen lights up with another unknown number. Naturally, my body tenses as I answer.

"Hello?"

"Is this Ace?" the young voice says.

"Yeah, who is this?"

"It's Cole. Sawyer's brother."

Ember loves Sawyer's brothers. I know none of this is their fault, so I try to hide the disappointment that it isn't Ember on the line as I try to figure out why he's calling.

"Hey," I say. "Is everything all right? It's the middle of the night."

"Yeah," he says. He takes a deep breath before continuing. "My life has been pretty messed up since my parents died."

"I know. I'm sorry for that."

"Ember really helped me through it at first. Then, Sawyer went missing. Or he left. Whatever. Either way, Ember had to leave too because they said she was in danger. I don't know what's going on, Ace, but I don't have anyone. I haven't for a long time now… Anyway, Brennon gave me your number a while ago while they were here asking questions."

"I'm sorry, man. This all must be hard for you. I'm glad you called."

"Yeah. It's really hard." He sniffles on the other end of the line.

"Sawyer's been gone for a long time. Ember was too while she was away with me. What made you call tonight?"

I don't know how much Cole knows, but Ember hadn't stayed in contact with the boys while we were at the safe house because of their connection to Sawyer. She'd had Brennon check up on them frequently. I wonder if he's calling because he found out Ember is missing.

"Sawyer called me a few minutes ago."

I sit up in bed, completely attentive. "What did he say?"

"He said that he and Ember are getting married. We still don't even know where he is. Why would he say that?"

I think back to the note. He says he is marrying her this week.

"Did you know she was taken?" I ask.

"What? He took her?"

"Yes. And now he's trying to get her to marry him."

"This is so messed up," he says, his voice nearly a whisper.

"What else did he say to you?"

"We haven't heard from him in months, then he called in the middle of the night out of nowhere. He wants Eric and me to come to their wedding. He said it would only be us because he wants us to be a *family* again." The way he says family is dull, like he no longer believes in the word.

"Did he say where?"

"No. He just told us what day. Tuesday."

Tomorrow is Tuesday. I grip my phone tighter. "Thank you, Cole. Thank you for calling. You did the right thing."

"Yeah," he sighs. "I can't believe he took her. I hope they find her."

"Me, too."

I hang up and text Brennon everything Cole told me. The wedding is tomorrow. That means he will have to contact Eric or Cole again to let them know where to go.

"I'm going to find you, Ember," I whisper.

chapter twenty-nine

Ace

I drive over to Sawyer's house first thing in the morning to sit with Eric and Cole while they wait to hear from Sawyer again. The boys have been alone ever since Sawyer disappeared over five months ago. I bring them breakfast from one of my restaurants, hoping the small gesture might ease the tension. The food steams as I open the containers and place them on the counter.

The boys dig right into the food. We sit around the table, mostly quiet as we eat. They hardly look me in the eyes before they finish their meals. I can understand why this situation might be uncomfortable for them, so I try to break the silence.

"Did you start college yet, Eric?" I ask.

He nods. "Yeah. I was supposed to go to Iowa, but I couldn't leave Cole alone. I've been taking classes at the community college for now."

Probably a sore subject. I move on. "Has your sister come to visit?"

"Yeah," Eric says. "Only once though."

That's shitty, I think to myself. "I'm glad Brennon gave you my number. If you guys ever need anything, I want you to call me, okay?"

They nod.

"Did you know I own a bar?" I ask.

Both of their faces look up in surprise, their eyes wide. I remember when I was their age. Anyone who has access to alcohol before you turn twenty-one is automatically cool.

"Which bar?" Eric asks.

"The Bungalow," I say. "Now I can't serve underage kids in my bar, but that doesn't mean we can't have a drink together sometime. You know, man to man."

They beam with excitement.

"That would be awesome," Cole says.

"Yeah," Eric agrees, trying to play it cool.

After I clean the table and wash the dishes we'd dirtied, I do my best to clean the rest of the kitchen. There are empty microwavable meals piled up on the counter, mixed in with some schoolwork that looks important. The kitchen is pure chaos.

After I clean the kitchen, I move on to the rest of the house. I can understand why Ember feels responsible for these kids. It isn't their fault their parents were killed. They don't deserve to live like this. This is all Sawyer's fault.

It is getting late, and I notice the rooms in the house growing darker as the sun disappears into the night.

I am taking a load of laundry out of the dryer when I hear someone's phone ring. I drop the clothes and run into the living room, where Cole and Eric are playing videogames. Cole's phone rings noisily in his hand. We all stare at it for a moment before he answers.

Cole accepts the call, putting it on speaker. "Hello?"

"Hey, sweetie."

Ember.

Ember's voice echoes through the phone's speaker, filling my ears with her presence and an overwhelming feeling of relief and despair.

"Ember?" Cole asks.

My heart feels like it drops into my stomach. Her sweet voice is on the other end of the call. But *why* is Ember calling him? Where is Sawyer?

"Yes, it's me. Your brother wanted me to give you a call about the wedding tomorrow. It's nothing big, as you can probably see, it's very last minute. But I...*we* are so excited to see you both. I've missed you boys so much. I hope you're doing okay. I feel terrible that you've both been alone all this time."

"We're okay." He keeps it short, the tone in his voice making it evident that they are anything but okay.

"Okay, then," she says. "Well, Sawyer is going to text you boys the address, but listen, please come alone, okay? It won't be safe for anyone else to be with you, do you understand?"

"Why wouldn't it be safe?" Cole asks.

The hesitation in her voice is all I need to hear to know that she's nervous. I realize Sawyer is probably standing right next to her telling her what to say. The thought makes me irate. Ember isn't safe. I'd promised I would keep her safe.

Fuck.

I have to find her. It takes everything in me to not speak, to not tell her that everything is going to be okay and that I *will* find her. That I love her. I'll be there tomorrow, no matter what Sawyer makes her say. Safe or not, there isn't anything stopping me.

"It would just be unfortunate to lose anyone else in our family," she finally says. "I don't want anything to happen to you or Eric...or *anyone*...and the only way to keep everyone safe is for you both to come alone tomorrow."

The way she says '*anyone,*' I know she's talking about me, but she has to know that nothing will stop me from finding her. And unfortunate to lose anyone else? Is Sawyer threatening the lives of his brothers now?

"Sawyer doesn't want Katie there?" Cole asks.

"No. She wouldn't make it in time anyway."

"Why do you have to get married tomorrow? What's the rush? Katie should be there. She's part of our family too."

"You're right. She is. But Sawyer…and I…don't want to wait any longer. We'll celebrate another time with your sister. For now, it'll just be us, okay?"

"All right, I guess."

Ember is quiet for a few seconds. "Hey, Cole?"

"Yeah?"

"Have you guys been talking to the police? Is anyone looking for us?"

I immediately shake my head, telling Cole to deny any involvement with the police. Sawyer can't know the police have been in contact with them. He might completely lose trust in his brothers if he knows the police are involved and may not confide in them anymore. Right now, this is our best shot. Our *only* shot.

"They haven't talked to us since Sawyer originally went missing."

I give Cole a thumbs-up.

"Okay," she says. I can tell she is disappointed, though she has to know he won't admit to that with Sawyer standing right there. "See you tomorrow, buddy."

I hear the click as she hangs up.

My eyes meet Eric's and then Cole's. "You guys okay?"

Eric stays quiet.

Cole shakes his head. "No. I don't want to go."

"I know." I place a hand on his shoulder. "We'll figure it out tomorrow, okay? For now, don't worry about it. The good news is they're both okay right now. I know you guys love your brother, but he could be dangerous, and we need to try and get Ember away from him."

"Yeah, okay," Cole says before he walks upstairs.

232

I take a seat at the kitchen table with Eric. I'm not certain what he thinks about all of this, and I know it isn't my place to ask, but I am all he has right now.

"You okay?"

Eric shrugs. "Pretty fucked-up, right?"

He's right. This whole thing is fucked-up. "Which part?"

"All of it." After a few moments he speaks again, "Did he really kill our parents?"

I look at him blankly. I didn't know that he had any suspicions about that. He is aware that the police are investigating their death, that it may not have been an accident, but Ember had made sure they didn't tell the boys that Sawyer is a potential suspect.

I decide to be honest about the situation. He is the man of the house now, after all. Things shouldn't be sugar-coated for him anymore. Ember is in trouble now, and I need him to understand just how serious this is.

"I hope not. But, yeah, I think he did."

"Just to get Ember back?" he asks.

I nod.

"That's so fucked-up. All he had to do was not be a jackass. She's always loved him."

"You're right. It is fucked-up."

Eric stands up and walks toward the stairs. He stops at the foot before taking his first step up. "You going to stay here tonight?"

"Do you want me to?" I ask.

"Yeah." Then he continues up to his bedroom.

I sleep on the couch, tossing and turning most of the night. Ember's been gone for two days. Forty-eight hours away, and it feels like a lifetime. I have to find her, and I have to find her *today*.

I can't let Sawyer force her into becoming his wife. I know this isn't what she wants. She would never want to marry someone she is afraid of, and though she still hasn't uttered those three words to me,

I know she loves me. It is my job to keep her safe, and I'm failing miserably.

Eric and Cole had come downstairs about an hour ago. I manage to cook us something quick for breakfast with what little groceries they have in the fridge. We all sit on the couch, a little on edge, as we wait for the address from Sawyer.

By noon, we still haven't heard from Sawyer or Ember. I can't get the thought of Sawyer marrying Ember out of my head. It makes me sick to my stomach. I never knew I could love someone the way I love Ember, until I met her. And now, she's missing.

The police are up to date on everything we know. They are aware of the phone call from Ember last night, and they know there is supposed to be a wedding today. Brennon is waiting for my phone call with the address. The boys don't want to see Sawyer today, and rightfully so, but Brennon says it is our best chance at finding them.

We watch TV for a little while before Eric and Cole's phones both alert them of a message. We immediately know it's from Sawyer. I can see on their faces that they probably feel what I am feeling right now: a little bit of nerves mixed with fear and nausea.

Eric opens the message first. Sawyer had texted them in a group thread.

Sawyer: Meet us in an hour at the curb.

I look at them both, confused. "The curb? Like, right outside in the driveway?"

Eric shakes his head. "No."

Cole glances in my direction. "I think it's where they first met."

"They met on a curb? There are millions of curbs."

"Sawyer took her to the same damn spot every year on their anniversary," Eric says. "It's by the high school. But I don't get how they could have a wedding there."

Cole looks back down at his phone. He doesn't say anything else.

"You okay?" I ask.

"I don't want to go."

"I know. But I'm going to go with you, okay?"

"How?" Cole asks. "Ember said it was too dangerous. What if Sawyer tries to kill me next?"

The fear in his eyes is undeniable. I don't know if Sawyer would kill his own brother. I would hope not, but he hadn't hesitated to murder his parents.

"He's not going to kill us, dude," Eric says.

Cole looks at him. "How do you know?"

"The only person he loves more than us is probably Ember. He would never let anything happen to us, you know that."

"I don't know that."

"Well, *I* do."

"Brennon and I are going to be there," I interject. "We'll make sure you're both safe. He won't know we're there."

"Okay," they both say in unison.

"Well, then, let's go to the curb."

Brennon picks me up a half hour later. Eric drives himself and Cole to the spot they believe to be the curb. It is near the parking lot of the high school, a small side street, nothing special.

Eric is right, they can't have a wedding here. It is out in the open, and Sawyer knows it would be too easy to catch them. Something doesn't feel right about the situation. What is Sawyer's end game? So, why did he lure his brothers to this place? What's his plan here?

Brennon and I park about a block away in an unmarked police car. You can't spot us from where they are, but we can see them perfectly. Brennon talked with them before we left, and they understand that we won't be able to hear them, but there are undercover cop cars parked around the entire perimeter of the school, and *all* eyes are on them. They are safe. I don't know how this is going to play out, but I know we won't let anything happen to those boys.

My body is jittery as the nerves start to set in. Sawyer will be here any minute. I have to pull it together. Ember is counting on me to save her, and I won't let anything stop me.

Eric and Cole stand on the sidewalk. Their car is parked a few feet away from them. Cole looks nervous. Eric, not so much.

We watch them closely, waiting for something to happen. Anything. It's been exactly one hour since they received the text from Sawyer, but there is no sign of him.

Eric takes a seat on the curb, and Cole follows suit.

I continue to examine every car that drives by, disappointed that I haven't seen Ember in any of them. I look at my watch for what feels like the hundredth time.

He's late.

Just as I am about to say something to Brennon, the back door to the car clicks open. The sound is followed by the feeling of something cold and hard against my temple. I don't move. I can't. Sawyer is in the back seat holding a gun to my head.

"Drive," he says.

chapter thirty

Ace

Sawyer doesn't pull the gun away from my head. It's still pressed firmly against me as my brother drives. Brennon looks calm. He's a cop, after all, and he's probably been in similar situations a lot more than I have. I think back to every memory I've ever had, and I can confidently say that I have never had a gun to my head.

All I can think about is Ember. What will happen to her if he kills me? And where is she? Why isn't she with Sawyer? I hope like hell nothing has happened to her.

"Turn left here," Sawyer instructs.

Brennon turns the wheel.

"How are you, Ace?" Sawyer says, jamming the gun deeper into my head.

I don't answer.

"Surprised to see me? I'll admit, I thought I'd never see you again, but circumstances changed. I told you not to look for us, but you didn't listen. So, I figured I would pay you a visit."

Still, I remain silent.

"Aren't you curious where Ember is?"

I ignore him and close my eyes. I picture her face and hope that she is okay. This is her biggest fear coming to fruition. I have to stay alive for her. Brennon and I need to make it through this.

"Fucking speak already," he yells.

"Where is she?" I ask calmly.

He laughs. "You'll see." I can sense the smile that spreads across his face. "Take the next right and park on the hill."

Brennon does as he's told. He puts the car in park, and we wait for Sawyer to make his next move.

I don't recognize the area. We aren't in the car long, but I have no idea where we are. There is a row of houses on our left with an open field on our right. The road is slanted, giving the neighborhood a lopsided appearance. This place gives off an eerie abandoned feeling.

Sawyer still holds the gun steadily to my head. "Do my brothers think I killed our parents?" he asks softly.

"No."

The last thing I want to do is antagonize him, though I know Eric has a pretty good idea that he did. But Cole doesn't have the slightest clue, which is ironic since he is the one so afraid of seeing Sawyer.

Brennon breaks his silence. "Ember made sure we didn't say anything that might hint at that during our investigation. Your brothers have no idea, even though I figured out as much."

"Ah, he speaks."

"Sawyer, where is she?" I ask again.

"She's right inside that house over there." He nudges his head in the direction of a small tan brick house down the street. "She's getting ready for our wedding. I'm finally going to marry my girl! How cool is that?"

I can't take my eyes off the house. She's in there. I need to get inside.

"Why did you bring us here?"

He ignores the question, but I see his smirk through the rearview mirror. I've never wanted to kill someone until this moment.

"Come on. It's time for me to become a married man! Let's call this the bachelor party, yeah?"

He slams the gun hard against my head. "Your cop buddy here better play it cool, or I'll shoot you before the nuptials even begin, got it?"

Brennon and I step out of the car. For a brief moment, Sawyer and I make eye contact. He's wearing dark jeans and a black T-shirt with a dark gray beanie over his trimmed hair. He keeps the gun pointed at me as we walk toward the tan brick house.

I glance down the street, looking for anyone that might see this psycho holding a gun to my head. How can there not be a single person outside to witness this?

He opens the dingy red door that leads us into the house Ember is supposedly in. When we walk in, I am instantly reminded of a house that would be subject to a drug bust in a movie. It's old and grimy and smells like mold might be growing inside the walls. This is where he took Ember?

He motions for us to sit.

"*This* is where you're getting married?" I question.

Sawyer laughs. "Of course not."

I let out a frustrated sigh, tired of his games.

The gun remains pointed at my head, its muzzle never losing sight of me.

"Sawyer?" I hear a female voice say from a back room.

Ember.

"In here, babe."

And then I see her. I finally find her, and she looks absolutely captivating. Her hair falls in loose waves down her back. She's wearing a white dress that has a deep neckline exposing just enough of her perfect breasts. The dress falls to her ankles and flows when she walks. When her emerald eyes find me, all I can see is hurt, pain, and fear. She looks breathtaking on the outside, but on the inside, she's crumbling.

"Wow," I whisper.

I have to look away. I can't look into those eyes any longer, not when there is a gun pointed directly at my head. She is living her nightmare, her biggest fear. I'd told her this wouldn't happen to me, that I will be fine, but I'd lied. Sawyer had come after me. She'd been right all along.

"What are they doing here?" she asks Sawyer.

"I wanted Ace to see how beautiful my bride looks on her wedding day."

Ember doesn't question him further. Instead, she turns around and walks away, clearly unamused with Sawyer's games.

"Where are you going?" he yells.

She doesn't respond.

Sawyer grunts, irritated. His back is to us as he's looking in Ember's direction. He isn't paying attention to where his gun is aimed anymore.

This is our chance.

I look at Brennon, and he gives me a slight nod.

chapter thirty-one

Ace

There is a loud crash.
    A gunshot.
    I hear her scream.
    Ember.
    My ears are ringing.
    I fall to the floor.
    My eyes close.
    Ember.
    I hear nothing.
    I see nothing.
    I feel nothing.

chapter thirty-two

Ember

Ace and I have spent every single day together for the last 180 days. There's so much you learn about a person when you spend that long with them. I fell in love with Ace, hard and *fast*, though I still haven't told him. I don't know what's taking me so long. I'm sure of my feelings, and I think he knows it too, but still, I can't seem to say it out loud.

Ace is the man I always hoped I would find. He doesn't fault me for my baggage or blame me when something goes wrong. I don't have to question his loyalty to me because I'm certain he would never do anything to hurt me. He's already done everything imaginable to keep me safe. He's the real thing. He's *the one,* and I've known it for a while now.

Last night was my first night back in my own house. In my own *bed*. Ace stayed the night. After we made love, I wouldn't let him leave. Despite the fear that still lingers with Sawyer nowhere to be found, I didn't want Ace to go home because the bed would feel empty without him. I had, in fact, spent several months in the same bed as him. How can I sleep without him now? So instead, I pulled him back under the covers and did that thing with my tongue I know he likes.

The next morning, I wake up with my body entangled in Ace. It is a familiar feeling, one that is even more comforting as I open my eyes and see the light streaming inside the bedroom.

My bedroom.

I need to buy groceries today so I can cook dinner in my own kitchen.

My own kitchen!

I plan to stop and visit with Taylor today too. She stopped by a few weeks ago when we first got back to Ace's apartment. She can't believe everything that is going on with Sawyer. She's never liked him, but she'd tolerated him because of me. Needless to say, she is thankful I found someone like Ace to look after me.

Ace and I have stayed at his apartment above the Bungalow for the last couple of weeks before we finally moved my stuff back into my house. There were a lot of nights spent in his bar, a few that I don't remember, but I always woke up in the morning next to the man I love. The once unfamiliar setting of his bedroom is now a safe haven for me.

Ace stands at the foot of the bed getting dressed before he leaves so we can start the day. He is still the most attractive man I have ever seen, and it takes everything in me to let him cover his perfectly sculpted body with clothing. I stay in bed, gawking at him.

He smirks when he catches me staring. "What?"

I trail my fingers over the spot where he'd lain just a few short moments ago and in my most seductive voice say, "Why don't you come back to bed?"

Ace buckles his belt that wraps around his jeans. "Babe."

"What?" I ask innocently.

"You're killing me. We're never going to get out of bed if you keep looking at me like that."

"Maybe that's my plan."

He laughs, walking over to the bed. He kisses the top of my head. "I love you so much, Ember."

I smile. "That's why you should come back to bed."

"What time are you supposed to meet Taylor?"

I glance at the clock. "In an hour."

"You should get going, don't you think?"

I grab at his belt buckle, the one he'd just put on, and slowly unfasten it. I unbutton his jeans next and pull at them until they lay in a puddle around his ankles.

"One more time before you go," I say as I kiss his defined abdomen.

He moans above me. "One more time," he agrees.

We make love again one last time before he leaves. I'm sure we will again tonight, but the thought of being away from him for the first time in six months leaves me wanting more.

Shortly after Ace leaves, I set the alarm to my new security system, and walk out the door. I am sure to lock and double lock the front door to prevent any potential break-ins and unwanted guests. You can never be too careful, and I don't want to take any chances, not with Sawyer still out there somewhere.

I step outside. It is a chilly morning, but still rather comfortable for this time of year. I walk to my car that is parked in the driveway, and just as I am about to unlock the door, something makes me glance up.

Call it déjà vu, but I see him. Again. Sawyer. At my house. He stands at the foot of my driveway, his car parked next to him.

My stomach falls to the ground. I look around, trying to plan my escape. My legs suddenly feel weak and my hands tremble, but I do my best not to look afraid. I'm sure he can still sense the fear radiating off me like hot lava.

He looks sad, but thankful. I can't quite grasp the exact emotion he's displaying as he walks up to meet me. I don't move. I *can't*. If I run, he will outrun me. If I fight, he'll win. So, I stay still, frozen.

"Hi, baby," he says softly.

He stands directly in front of me now, his hands cupping my cheeks as he gently strokes one side with his thumb.

I don't say a word.

"I was so worried about you. Are you okay? Did he hurt you?" he asks.

My eyebrows crease as I look at him, confused. *Seriously?*

"No, Sawyer, he didn't hurt me."

"He kept you from me for so long, baby. I tried to get to you. I'm so sorry it took me this long." He kisses my forehead before he wraps me in his embrace. I remain stiff. His hug no longer has any effect on me. In fact, it makes me sick.

He kisses me again, this time on my cheek. "Come on, babe. Let's get out of here."

When he senses my hesitation, he continues, "I don't want to hurt him, Ember, but if he shows up while we're here, I'll have no choice but to do just that. Let's walk to the car now. There's no need to cause a scene."

I don't want to leave with him, but what other choice do I have? If something happens to Ace, I don't know what I would do. If I try to call for help, or cause any scene at all, he'll go after him just to spite me. I love Ace more than I love myself, and if I have to leave with Sawyer to keep him safe, then that's what I'll do.

Sawyer opens the car door for me, and against my better judgment, I get in. As we sit inside a car I don't recognize that is noticeably *not* white, I keep my eyes fixed on the road.

Out of the blue, he holds out his hand to me.

I look at it, confused.

"Give me your phone," he says.

I don't falter as I reach into my purse and hand it over. He powers it off and puts it in his pocket. Then, he picks up his phone and dials a number.

"Hi there," Sawyer says into the phone.

I can't hear who is on the other end of the call.

"Ace! Old friend. Glad you can recognize my voice. How've you been? Did you have fun playing house with my girlfriend?"

Shit.

Shit. Shit. Shit.

"Oh, it's a little late for that. You kept me from her for months, Ace. I waited *years* to be with her again, and when I finally got her back, you took her away. How could you expect me not to be there the second you finally left?"

Ace is going to blame himself for this.

No. This is not his fault!

"I just want my girl. And I want you to leave us alone."

Ace says something I can't understand, but his voice is noticeably louder on the other end.

"Oh, but it is, Ace. You wouldn't want something to happen to her, now, would you?"

What? Something happen to *me?* Would Sawyer hurt me? The thought has never crossed my mind. I am more afraid of what he might do to others, what he would do to *Ace*, but now he is threatening my life?

"You're right. I'd never hurt her. But I can make sure that she never sees anyone else ever again. Kind of like what you did. I think it's my turn to play house now. Goodbye, Ace."

Then he hangs up.

We pull into the Bungalow's parking lot. The familiar place fills me with both fear and relief. Maybe Ace will be home and will help me. Or, I think about it again, maybe something bad will happen to him if he is. Suddenly, I hope he isn't here.

Thoughts flood my head. Why did Sawyer bring us here? Why did he risk taking me to such a public place? What will he do if Ace is home?

"What are we doing here?" I ask.

"Just want to stop by quickly. You have a key, don't you?"

How does he know that? I only nod.

Sawyer walks closely behind me as we enter the bar. There are only a few people here, but not too many, seeing as it is early in the day.

I eye the bartender, hoping he will say something to prevent us from going any farther, but unfortunately, he doesn't question me as we make our way up the stairs to Ace's apartment. Why would he? I've practically lived upstairs for the last month.

Dammit.

I shove the key into the wooden door and turn it until it clicks. The door unlocks, and I push it open.

Please don't be home. Please don't be home.

"Ace?" Sawyer yells.

Silence.

Good. He's not home.

"Make yourself comfortable, baby. We shouldn't be expecting any company."

I sit on the couch. It smells like Ace. Lemon and wood. Clean yet manly. It is comforting.

Sawyer grabs a pen and starts writing something on the countertop. I can feel my pulse quicken in my pressure points. I don't know whether to run or stay quiet and see what Sawyer has planned. I'm scared that if I make the wrong decision, he will hurt Ace, so I do nothing. I sit there like an obedient child waiting to be told what to do.

"*Fuck*," Sawyer moans.

I turn my head to see what is wrong, but his eyes are heavy lidded as he stares at me with thirst. Nothing is wrong, but it will be very soon. I know exactly what that look means.

I feel a sharp pang in my stomach as he walks toward the couch and kneels in front of me.

"I missed you, Ember. I missed you so much," he says as he caresses my leg.

Goosebumps emerge on my legs, but not the good kind. They are the kind that appear when the hair stands up on the back of your neck out of fear.

His hand makes its way up my leg until it rubs between my thighs. I close my eyes, willing the tears back. I feel them as they pool in my eyes. I squeeze my eyes tighter, trying to prevent any from falling. He can't know what he is doing to me. I can't let him see that I am afraid.

Suddenly, his lips find my neck, kissing and sucking, no doubt leaving marks. His tongue glides over my skin. His lips eventually find mine, and his tongue pushes through. I don't kiss him back, but his mouth leaves mine too quickly to notice. He works his way down my neck again, his tongue ultimately finding my chest.

He unbuttons my top, one button at a time, until my breasts are exposed yet covered by the cotton of my bra. I can't stop the tears from spilling anymore. I tilt my head back, focusing on the ceiling, wishing for a distraction from this nightmare.

Please let this be over soon. Please.

His mouth falls to my bare skin as his hands reach behind my back and unclasp my bra. Tears fall uncontrollably, but Sawyer never notices. He is too busy sliding his tongue over my nipples, slowly circling each one.

He stops for a brief moment, but only to pick me up. He carries me into the bedroom, into *Ace's bedroom.* He lays me on the bed, staring hungrily at me, at my body.

"Sawyer, please. Can we not do this here?" I beg.

"Baby, I've waited so long. I can't wait any longer. I'll be quick, I promise."

I squeeze my eyes shut again and cry. I cry as he takes off my pants. I cry as he pulls down my panties. I cry as he pushes himself inside of me and fucks me on Ace's bed.

"*Fuck.* You feel so good," he moans.

I try to imagine Ace. I try to picture him walking in and beating the shit out of Sawyer for raping me. Raping me on the bed Ace and I made love in countless times. Sawyer is taking something from me. He doesn't respect me or my body. He is taking what he thinks belongs to him.

Sawyer is right about one thing, he is quick. It only takes five excruciating minutes before he comes inside of me, but it feels like all of eternity. When he pulls out, he collapses on top of me, out of breath.

Sawyer raped me.

That is all I can think about. Sawyer raped me as I sobbed beneath him. I don't have any more tears left. My eyes are dry as I realize I have no idea what he will do to me next. I'm numb. Numb to him, numb to the situation, numb to the world.

He puts his clothes back on, then hands me mine, but before I can move to dress myself, he lies next to me, drawing circles on my stomach with his finger.

I stare blankly at the ceiling.

"I love you, Ember. That was amazing."

I lay there naked, still staring into oblivion. My eyes are still swollen and raw from crying. How can that have felt amazing? What a piece of shit.

"Get dressed. Time to go," he says, watching as I put on my panties, followed by my jeans. "Baby, if you move any slower, I'm going to have to fuck you again. Do you have any idea how attractive you are? I'm getting hard again just watching you."

I turn around. That is the last thing I want. I quickly dress, covering the rest of my body with my clothing. I follow him out of the bedroom and down the hall until we are back in the kitchen. He grabs the piece of paper he'd been writing on earlier off the counter and tapes it to the door before we walk out.

"What's that?" I mumble.

"A goodbye letter," he says.

I catch a glimpse of the last part of the letter.

See you never.

I repeat the words in my head, then swallow the lump in my throat.

chapter thirty-three

Ember

Sawyer takes me to a small house on a slanted street. The neighborhood is eerily quiet and when he leads me into the house, I almost gag. The place smells like shit.

"Whose house is this?" I ask, disgusted.

"We're going to be staying here temporarily. Don't worry, I've already found the perfect house for us. It's going to be my wedding present to you."

Wedding present? "What?"

Sawyer reaches into his back pocket and gets down on one knee. He opens the small velvet jewelry box and displays a giant diamond sitting on a silver band. Is he really going to do this? In the entrance of a crack house?

"Baby," he says. "I have been in love with you since the moment I first saw you. I'll admit, I've messed up a lot, but I've tried so hard to make up for it. I'll do whatever it takes to make a future with you, Ember. I can't live without you, and I never want to again. The last couple of months have been so hard for me. *Hell,* all the years that we weren't together were hard. I know you missed me like I missed you. There's no denying the love that we share. We're *unstoppable*, baby. You and me. I know this might seem sudden, but we've known each other for so long. We belong together. I've never been so sure. I will love you for the rest of my life, and I'll do whatever it takes to prove that to you." He takes a deep breath. "Will you marry me?"

I feel like I'm living someone else's life. I'm a bystander, watching this dumpster fire of a proposal from a man who just *raped* me. A man who *murdered* his own parents. Words don't escape me. My hands tremble as he holds them. If I didn't feel so numb, or if I had any tears left to cry, I am sure I would be curled in a ball on the floor bawling my damn eyes out. Why is this happening to me?

I almost collapse, my legs suddenly feeling weak, but Sawyer catches me in his arms. The familiarity of my racing heart and shortness of breath indicates I am likely having another panic attack. This time, Ace isn't there to comfort me. My body collapses further against Sawyer. He holds me up in his arms, but my head is buried in his neck. The only thing keeping me off the ground is him.

"It's okay, love. I know. This is a lot. You don't have to say anything. I know you love me," he whispers into my ear.

Somehow, I find more tears. My sobs grow louder, and it becomes harder and harder to catch my breath. Sawyer strokes my back in his attempt to comfort me, but it doesn't work. It won't work. *He* is the reason for my panicked state. *He* isn't Ace, and he never will be. Sawyer is a murderer, and as long as he is in my life, I am in danger. Ace is in danger. Everyone I care about is in danger. The only way to guarantee their safety is to give into him, to not give him a reason to hurt anyone else.

He takes the ring out of the box and gently slips it onto my finger. I don't have the strength to fight him. I'm too weak. Too numb.

He carries me into a back room and places me on the bed in the corner. Thankfully, the room is noticeably less grimy than the rest of the house. The king-size bed topped with a white down comforter doesn't look like it belongs in a dirty place like this. The pillows scattered across are cold and soft, the feeling soothing as I press my cheek against one. He pulls back the covers, tucking me in.

It is the middle of the day, but I am exhausted. So many emotions and so much fear. If it's even possible, this is the safest I've felt with Sawyer since we left my house. I am in an unfamiliar bed, but it somehow helps me to relax.

"Shhhh," he says as he rubs my face. He places another soft kiss on my forehead. "We're getting married on Tuesday. I've already picked out your dress. It's in the closet. I'll call my brothers later and invite them. I know you'd want them to be there. I love you, Ember. We can finally be a family again."

I continue to stay quiet, though it's not hard in my shocked state. I have nothing to say to him. I only hope if I do what he says, everyone I love will stay safe, including Eric and Cole. Sawyer killed his parents, and I have no doubt that he will stop at nothing to get his way.

I shut my eyes, wanting to wake up from this nightmare. Sawyer kisses my lips before he walks out of the room.

"I'll be back in a little while to join you. Sweet dreams, love."

He shuts the door behind him, and I cry myself to sleep.

I wake up the next morning after somehow having slept through the entire rest of the day and night, disappointed everything that has happened is real. I don't get out of bed, even after Sawyer has sex with me again while I pretend to be asleep. I cry, keeping my head buried in the pillow. When he leaves the room, I cry harder.

I spend as much time as I can in bed. Sawyer brings me breakfast and lunch and eventually requests my presence in the kitchen for dinner.

When I walk out of the bedroom, I take another look around. The smell permeates around me. This house is *disgusting*. As I enter the kitchen, I notice rodent feces speckled on the counters.

"I don't want to be here anymore, Sawyer. This place is nauseating," I say as I take my seat. It is one thing for me to be stuck with Sawyer, but for me to be stuck with Sawyer in *this* place is even worse.

Sawyer places a mound of spaghetti and meatballs in front of me. "I know. We're going to leave tomorrow."

"Where are we going tomorrow?"

"After the wedding, I'm taking you on our honeymoon." He smiles. "We'll move into our new house when we get back."

"What about the home I already have?"

"I want to start fresh. Besides, it's not big enough for us and kids. You know that, baby. We'll sell it."

My face falls flat. *Good luck making that happen.*

"Babe?"

"What?" I say flatly.

"I need you to call Eric and Cole and let them know I'll text them where to meet me tomorrow. I'll pick them up right before the ceremony."

"Why do *I* need to call them?"

He grabs my hand. "You're like a mother to those boys now, Ember. We've both been absent from their lives, and it's time we start making up for it. That includes you."

I can't hide my disgust. Everything that has happened to them is *his* fault. Though I feel a responsibility for their well-being, it is Sawyer who did this to them in the first place.

"Ember, if they try anything funny, I won't be afraid to do something about it. Do you understand me? It was an unfortunate accident with my parents, but on the bright side, it brought us closer together. I would hate for this family to suffer another devastating loss."

I swallow the saliva that builds up on my tongue and almost choke. Now, he's threatening Eric and Cole.

"You'd hurt your own family…"

"Baby, I would never hurt you. I don't want our family to lose anyone else, so I need everyone to cooperate to make sure this wedding goes as planned."

"Don't I get any say in our wedding, Sawyer?"

He stands to grab something out of the fridge. "I already have everything that you could ever want ready, Ember. I know you. I understand your wants, your needs. Everything you desire." He sits back down. "Unfortunately, I don't see how Ace could fit into all that, but I'm willing to look past your indiscretions because I love you. I know how you feel about me, and your being here is enough for me. Everything is ready for you. I'm prepared to make you my wife, babe. It's going to be the best day of your life. I've made sure of it."

"I'm not hungry," I say as I push away the plate he made.

"Ember, you've hardly eaten anything all day."

I look around. "Look at where you've brought me! How can you expect me to eat when there are dead bugs and rodent shit scattered everywhere?"

He nods in understanding. "I'm sorry, baby. You're right. Tomorrow will be better."

"Why can't we leave today? I don't want to spend another minute here."

"I know this is less than ideal, but I cleaned the bedroom for you myself. If you feel more comfortable in there, then we can go back to bed."

We. I know what happens when Sawyer and I are in a bed together. "I'm fine."

"Call them before you rest tonight, please."

"You took my phone, remember?" I say harshly.

He pulls out a phone from his front pocket and hands it to me. "Here."

I call Cole with Sawyer lurking over me. It is hard to hear his voice. He sounds sad, maybe even nervous to speak with me. I say what Sawyer tells me to say. I can't let Sawyer hurt them. This is just another way he's forced my hand into doing something I don't want. Sawyer is devious, manipulative. How did I not see that before?

"Have you guys been talking to the police? Is anyone looking for us?" I ask Cole before I end the call.

Sawyer looks at me, his eyebrows scrunched. He hadn't told me to ask that. In fact, I'm not sure why I did. Maybe I am hoping there might be a hint in his voice that will leave me a glimmer of hope. Will they find us? The only way I am getting out of here is if the police find me and arrest Sawyer before he can hurt anyone else.

"They haven't talked to us since Sawyer originally went missing," Cole says.

My heart sinks, but what did I expect? I have to put my hope in Ace and Brennon. Ace would've had the police on it the second Sawyer called him. But how can they find me? Their only hope is Eric and Cole ratting out their brother. Will they do that? I'm not sure. They don't know that Sawyer killed their parents. Right now, I'm sure they're only concerned about seeing their brother again.

"Okay," I say. "See you tomorrow, buddy."

I hang up.

Sawyer looks at me annoyed. "Why would you bring up the police?"

"I wanted to make sure there wasn't a threat that someone might follow them. If the police are looking for me like they were looking for you when you disappeared, there's a good chance they wouldn't come alone. I don't want anything bad to happen to them, Sawyer."

I grab his hand, hoping he'll believe my reasoning for involving the police in the conversation. It is partly true. I don't want anything to happen to them.

He smiles. "I love you."

I give a pitiful smile in return. "I'm going to lie back down now."

chapter thirty-four

Ember

I'm supposed to get married today. It should be the happiest day of my life. And it would be, if I'd been marrying someone I am actually in love with, someone like *Ace*.

Sawyer left an hour ago, leaving me with the instructions to be ready by the time he gets back. He has everything laid out for me: shoes, wedding dress, jewelry.

I should run away. I should leave. He clearly isn't afraid to leave me alone.

Why?

He knows no one will find me here. He knows I won't run. He'll kill them if I do. I can't let him hurt Eric, Cole, or Ace in exchange for my freedom. My freedom isn't worth that.

So, I prepare myself for the big day. My *wedding* day.

I curl my hair in long, loose waves and pin half of it up. I brush my eyelids with a shimmering eye shadow and put a touch of mascara on my lashes before I pucker my lips in preparation for lip gloss. Once my makeup is finished, I slip on the dress Sawyer bought me.

I look beautiful. The dress is breathtaking. It is exactly what I would have envisioned myself wearing.

Sawyer has always paid attention to the small details. He knows what I like. That sort of thing would have been attractive in a partner who didn't stalk you.

Now, I look at the dress with disgust. He knows so much about me because he *watches* me. He observes my every move. He keeps me from forming any relationships so he can have me all to himself. It is all part of this grand plan he has.

I am about to get married to Sawyer, the occasion only solidifying the fact that I will never see Ace again.

The thought that haunts me the most is that I still haven't told Ace I love him. What I would give to go back to those days in our small, secluded shack. I had so many opportunities to tell him how I felt, but still, I never let those three important words slip. I knew I loved him then. I've known it for a long time. And now, I'll never have the opportunity to tell him.

A single tear falls down my cheek.

This is my life now.

I'll be happy to see Eric and Cole today, though I wish it could be under better circumstances. I haven't seen them since Eric's graduation. I have been flooded with guilt since I left with Ace. Brennon had been wonderful during that time, always checking in with the boys while the investigation continued.

I don't know what the boys thought of Sawyer after he had left them, but I made sure they didn't know he is a murderer. That sort of news would devastate them, and they have already had it pretty rough as it is. How could they live knowing their own flesh and blood had been responsible for the death of their parents? Sawyer leaving them had been the icing on the cake. It only proved that he doesn't care for anyone's well-being other than his own, and *maybe* mine. I have no doubt they are angry with Sawyer for abandoning them. I'll bet they're furious, as they should be.

Eric and Cole won't miss our wedding, of that much I am certain. Though they have every right to turn a cold shoulder on their brother, I know they would still do anything for him. It's sad, really. How unfortunate for them that he is their role model. I need to do better for them. If Sawyer thinks we are going to become one big happy family after this is all said and done, then I'll be damn sure to make those kids the happiest they've ever been.

I want to give them everything, even if my life is the cost. I know I am giving up a lot: *my* family, *my* friends, *Ace*. But those boys are innocent in all of this. Sawyer has done everything as part of a sick and twisted plan to win me back, and I can't help but feel like this is all my fault. They don't deserve any of this.

I take a look in the mirror at myself, at my life. It is all going to end today. I will be married to Sawyer by nightfall, but Eric and Cole will be safe. Ace will be safe.

The front door opens. My heart races with anticipation. I hear voices from the front room.

"Sawyer?"

"In here, babe," he yells.

I open the door to the bedroom and walk toward his voice. When I enter the living room, I don't see Eric or Cole. Instead, Sawyer is holding a gun to Ace's head while Brennon sits next to him on the couch.

Ace.

Ace is here.

Ace has a gun pointed at his head.

I have done *everything* Sawyer has asked. Why the hell did he bring them here?

Brennon doesn't move a muscle as he stares at the gun in Sawyer's hand, helpless.

Ace glances up. When he notices me, his entire demeanor changes. They are subtle changes, but still, I notice. His eyes soften slightly, his shoulders relax.

"Wow," he whispers, holding my gaze for a few seconds before looking away again.

My eyes go back to the gun in Sawyer's hand. "What are they doing here?" I ask Sawyer.

"I wanted Ace to see how beautiful my bride looks on her wedding day."

What the fuck?

I turn around, disgusted and no longer able to look at the man I love with a gun to his head. I walk back toward the bedroom, not bothering to fight the tears streaming down my face. I want to be anywhere but in this house. I have done everything Sawyer asked. I left with him. I let him fuck me on Ace's bed. I've stayed with him in this disgusting house. I even got ready for a wedding I want no part of. I am ready to give up my life to him in order to protect the people I love. To keep Eric and Cole safe. To keep *Ace* safe.

At this point, none of it matters. I can't look at Ace again while his life is in Sawyer's hands.

Sawyer is going to kill him.

I have never been more sure of anything in my life. Sawyer has brought Ace here with the intention of killing him.

My sobs grow louder. What can I do?

I retreat to the bedroom as I hear Sawyer yelling for me. His voice is harsh, the angriest I have ever heard him speak to me.

I know I have to do something before his temper blows things even more out of control. I can't leave Ace out there at Sawyer's disposal. I turn around and move back toward the living room, certain that I will do whatever it takes to protect Ace.

Suddenly, there is a loud crash. I instinctively pick up my pace, eager to reach Ace. My need to keep Ace safe trumps the emotional turmoil I had previously felt.

When I reach the living room, Brennon is wrestling on top of Sawyer. They fight for the gun that had been held to Ace's head. Then, a shot is fired. The unexpected dismissal causes me to scream. My ears ring as I frantically search the room for Ace.

Brennon has the gun now and Sawyer is lying unconscious on the floor. The gun has sounded, but there is no blood on Brennon or Sawyer.

Brennon looks up at me, panting. "Are you hurt?" he asks.

"No," I say, hardly hearing the sound of my own voice over the ringing noise in my ears.

Brennon turns and fixes his eyes on Ace. For the first time since the initial crash, I find him. Ace is no longer sitting, but lying over a pool of blood.

"Shit!" Brennon yells.

He immediately pulls out his cell phone and dials 9-1-1. I run to Ace, falling to my knees next to him. Everything after that happens so fast.

I remember Brennon motioning for me to take his shirt and press it over Ace's abdomen. I remember crying hysterically as tears fell from my face onto him. I remember not taking my eyes off him, as his skin paled and blood soaked through the T-shirt. I remember repeatedly telling him that I love him, wishing it would wake him up. I remember how peaceful he looked. I remember thinking that he doesn't look like he is in pain. I remember Brennon checking his pulse. I think he was still breathing at that point.

Soon, the paramedics arrive and rush Ace into an ambulance. Brennon and I climb into the cabin once Ace is lifted in. I don't remember anything after that. Not the ride to the hospital. Not how I ended up in the familiar pale blue waiting room with uncomfortable chairs.

Once I snap out of my daze hours later, I turn to Brennon. Had either of us said a word since we left? Is everything a blur to him as well?

"What's going to happen to him?" I ask.

Brennon looks at me, and I can see the devastation in his eyes. Ace is his brother and whatever I am feeling, he is feeling it too.

"He's in surgery," Brennon manages.

"Is he going to die?" I ask softly.

Brennon doesn't answer. He grabs my hand and bows his head. I think he's praying.

chapter thirty-five

Ember

I walk down the dark, unoccupied hallway. It is cold. The gray
cement walls close in on me. I have never been to a place like this
before, a place so murky and unwelcoming. I reach a small window
that is enclosed in metal bars. A woman with short yellow hair looks
up to me as I reach her. Her face is expressionless.

"ID please," the woman asks.

I reach for my ID and slide it through the small opening in the
glass. She snatches it and scans it, all while never taking her eyes off
me. She really gives me the creeps.

"Do you have any of these items on you today?" The woman
points to a laminated piece of paper that is taped to the glass window
listing several objects ranging from sharp knives to over-the-counter
drugs.

"No."

She returns my ID and pushes a black button. "Through those
doors."

The heavy black doors to my left open, accompanied by a loud
sounding alarm.

On the other side of the door I am greeted by a gentleman. His badge displays the name Frank. Frank smiles and nods his head in a much more welcoming manner.

"This way, ma'am," he says. His arm opens to another hallway, and he motions me in the direction I need to go.

I walk down another dreary corridor until I am stopped at a titanium door. There is one small window opening in the center made of a thick opaque glass. I hear an overhead sound buzz and the door opens in front of me. I walk through.

"Who are you here to see?" asks another guard.

I swallow before I speak. "Sawyer Christensen."

"Take a seat over there." She points to one of the tables in the room. "He'll be out soon."

I make my way over to the table and take a seat on the cold metal bench. The room is spacious with several tables resembling the one I occupy. There are a lot of other people visiting. I wonder how many of them are here to see rapists or murderers. The thought sends a chill down my spine. This is a first for me, visiting a *jail.* I've never had a reason to until now.

Another overhead alarm buzzes, and I watch as a different set of doors open. Sawyer walks through wearing an orange jumpsuit. It is the first time I've seen him since court. His hands are cuffed, but the guards are removing them. I wish they wouldn't.

Once the restraints are removed, Sawyer glances around, his eyes searching the room until they find me. They hold my gaze for a few moments before he smirks.

He walks in my direction. I remain tranquil as I pick at my nails. I would be lying if I said I'm not nervous.

He takes a seat across from me, his elbows resting on the table. He leans in closer. His smirk soon turns to a full out grin, exposing his perfectly white teeth.

"Ember," he says with longing. "I've been thinking about you."

"Hi, Sawyer."

"It's been a while."

"Three years," I confirm.

Sawyer had been sentenced to ten years for the attempted murder and kidnapping of Ace and an officer. All the charges Brennon tried to place that involved me had been dropped because I left with Sawyer willingly: the kidnapping, the rape, *all* of it. I had done nothing that would convince the jury otherwise, so my lawyer advised against pursuing the charges, said it would only draw out the long proceedings as it was a winless battle and not one that he felt I really wanted to fight. I felt like shit for months knowing I was the reason Sawyer wouldn't be locked up longer.

Sawyer had never been charged for his parents' death. There hadn't been enough evidence to tie him to that either. Basically, the only charges Brennon could put him away for were the events he'd witnessed himself with clear evidence.

I hadn't seen Sawyer since the trial, and even that had been three years ago. He looks mostly the same, outside of his shaggy hair that reminds me of the boy I dated in high school. How long ago that seems now.

"You look more beautiful than ever." He winks before he relaxes into the bench. "What brings you here today?"

"I think you know, Sawyer."

"You couldn't wait just a few more days to see me?"

Sawyer is getting out on parole this week.

"No," I say. "This couldn't wait."

"You know I sent you letters?"

"I asked them to stop sending me the letters."

"Did you read any?"

"No."

Sawyer sighs. "Damn shame."

"Why's that?"

"Those letters outlined everything I ever did for you. Every time I watched you sleep, or when you undressed yourself in your high-rise apartment in the city. I watched it all, Ember. Call them *love letters*, if you will."

His words give me chills. I already know he'd watched me. To what extent, I didn't know, nor did I care to. It had happened, and it is something I have to accept. I can't change the past. at least, that's what my therapist tells me.

"You know, sometimes just the sight of you would make me hard?"

"Sawyer, stop. I don't care."

"Do you even know how beautiful you are, Ember? There was never a time I couldn't get off by just thinking of you. How do you think I survive in here?"

"I'm moving," I blurt out in a desperate attempt to shut him up.

He cocks his head, his eyes searching mine. "Moving where?"

"Out of Illinois," I say ingenuously.

I've filed a new restraining order against Sawyer that will go into effect the day he is let out. He is confined to the state of Illinois, and therefore, I want to leave. His parole officer and I have reached an agreement that will not allow him to travel anywhere I might be, even if it's within the state. If he comes within a two-mile radius of me or violates any other detail of his parole, which includes leaving the state at all in the next three years, he will immediately be sent back to prison.

"Now why would you do such a thing?" he asks. "This is your home."

"*Was* my home, Sawyer."

"So, you came to say goodbye?"

I look down at my hands and the nail beds that I have already caused to bleed. "Look, I know you loved me. Maybe you still do. But I need you to know that you caused me more pain than happiness. I don't want to see you again, Sawyer. I hope I *never* see you again. Figure out your life, but you need to do it without me. Do better this time."

"Ember, you don't have to leave." I ignore the obvious disappointment in his voice. "Please, don't leave."

"Don't fuck this up, Sawyer. Don't violate your parole. And you better leave me the hell alone."

He glares at me, hard, but doesn't say anything more.

I stand up and scoot myself off the bench. I take one last look at the first man I ever loved. "See you never," I say.

Ace is waiting for me in the visitors' lot. He steps out of the truck to open the door at the first sight of me. I remain quiet. Once I am in, he shuts the door behind me and makes his way back to the driver's seat.

After he is situated in the front seat, he looks over in my direction. I can tell he is studying my face. Ace is always so concerned about me. He accompanies me to *all* my therapy appointments and remained strong for me during the trial. He is my rock and will be forever.

I give him a reassuring smile. "I'm okay."

He grabs my hand and brings it to his lips. He kisses it softly. Even after all these years, his touch still gives me butterflies. His kiss sends waves of shivers up my arm.

"Ready?" he asks.

"More ready than I've ever been."

The truck is filled to the brim with all our belongings. The movers are set to meet us at the new house tomorrow. We will be in Colorado in less than sixteen hours.

Ace and I found the perfect house that is seamlessly placed in the mountain tops. I have read that there are hiking trails nearby, and we will only be a few miles away from Ace's new bar and grill. The neighborhood is in a wonderful school district and even has several parks where kids can play. I know Brady will love it.

I turn my head to look back at the faultless human sitting in his car seat. "You ready to go home, buddy?" I ask as I tickle his feet.

He giggles. His smile reminds me of his dad's, but he has his mom's green eyes.

Ace starts the truck, and we begin our journey home.

epilogue

Ember

Colorado is everything we hoped it would be. We've built a life here, a life I never thought I would have. When Sawyer's parents died, I thought that was it for me. I didn't know I had a chance at the life I truly wanted. I had never been given that opportunity in the past because of Sawyer. I know that now. Ace makes sure I know every day how special I am.

Ace and I got married a year after he was released from the hospital, right after the trial. Sawyer had shot him in the stomach. The bullet had lodged in there deeply, causing him to bleed internally. He had emergency surgery and was released two weeks later. We've been inseparable since. He moved in with me shortly after his release but kept his apartment available to us on the nights he had to work late.

My mom became a grandma. Our little Brady was born shortly after our wedding. He's been the perfect addition to our family. My mom also decided to move to Colorado to be closer to us.

Brady is such a blessing. Before he turned one, there was already talk of baby number two. Unfortunately, we suffered a miscarriage last year. That was hard for us. Ace was of course supportive throughout it. He really is one of a kind. I'll never know how I got so lucky.

Ace's parents still live in Florida. We visit them frequently throughout the year. It is so easy to understand why Ace and Brennon are such good guys. They were raised by some truly amazing people. Ace's parents quickly took me in as their own and made me feel like I was part of their family. They're the kind of in-laws you refer to as *mom* and *dad*, even if they had no part in making you. Ace's dad even walked me down the aisle on our wedding day.

Brennon and Taylor met at the wedding, but they really started to hit it off after Brady was born. I think they bonded over the fact that they were both Brady's godparents. They've been dating ever since. They both still live in Illinois but visit us all the time. Brennon isn't at all Taylor's type, but he is exactly what she needed.

Eric and Cole have visited too. They moved to Michigan a couple of years ago to live with Katie and her husband. Eric ended up going to Iowa for college and graduates this year. Cole just started his freshmen year at a college in Michigan. Life ended up working out for them, though in an almost perfect world, the boys would be in Colorado with me. Katie feels terrible for not being there for them when Sawyer was missing. She blames it on the fact that she was trying to get pregnant, and she couldn't deal with the stress of the situation on her fertility. If you ask me, there is no excuse for what she did. However, all that matters now is that she stepped up for her brothers. Katie has recently announced that she is pregnant after two rounds of IVF treatment.

Overall, life seems like it can't get any better. I have the perfect life with the perfect family. I love my husband and son more than I could ever love another human being. I would go through it all again, because it led me to them.

Today has been a good day. I sit outside on the deck as I watch the sun set effortlessly behind the Rockies.

Brady fell asleep about an hour ago. We've just celebrated his third birthday. We had a zoo-themed party that wouldn't have been complete without the in-house petting zoo. Ace's parents flew in, as well as Brennon and Taylor. Eric and Cole sent Brady a birthday present that is by far his favorite: a remote-control car that can drive on walls. How does that thing defy gravity? I haven't a clue, but Brady absolutely loves it.

Ace walks toward the gliding door that leads to our patio. He opens it, and I watch as it slides across the tracks.

Ace pokes his head out. "It's time," he says.

I look at him nervously, then take a deep breath.

"Okay," I say softly.

I slowly get out of my porch swing and walk into the house, Ace following closely behind. It is lying on the counter, too far away to see. I can't look at it yet, so I fix my eyes on Ace and his comforting demeanor. He grabs my hand and gently squeezes.

"I love you," I say.

He smiles. "I'll never tire of you saying that."

"I'll never tire of saying it."

"You ready?" he asks.

Am I ready? I've been ready for a long time. But am I ready for that devastating heartbreak again? That, I can never be ready for.

But this isn't the time to be uncertain, so I nod.

My heart feels things it hasn't felt in a long time. Since last year. Since last time. With our hands intertwined and our breathing shallow, we both look at the pregnancy test at the same time.

My heart skips a beat.

Positive.

My eyes swell with tears at the news.

I am pregnant!

It took us a while to be ready to try again, after the loss we'd both suffered. The pain of the miscarriage still lingers in my heart. It is one of the hardest things we'd ever had to go through, and Ace and I have been through some shit. I hope this time will be different.

Ace wraps me in his arms. I know that losing our baby was hard for him, too. We both need this, a blessing.

Ace's phone vibrates against my belly as he holds me. He tries to ignore it, not wanting to ruin the happy moment.

I step away and wipe at my eyes. "It's okay," I say. "You can answer it."

When I look at Ace, I see the glassiness of his eyes. But as always, he tries to keep his cool.

Ace keeps his gaze locked with mine as he pulls his phone out of his front pocket. He turns the screen to show me who the call is from. "It's Brennon," he says.

I smile. "Good. Let him know he's going to be an uncle again."

Ace returns my smile before answering the phone. "Hey, man."

His face drops almost instantly.

"What is it?" I ask.

Ace's eyebrows furrow. He doesn't speak. He only listens. After a few seconds, he ends the call.

"What did he say?" I ask. "You didn't tell him we're pregnant."

"Ember."

"What? What is it?"

After a few beats, Ace finally answers, "It's Sawyer. He's violated his parole. He's left Illinois. They think he's on his way here."

I hope that you've enjoyed reading *See You Never*. I invite you to please leave a review.

.

acknowledgments

Firstly, thank you so much for reading *See You Never*! I never thought I would write a book, but these characters allowed me to get through some pretty scary times in our world. Thank you for diving into this story and sticking with me until the end.

Huge thanks to everyone who helped make this book possible. The list could go on and on with all the amazing support I received while writing it, especially from Kirsten Iversen and Michelle Bentkowski. Several others kept me motivated along the way, always demanding the next chapter as I was writing. It was all the inspiration I needed to continue the story. Thank you, Lexi DeAngelis, Jessica Campione, Donna Zeigler, Paige Plewa, Alexis Marrs, Amy Gerald, and Amanda Wells. And to all my other friends and supporters, who read the very scary rough draft of this book, thanks for lying to me and telling me it was good. I read it too, and I know it was far from suitable. But you stuck with it and supported me in this new endeavor. You know who you are, and I thank you.

To my family, who I wouldn't allow to read this story until it was published, here we are! We've made it. Or rather, you've made it. Thanks for waiting this one out with me. I'm excited to finally get to share what I've been working on for so long with you and the rest of the world.

A very special thank you to Justin McClain who set me up with Fred Heidbrink who did an amazing job designing the book's cover. We went from nothing to a whole lot of something. Thank you for giving this book character.

To my husband who had to give up spending several days and nights with his wife, thank you. This was an unexpected dream of mine, and you stuck it out with me, despite it all. Your support is the most important thing I could ever ask for. I will always support your hopes and dreams as you've supported mine. I love you the most.

There are so many of you who have asked me when this book was going to be published out of pure excitement to order, and I am so happy to say the day is finally here. Thank you to those who have followed my journey of becoming an author. And my friends, especially Pat Lindgren, who continued to share my personal updates and help get the word out about See You Never.

Thank you to everyone at The Pro Book Editor, especially Debra L Hartmann, for guiding me on this new adventure and turning my typed pages into a true novel.

Thank you to my glam team for getting me photoshoot ready for head shots. Jenna Brooks (@jennakbrooks) is a hair goddess, Erin Fahey is my skin/makeup guru (@erinfahey_), and Sydney Schleicher (@snappedbysydney) is the talent behind the lens.

And thank you to my readers. To anyone who happens to pick up this book and read it from start to finish, thank you for following along with Ember, Ace, and Sawyer.

A special thank you to my favorite book club The Lady Bookers for the amazing community of women, and some men, who also love to read! I hope this book finds you all.

I've written two additional standalone books: *Rocky Love* and *Give Her the World*. Stay tuned, as I'm excited to share these stories with my readers in the near future.

about the author

Delaney Lynn is a Public Health Nutritionist and avid romance reader. She currently resides in the suburbs of Chicago with her husband, four cats, and dog. She started the Lady Bookers Book Club via Instagram in 2019, frequently sharing her favorite authors and novels. We invite you to follow Delaney's book club @ladybookers on Instagram and connect with the author @laneyylynn on Instagram.

Please enjoy this sneak peek of Rocky Love

chapter one

I'm the new girl in school. The one you remember showing up in the middle of the year with no friends, doomed to be a loner, eating meals alone in the cafeteria, and spending Friday nights at home while the rest of the student body takes advantage of fake IDs and open houses. It's my senior year and my dad's job brought us to the middle of nowhere, Indiana. I grew up on the beaches of Orange County, where the sun was always shining and everyone knew how to surf. I can't remember the last guy I dated who wasn't a surfer. I spent most of my free time at the beach with my friends, sun-tanning in our bikinis while the boys showed off their skills inside a barrel. I guess I can thank them for my nice bronze skin in the dead of winter. *Winter,* that's another conversation. The ground here is covered with white powder snow. The warmest coat I owned up until a week ago was a cropped leather moto jacket. That's how I found out we were moving to Indiana. My dad walked into my room and surprised me with a coat so heavy and full of fur I was sure we were going to be Eskimos. But I wouldn't be that lucky to live amongst the indigenous circumpolar people in Alaska, Canada, or even Greenland. No. I get to live in Indiana!

My dad's job is what allowed us to live the expensive lifestyle California had to offer. He couldn't refuse the opportunity to take over a law firm that would nearly double his salary. But what good does all that money do in Portlet, Indiana? Sure, it bought us a house that is five times the size of our old one back in California. But is a big house really worth it when I had to leave all my friends and my entire life behind? No, it's not. Especially in my senior year.

I guess you could say that I'm bitter. There's only one semester left in the school year. Six months until I'm a high school graduate and can move back to California for college. College was the only way my parents were able to justify the move.

"But, Harlow, it doesn't need to be permanent for you. You'll be able to attend whatever college you want with my new income," my dad had said when I threw a temper tantrum the second the word *Indiana* left his mouth.

I'm a daddy's girl. Being an only child, my dad has spoiled me rotten. My mom is a stay at home mom who does anything but stay home. She frequents the shopping malls, but only the ones with valet parking. How dare anyone make her walk all the way to her car in a parking lot when she is holding heavy shopping bags full of the newest Versace trends and red-bottomed stilettos. When my dad said his salary would double, her eyes nearly fell out of their sockets. My mom was all for the move, but for all the wrong reasons.

My dad keeps me grounded. I don't have the expensive taste my mom has. I don't care to follow trends or be that basic bitch who orders Starbucks for an Instagram picture. I may be a bitch, but I'm one who sets her own trends and avoids Starbucks at all costs. I would describe my style as rocker-chic. Most of the clothes I own are black. Black makes you stand out in a world of pastels and patterns. Everyone in California dresses the same. There are no unique styles—everyone and their mom wears floral printed skirts and flowy crop tops that hardly cover the skin beneath their breasts.

"Harlow Brooks," the teacher calls out in first period.

I raise my hand, acknowledging my presence.

"Class, we have a new student joining us for the rest of the school year. Harlow, can you come join me in the front of the classroom for a moment?"

I roll my eyes. The classic first day of school introductions. I've been watching new kids do this since first grade, though I've never moved, never been the new girl, until now. My friends used to joke at the inelegance of the situation. Who wants to introduce themselves in front of a group of people they've never met? It's always made me uncomfortable. I hate awkward situations, and here I am being put into one. I already hate Indiana.

I walk to the front of the classroom. It's cold outside today, so I chose to wear my classic black jeans with rips in both knees and black booties. It's my go-to Harlow look. I didn't want people thinking I was gothic, not that I even care what these people think, but I chose an edgy mustard yellow sweater with puffed sleeves for a pop of color. I always line my lips with ruby red lipstick, my signature back in California. Girls always knew which man I had my eyes set on because there would be the perfect outline of my lips placed in the center of their cheek. Guys swoon over my lips. They're full and plump. My mom doesn't go a day without complaining about her need for filler. How had I gotten the perfect lips when I came out of her? Jealousy doesn't look pretty on Erica Brooks.

Every eye in the classroom is on me. I see girls gossiping in the back corner. I'm used to that. It wouldn't be high school without some cattiness. Pretty girls love to hate pretty girls. My dirty blonde hair falls just below my chest. I was born with my mom's bleach blonde hair but make it a point to add lowlights to give it some edge. It's another point of conflict between my mother and me. I had no desire to look like every other girl in California with blonde hair. I work hard to keep my blonde dirty. No one in this classroom has hair like mine. I already like that I stand out.

"Why don't you tell us a little bit about yourself," the teacher says.

I keep my gaze straight ahead until I begin to speak. When I'm about to open my mouth, my eyes fall to the person sitting in the second to last row. His hair is dark. I love dark hair. It was so hard to find a man in California with dark hair. They all had shaggy blond, the typical beach boy surfer look. It got boring. I mostly settled for light brown hair as a last resort. But his hair is so dark it is almost black. He styles it differently than I've ever seen. It's long but doesn't fall under his eyes. It's practically in a perfect mess on top of his head. His eyes are as blue as the Pacific Ocean. The one thing I loved about California, the ocean. I love it even more in his eyes. His lips are curled in a slight grin. When I realize I've been staring at him for far too long without speaking, I look back up to the class but not before we make eye contact. He's looking directly at me, almost through me. I know he caught me staring. I need to play it cool.

"Hi. I'm Harlow. I just moved from California last week to the wonderful state of Indiana," I say sarcastically.

The class laughs.

My eyes fall back to the boy in the back. His smile when he laughs is mesmerizing. His teeth look perfectly imperfect, and I love them.

I'm done with my introduction, so I take my seat. He's sitting directly behind me, and I can feel the heat of his gaze on my neck. He smells of fresh pine. I'm distracted for the entire rest of the class.

I quickly walk out of the classroom when the bell rings, having no desire to make friends in this state. I want no ties to Indiana, nothing that can hold me back. It's only six months. Six months and I can be free of this stupid state, with its stupid snow and the stupid hot boy in my class.

I find my locker for the first time after first period, the piece of paper they gave me with the number and combo in hand. I twist the lock, entering the number sequence. When I attempt to open my locker, it doesn't budge. I try again and it still won't open.

"Shit," I mumble.

"Need some help?" I hear from behind me.

When I turn, I'm immediately taken back. It's him. Cute boy from first period is standing next to my locker, asking if I need help. Did he follow me here? Are the boys in Indiana that clingy?

"It's stuck," I say.

"Wrong locker."

"What? How would you know?" I look at the piece of paper in my hand and look back up at the locker number. *Shit.*

"This is my locker," he says smugly.

Of course. His locker would be next to mine.

"Sorry," I say as I move over one locker.

I enter in the combination and it opens without difficulty. As I'm shoving things into my locker, I can feel his eyes on me. I pretend not to notice, shut my locker, and walk away. I don't look back, even though I know he's watching me walk away. His presence does something to me, makes me nervous. And it doesn't help that he is the definition of hot in my book. It might be harder than I thought to make it through the school year without a fling. If I had to break my rules for anyone, it would be him.

I manage to make it through the rest of the day only having to introduce myself in three other classes. Cute boy from first period wasn't in any others. I didn't go to my locker again in an attempt to avoid him, having decided somewhere between lunch and sixth period that it would be best to not break my rules. I can make it the next six months without any sort of fling. The beautiful state of California is waiting for me. I'm sure whatever college I attend there will have plenty of dark-haired men to choose from. I don't need to drop my panties at the first one that makes my mouth water, especially if he's from Indiana.

When I get home and pull into the driveway of my new giant house, I sigh. There's at least a foot of snow on the ground. My mother didn't shovel, my dad's been at work all day, and they probably haven't hired any services yet. I open my car door and put my feet in the snow, feeling it seep over the top of my booties and down to my ankle. It's cold, really cold. I grab my backpack from the passenger seat and make my way to the front door.

Mom's sitting at the counter, online shopping. "There's no Chanel at this mall, Har! Can you believe that?"

"What a shame," I say sarcastically.

"The neighbors invited us over for dinner tonight."

"I think I'll stay home. I have a lot of homework already." I don't care to make nice with our neighbors. I want to get this school year over with and get back to the beach.

"Harlow, it's not until seven. Get started on it now. Your dad will want us to go as a family."

"Fine."

I spend the next several hours finishing assignments before it's time to get ready for dinner with our new neighbors. My mom makes me change for dinner, so I wear a short black dress that accentuates my curves and displays my long legs. It's one of the few expensive pieces she has bought me that I wear. I appreciated her finally buying me something in black. She often buys bright colored dresses in an effort to make me look more girly. I keep those in the back of my closet.

My dad gets home from work shortly before it's time to leave. "How was your first day of school, sweetheart?" he asks me as he kisses my forehead.

I shrug. "It was okay. People are already talking about me."

He laughs. "Never fails."

We walk outside, to the house next door. I silently praised whoever shoveled our driveway and sidewalk. Our next-door neighbor's home slightly resembles ours but is noticeably smaller. It would be unlike my parents to not have chosen the biggest house on the block.

My dad knocks on the front door, and we are greeted by a petite older woman wearing an apron. She must be their housekeeper.

"Come in," she says. "They are waiting for you in the dining area."

We step into the foyer. The house is exquisite, decorated with beautiful modern furniture and has floor to ceiling windows throughout. We're led into the dining room and met by the homeowners. My parents introduce themselves before they step aside to introduce their only child. I step forward.

"This is Harlow," my dad says. "Harlow, this is Mr. and Mrs. Walton."

"It's very nice to meet you both," I say as I take their hands one by one to shake them.

"Jeff, your daughter is lovely," I hear the man say.

I smile politely. I hear in conversation that Mr. and Mrs. Walton go by David and Monica. As we are about to take our seats, I hear footsteps coming down the stairs toward us.

Monica's face lights up. "Aiden, our guests are here," she says.

I turn my head in the direction of the newcomer. My mouth falls open. I can't hide my shock.

"Sorry I'm late. I was just finishing up one of my assignments," Aiden says as he kisses his mom on the cheek. He turns to face my father. "Hello, sir. I'm Aiden."

My dad takes his hand and shakes it firmly. "It's nice to meet you, Aiden. I'm Jeff, this is my wife, Erica." Then he turns to face me. "And this is our daughter, Harlow."

Aiden smiles. "Harlow."

"Hello," I say as I take my seat.

Aiden walks around the table to the only empty seat directly across from me. His eyes don't leave mine.

"Aiden is a senior at Liberty," Monica says.

"Harlow just began her last semester there today," my mother responds.

My dad turns to look at me. "Did you have any classes together?" he asks.

I shake my head. "I don't think so. I wasn't paying much attention," I lie.

David turns his attention toward Aiden. "Son, you should introduce Harlow to your friends. Make her feel welcome."

Aiden smiles. "I intend to."

I can't take my eyes off Aiden. He intrigues me. The boys back home acted nervous around me, but not him. He's almost arrogant, maybe even a little cocky, and that makes me uneasy. He's so different. I want to know more, but I've already told myself no dating in Indiana. I have no desire to meet his friends or spend any more time with him than I have to. His locker is next to mine, we have first period together, and apparently, he's my next-door neighbor, so I have a feeling we will run into one another quite often over the next six months. I take my gaze off him and bring it to my plate that was just served a decadent lamb chop with roasted potatoes and asparagus. Rich people food. I'm used to this by now, but I would be lying if I said I wasn't more of a 'burger and fries' kind of girl.

I make it through dinner without glancing up at Aiden again, then to the front door where my parents say our goodbyes.

"Dinner was marvelous," my mom coos. "You must join us for dinner at our home once we are settled."

Aiden's parents smile and agree.

Aiden walks over to me and places his hand on my shoulder.

My eyes are instantly brought back to his as a result of his unexpected touch.

"I'll be seeing you around, Harlow," he says.

"I suppose you will, Aiden."

Made in the USA
Middletown, DE
14 September 2021